Prodigal

By

Willard N. Carpenter

This book is a work of fiction and any resemblance to persons, living or dead, or places, events or locales is purely coincidental. The characters are productions of the author's imagination and used fictitiously.

PRODIGAL. Copyright 2012 by Willard N. Carpenter.

Dedicated to Jacinda

"And not only that, but we also glory in tribulation, knowing that tribulation produces perseverance; and perseverance, character, and character, hope.
Now hope does not disappoint, because the love of God has been poured out in our hearts by the Holy Spirit who was given to us." - **Romans 5:3-5**

God brings people into our lives for a purpose; mine is to touch as many lives as my Lord would have me. You have touched many more than that; you teach us.

Keep in touch with Samuel and his family on facebook.
http://www.facebook.com/people/Samuel-
Hersberger/100001879866459

Keep in touch with the Author
http://www.facebook.com/Will1953

Web Site 'Secrets of the Son'
http://secretsoftheson.webs.com/prodigalexcerpts.htm

CONTENTS

ACKNOWLEDGMENTS

❖ Shelley, for inspiring the writing of this book. For believing in me.

❖ Tina, for volunteering your time to the editing of this book.

❖ Pastor Matt, for your sermon and help in biblical texts. For your love as my son.

❖ My wife Michele, daughter Lindsay, and youngest son Mark: For being there for me when I needed you, and for your love.

Thanks can never say or mean enough for how y'all allowed God to move you in my life.

Foreword

I own an old Ford Ranger pickup truck. After all, what is an ole country boy to drive? From the time I had got it until now, the gas gauge has not worked. As I drive, I watch closely to see how many miles I log to determine when it is time to 'gas up'.

It was on a bright and sunny day on the 4th of September, 2009 that I went to visit my wife at work to have lunch. Afterwards, as I had done many times before, I took a side trip west on 322 (Horseshoe Pike) then south on route 10 to two of my favorite Amish stands. The first one, I picked up bakery items; the second, vegetables and freshly canned jams.

After some pleasantries with the young Amish folks at the stands, I was on my way home. Not paying as close attention as I should have, I ran my truck out of gas.

Slowing, I was able to maneuver my sputtering Ranger off the road, just clearing the driveway of a farm. I was just off the shoulder and had to watch the traffic of busy Horseshoe Pike when I got out.

Putting up my hood to signal that my truck had 'broken down'; I called my brother who lives in the area only to find he wasn't home.

Undaunted, I decided to wait a short while before calling him again and thought I would settle myself on the tailgate. Lowering the tailgate, I noticed a buggy approaching; the same one that I had passed a short time before.

After sitting down, that same buggy turned into the driveway in front of me. The solemn man and woman in the front had not made eye contact with me, choosing to enter the drive without interaction.

While I was thinking about how I needed to fix the gas gauge, the same Amish man who had turned into his drive came out and greeted me. He introduced himself as Samuel Hersberger.

I introduced myself as Samuel took in the situation and commented on my truck. "Gut truck," he says as he then smiled and asked me what seemed to be the problem.

"Out of gas," I told him simply.

In his Pennsylvania Dutch accent he told me, "come!" At the same time he is motioning for me to follow.

Walking up the blacktopped drive I noticed how neat and orderly this farm was. I also noticed that it was not typical for a farm. There were no cows, hens, or pigs, just horses.

Arriving behind some stables we came upon, yes, a black Ford Ranger pickup. It was in good condition with a current inspection sticker.

As I did a double take, I snickered and commented, "Good truck!"

He looked and with a laugh said, "Jah." He reached in the back and pulled out a red five gallon plastic container filled with gasoline.

We began to speak while bringing the filled plastic container back to the road side. Arriving, Samuel stood in the grass behind the truck as I began pouring in the gasoline.

I guess he was looking at the stickers on my back windows as he continued speaking to me, asking if I knew the school. Looking up from what I was doing I asked, "which one?"

"Gut school!" he said, while pointing. I shook my head affirmatively and told him my son was in his second year there.

By this time, Samuel had caught my interest. I suppose I caught his also. After putting in about a gallon of the fuel, I went around to the driver seat. Turning the key, the truck started right up. Getting out of the truck, I offered to pay him. He waved me off, taking the gasoline container, which I'd laid in the grass.

Samuel invited me in for coffee. Always looking to meet new people and being a little curious, I accepted. I pulled the truck into the drive and followed him to the back door of the kitchen and went in.

3

Samuel pulled out a chair telling me to, "sit, sit!" I did as he put two mugs down on the table, and continued to talk about the school. "Class of 1981, I went to that school," says Samuel then pausing before asking, "are you shocked?" He was looking at the surprised look on my face.

We continued with more small talk as he spoke about things never being what they seem when a young woman came through the back door wearing a black bonnet and a large heartfelt smile. She greeted her Uncle Samuel as she looked over at me. Samuel introduced Mary to me and she said, "Hello." Samuel continued.

"Mary now is a gut example. She grew up English. She became Amish within the past decade." Mary smiled down again at her Uncle.

"Uncle, I must go; Aunt Mary is visiting with my mom."

Samuel answered her as she left, and continued, "The other Mary is my wife. Many Mary's; I keep them separated by calling her young Mary," says Samuel laughing. I continued to smile as I picked up and took another sip of the piping hot coffee in front of me.

Samuel appearing to have the need to talk, continued, "How I know that school!" He continued with his walk through his past and thanked me for bringing back, "gut memories" to him. We continued with the small talk as Samuel sat to my left near the stove.

"Things aren't always what they seem. Now you would not think that most of half my life up to now has been amongst the English? Ach! I was English for 25 years!" He looked over at me with his mug in hand and shook his head. "We all have our stories, I'm sure you have yours, yes?" I nodded affirmatively while I looked at him.

"I have mine also," he said to me.

With that, he began to tell me the most incredible story of one Amish man's journey. It's been nine months; in that time, Samuel and I have become good friends.

4

After these many months of looking for something to write about, I find my story. It is Samuel's story. It is the story of a sensitive, but strong, faith filled family man with many loves and many secrets. Many of his secrets have unfolded within his community but are largely unknown amongst the 'English'. The words that I put down do him no justice as to the person that I have gotten to know; he is a person that I now call my friend.

Prologue
Change

February 2, 2001, Friday, it's been twenty five years, a lifetime away from home and the Amish community that I refused to join. I had decided at that time that I wanted more in my life. I wanted an education and a sense of adventure amongst the English.

Rumspringa, my running around time, had brought me to this. It wasn't supposed to. In fact, it was supposed to show me what not to like amongst the English and keep me within the fold of my family and my faith.

Twenty five years later and I am being brought home to my dying father; my father with whom I had very little dialogue while growing up. My father, even though we spoke little, I knew loved me very much as I did him and who, despite all the arguments, understood me. It was as though he could see into the future and was trying to protect me, but he also knew he had to let go.

To this day, he does not understand why I left and what I did while I was away. There is only one family that knows my 'secrets'; my good friend John, and his mother and father, Mary and William Dietrick. They were the ones who, for all intents and purposes, 'rescued' me from my Amish life. The same Amish life I find myself running back to now.

Home, stone walls which were built during a time when all traversed the countryside with horse and buggy, both English and Amish alike. Our home had been passed down three generations to my daed. He cared for it as though God watched him specifically from a hay loft above.

The care of the land and livestock was meticulous. Each care was given its time, from livestock being fed to seed being planted.

Inside the walls, our true home was made of love and all the warmth that any child would need to convince them that they were loved and needed.

On any given day, my youngest schweschder Becky would be with our Mamma in the kitchen. The smell of breads, cookies, cakes or pies would make its way through our home. A smile could always be seen on their faces. I can still see Becky with that heavenly smile of hers, enticing me with a sugar cookie. They were in perfect pace with the entirety of farm life.

Each meal was planned and timed to fit into the seasons down to the month, day and hour, from the growing in the fields, the processing of meats, and the canning of what was grown.

Though they had moved out, having taken on families of their own, my *bruders* and *schweschders* had found harmony within those walls. There was my oldest *bruder*, Jeremiah. He was born August of 1952 and is forty-nine years old. The most rigid of us, he has a wife, Erica, and three kinner. They are Jeremiah, Catherine, and Daniel.

Emma, who is forty-seven, was born May of 1954. She was next to add to the warmth of our home. Mamma says she was born at a time when the birds could be heard outside of the windows, blending in with her whimpers from the cradle.

A time when the fragrance of spring flowers was noticed coming through open windows which had been closed during a long winter of whiteness and gray.

Emma married Solomon and the two of them have the largest of all our families. Their daughter Katie is the oldest of six. She is pregnant with the next generation of God's carefully kept people.

Then Amos, we played together often, as well as worked together. He was the one who tried in earnest to talk me into staying. He had just gotten married after being baptized into the church.

God had come so easy for him. I can't say he even had *rumspringa*. It was as though he went directly from childhood to God and adulthood within family and church and skipped his years in between. He is forty-five, being born March of 1956. He married Elizabeth and they have five *kinner*.

Then there was my little *schweschder*, Becky. She is forty-one and the only reason I almost stayed at home and joined the church. She so looked up to and adored me. From the time she could talk, it was all I heard from the lightly freckle-faced little girl, *bruder*. I can still feel her little hands in mine today as she would look for any reason to hold it as we walked across fields or along the roadside.

She cried so much the day I left. She was the one who wrote constantly through John. It was as though a piece of her soul would not be whole unless I was a constant in her life.

Though I missed them all, it was Becky, *daed* and mamma which made my heart ache so at times. It was those three that made me recognize loneliness, though I was amongst many. It was the memory of Becky and mamma that would come flashing past me in my senses when I would smell cooking or baking.

It is, however, daed who brings me home to the four stone walls, the rich earth, the smell of the kitchen, and the warmth of family.

Chapter One

At forty-five thousand feet, the Lear jet 35 was settling in for a smooth flight up the east coast. A gentleman in a dark blue three piece suit sat in the front left seat.

Samuel Hersberger was tired from a long day of meetings the previous day before seeing some of his men off at 1 a.m., as they left for South America on business. After arriving back at his home at 2 a.m., he briefly flipped through his mail and listened to his phone messages.

Pushing the button of his answering machine, he heard the familiar single beep, and then...

"Samuel, it's John. I'm sorry to have to call you like this, but your brother, Amos, was over and asked me to contact you. It's your dad Sam; he's dying and your family needs you home." Samuel spent the next five minutes just staring at his machine as it made the single beep again at the end of the messages. He reached up and wiped away a single tear before spending the rest of the night packing and moving his personal belongings for the flight he is now on.

It seems the older I get, the more easily I tire...Daed, I can't believe this; last I heard he had beat the cancer. Why did it come back? Why daed? I wonder how mama and Becky are. Dang, I am so tired. Think I'll get some sleep...Daed?

Sohn, remember the commandments. You shall have no other gods before me. Daed? Sohn remember the commandments. Honor your father and mother. Daed? Sohn, remember the commandments. Do not murder.

Do not murder...SIR...There is nothing you can do! They're all dead! All dead! There was nothing we could do, nothing. All the...Who could do such a thing? Do not...murder...? The one's who did this are where? The innocence. The babies. The women. The children. They're all dead.

Sohn, remember the commandments...I am so tired...Do not murder. Do not lie. Keep the Sabbath holy, Sohn...I am so tired...So...

"Sir...Sir!" called the flight steward, gently shaking Samuel, "Wake up sir!" He woke to the steward and co-pilot standing to the right of his seat.

"Sir, you were screaming out and you're sweating. Are you alright? Can I get you anything? Maybe some water?"

"Ahh, Yeah, Yes! I'm Ok. Thank you just the same. Where are we?"

"We are at about 25,000 feet and descending. About thirty minutes from Reading, Pennsylvania. You must have been having some nightmare." They shudder from the turbulence of the light plane as it makes its way down through the clouds on the way to its destination. As he reaches up to take the bottle of water, he answers.

"Yes, a lot of those lately. I'm looking forward to this break. Maybe it will help."

"Yes Sir," says the co-pilot as he returns to his place and the steward sits down in the seat across from Samuel. After fastening his seat belt for the upcoming landing he takes a drink of his own water and continues to watch Samuel in his three piece suit as he stares out the window.

Reading, I remembered picking Reading as a destination for my flight so I could arrive unnoticed. It would be out of view from the folks in the big city, Philadelphia. The plan is to take a cab and not a limo down Route 222 into Lancaster. I'll stay at a local hotel in Lancaster, near enough to the family farm outside of Honey Brook and yet far enough away to be alone and away from everyone.

Don't fall asleep again, Hersberger. Still don't know if I'll be Hat willkommen gehei Ben. But welcome or not, I have to face them. February 2, Erdschwein Tag, it's that day I wonder if that stupid groundhog will see his shadow? I wonder how cold it will be. Is there snow? Hmmm...

German, the one thing I held onto. It had come in handy over the years. Takes me back to college. John's family had taken me in the day before my eighteenth birthday. There was so much to do. I remember studying for my GED, taking the test, and passing it. Then to community college in Reading, full time, straight A's. That is when Mr. and Mrs. Dietrick suggested I move onto a better school.

When did I start college? Was it seventy-six? No, September nineteen seventy-seven. How I hated to love that year. It was bad enough not having any support from my own family. They had all but forgotten about me. Except Becky. I can only picture two faces of hers; that smile which angels put in place and the tears when I left.

*Then, I had to pick a school so dang far away. South Carolina of all places, but then the scholarship; couldn't pass that up. I was off on my adventure amongst the English. The Dietrick's were great. My new family, they had visited as often as I could see them and they could come down. John had stayed near his home for his education, choosing to study science at Gettysburg College. Where had all the time gone? Well, I'll use up all the vacation time I have saved up and...*A sudden lurch and squeal of the wheels startles and brings Samuel Hersberger out of his day dream.

Day dreaming.....sight of a lot better than the nightmares I've been experiencing. As the Lear jet taxis along the runway, Samuel looks out at the small mountains surrounding the one side of Reading. They are gray with white hanging on the trees. Snow left over from a not so long ago storm.

I already feel as though a huge weight has been lifted off of me from my past. No other aircraft here. Hmm, there are a couple of single engine planes.

"Sir, we have arrived," says the steward who is now standing and looking out the door's window, occasionally looking back at its lone passenger.

"That we have," answers Samuel as he begins to stand while the small jet taxis to its final stop. The plane comes to rest just inside one of the fences facing the parking lot.

The door to the Lear jet is opened from the inside and the steps go down on the left side of the aircraft. As the steward steps down, a rush of cold comes into the warmth of the aircrafts interior. The copilot remains seated in the right seat and is writing in a log. The pilot, who is on the tall side, stoops facing the rear of the aircraft.

"Captain," exclaims Samuel Hersberger.

"Yes sir," answered the pilot, diverting his attention from outside of the Leer's door.

"Nice flight," Samuel says as he smiles, almost chuckles in relief at the pilot.

"Thank you sir," the pilot responds. "I like these short hops," he continued.

"Well, now to get all of my stuff off this aircraft," says Samuel with a smirk.

The Captain nodding his head responds, "Yes Sir," and they both laugh.

"Captain, are you flying right back?"

"No, not today, 6 a.m. tomorrow. The three of us are going to check into a hotel, then see about getting something to eat. Care to join us, sir?"

"Ohh, noo, thanks, my day is just beginning. What time is it?"

"Three-forty-five sir. Jim's getting your gear together on the airport's flat hand truck." The pilot looked toward the left and made his way down the short steps to the tarmac.

"Good, good! Well you boys, thanks a lot now, and have a good evening." Samuel is now standing on the cold of the tarmac. A slight, but very cold wind is blowing and Samuel can feel it through his top coat as he pulls the collar up and closes the top of it.

"Thank you sir, and you also have a good evening," says the pilot.

Just as he said, there are five footlockers and four suitcases on the flat truck. And now I'm awaiting a cab. I can only hope that I can get all of this into the car. I should have hired a truck.

The yellow cab out of Reading comes quickly around the turning circle of the Reading Airport and to an abrupt stop.

Just as quickly as the cab comes to a stop, a slight young woman jumps out. She is in her early twenty's with shoulder length black hair, which at the moment of stepping out of the car catches a breeze and is whipped into her face.

"Are you Mr. Hersberger?" She quickly brushes her hair back with her fingers.

"Yes, I am. I take it you're my ride." *Pretty girl!*

"Yes sir, that would be me. I don't understand. There weren't any flights due in at this time. How'd you get here?" She began to look around. Spotting the small jet with its markings just off to the other side of the fence and parked on the tarmac, she looks at Mr. Hersberger, "Is that yours?" she asks inquisitively.

"A little nosey aren't you?" Rebukes a tired Samuel as he stares at her a little put out.

"I'm sorry," says the driver, again fighting the breezes, she pulls the hair out of her face again.

"Well, now that we've dispensed with the formalities, maybe you can tell me if we can fit all of this in the car."

The back seat is full, as well as the trunk. Samuel Hersberger is sitting in the front seat, which he'd rather anyhow.

Feeling a little more renewed, he begins speaking again, "Hi, shall we start again? I'm Sam Hersberger." There is a pause as the cab pulls right out of the parking lot heading for Route 222.

"And you are?" Samuel questions again trying to get the young woman's attention.

"I'm sorry, Amanda, Amanda Russo," responds a hesitant Amanda.

"Amanda Russo, how are you?" questions Samuel now smiling and looking directly at his young driver. She responds quickly returning his gaze and smile, "good, fine, thanks."

"Good. Has the cab company informed you as to my destination?"

"Yes sir, the Dutch Inn on East Lincoln Highway."

"Very good, Amanda," responds a surprised Samuel. Driving quickly down the highway, he notices snow all around. He cracks the window a bit to let in some of the cold, clean air. Looking out the window, he notices the landscaping of brown peppered in white with a background of gray outlined in white.

The countryside begins to look familiar to him as they close in on Lancaster. Samuel begins to remember how pretty the Pennsylvania countryside can be when his sightseeing is interrupted by Amanda making an attempt at small talk.

"They're calling for more snow on Monday."

"How much?" asks Samuel.

"Don't know but should be a lot; it's a nor'easter. You know how they can be," says Amanda, glancing over at Samuel.

"No, don't recall actually," Samuel responds, looking back at his driver.

"Where'd you come from?" Amanda, now smiling, picks up the conversation.

"North Carolina," responds Samuel again.

"What's in North Carolina?"

"I have a ranch there. I raise horses. Well, I should say I have people who raise my horses. I own them though. When I'm in the country and have time off, I stay at the ranch. I go riding. Up to five years ago, we, my wife and I at that time, would go riding some."

"I hope you don't mind my asking. Where is your wife, Sam?"

"No, I don't mind. My job takes me out of the country a lot, or it used to. One day I came home and she was gone. Same old story, no forwarding address, no phone, just divorce papers from her attorney a year later. Shortly before this past Christmas, I heard she died."

"I'm sorry. Sounds like it was rough," says Amanda, looking over at Sam with concern in her eyes.

"Thanks, it's ok now," he looks back and smiles. The cab pulls up to the front lot of the Dutch Inn.

"Wait here a moment Amanda, will you please, while I see where they have me." He checks in, getting two adjoining rooms, one with a king size bed. The other is for all of his belongings, so he doesn't trip over them. The cab pulls around to the first two rooms on the first floor. Amanda helps with the luggage while Sam unloads the footlockers into the second room.

"Amanda, it's been a pleasure meeting you," Samuel says, making eye contact with her.

"Same here," Amanda responds respectfully as Sam hands her a generous tip. "Thanks for the chat also," says Amanda as a final note. Samuel nods again at her and she smiles before returning to the cab and leaving.

℘⫯℘

"*Jah Daed.*" And with those words, Jeremiah acknowledges his respect for his father while he lies in his bed in the first floor front bed room. It was his *daed's* way; the cancer had come, had been fought, and now had returned. He had chosen to leave, to go to his eternal home and be with his heavenly Father. What had been missing was Samuel, his youngest, his head strong, Samuel his beloved, Samuel his 'prodigal son'.

The contention between Jeremiah and his father lasts but five minutes. Jeremiah felt it was truly wrong to pass onto Samuel what the family and he, his Father, had worked so hard to maintain. While his *bruder*, Samuel, was out enjoying himself amongst the 'English'. His father reminds him of Luke 15, likening Samuel to the prodigal son, and in a low voice tells him, "Jeremiah, what had any of us given Samuel when he left? Had he taken anything? Did any of us even send our love with him? Would you agree that your *bruder* is better than the prodigal son? This is my wish," spoke *daed*.

With tears in his eyes, Jeremiah says in a whisper, "I miss my bruder. I miss Samuel. It will be as you wish. *Jah Daed.*"

"*Danki*, Jeremiah, *Danki*," responds his *daed*, now struggling to get the words out.

Jeremiah walks into the kitchen; he is stoic, hardened from a near lifetime of what he felt was picking up after his youngest brother. Now, accepting what he felt was the inevitable, he prepares for the possibility of his brother coming home in the future. Jeremiah, the oldest son, after his discussion with his father is resigned to doing the right thing for the family.

Slowly entering the kitchen he looks over his family and in a quiet tone of voice reflects his fathers, and now his own, wishes, "We will *willkum* our Samuel home." His mother, with welled eyes herself, smiles as she wipes her hands on her apron.

"*Jah*, we will." She swallows hard. They all look at each other; Jeremiah at his mamma, who is looking at Samuel's other brother, Amos, and his sister, Emma. And they all smile amongst the anguish of the nearby room where *daed* now lay sleeping restlessly.

The father did not know where his son, Samuel had been. For that matter, where Samuel was now, all he had known was how to get word to him through John Dietrick. Faithful to his word, John had gotten hold of Samuel while he was at his ranch in North Carolina.

Upon hearing of his father's plight, Samuel decided enough was enough.   He told his boss it was now time to retire. He couldn't sleep anymore and his father was dying. His longtime friend and boss simply told him, "You have a lot of vacation time, take it! I'll be in touch!" Now, less than twenty-four hours later, and unbeknownst to his family, Samuel was just a few minutes away from his childhood home in a Lancaster hotel.

ℰℭ

Mary Stutzman was preparing her children for a walk to the Hersberger's. She had spoken with Emma's daughter,

Katie, at the quilting bee. She had heard from Katie that her *dawdi* was much worse.

It had been almost seven years since Mary lost her husband, David, from a farming accident, and Katie had been a *gut* friend at that time by helping her with the kinner and more importantly with her grief.

Mary had moved back to her *dat's* house and farm, off of Horseshoe Pike on Pleasant View Road. On a clear day, she can see what had been her and David's home through the trees in the distance.

Sold to David after their marriage, the home remained on her *dat's* farm. It has good acres behind Rebers Lane and borders some homes off of Horseshoe Pike about a mile from Honey Brook.

They had planned to have more children before he was taken home to God. Now, she was on her way with her kinner to give comfort to her friend Katie and her Mamma Emma at their most trying time.

₮Ↄ

John left his wife with her guests at home on Horseshoe Pike to meet Samuel at the Dutch Inn. John had just gotten off the phone with Samuel and was recalling his conversation. "John? It's Samuel," a somber Samuel begins.

"Sam!" sounded the reply in a near yell, "Where are you at?"

"I'm in town, well almost in town, in Lancaster, at the Dutch Inn, off of East Lincoln Highway. Do you know of it?"

Without thinking, John replied quickly, "I'll find it! What a surprise. This is really exciting having you home and all. It's really good. Does your family know?"

"Not unless you told them." Samuel is a little short on the phone from having very little sleep. He is sitting at a table in his hotel room looking out the window at the sun, now low in the winter sky. The electric heat in the room is at his knees blowing welcomed hot air.

"That's right; I'm talking to you on your cell phone. Sometimes I forget you're Amish." John is unfazed by his friend's shortness and just continues speaking.

"Well if they accept me back I will be," quips Samuel at his friend.

"Sam they will, they will, just wait n see," says John.

Samuel continues, "We will see John, we will, heh, can I trouble you for a ride home?"

"Well, that's why I thought you were calling. I actually expected for you to call from the airport. So Sam, what room are you in?"

"I have adjoining rooms, 102 and 104, my stuff is in 102 and I'm in 104."

"Well, I'll see you and your stuff inside a half an hour."

"That's great buddy, thanks a lot." Samuel ends the call on his blackberry and places it back in his coat pocket.

The sun hangs low in the winter sky over Lancaster County as John arrives in his glossy, black, crew cab pickup. He parks just in front of room 102 and hops down out of his truck as Samuel exits his room off to his right. Both old friends spot each other instantly and move quickly to a handshake turn hug.

"It's been too long John, too long." As he holds his closest friend at arm's length, looking at him, Samuel shakes his hand again, this time clasping John's right hand with both of his.

"I know, Sam," says John, now shaking his head.

"We have a lot of catching up to do John, but first I have to get to my folks." John points to his truck.

"Big enough for all that stuff you needed a separate room for?" He says with a chuckle. Sam laughs along with him.

"Yep, but I won't be taking any of it with me yet. Have to check the climate first." John smiles slightly again.

"Gotcha, you ready to go?"

"Yep," responds Samuel quickly in return.

"Well, get in already old man," John says as Samuel climbs into the truck at the same time as John is shutting his door.

A moment later they are on their way down East Lincoln Highway and turning right onto Route 23. Then, in what felt like a few moments, they are on Route 322 and on their way to Samuel's childhood home.

They pass little hints to Samuel's past, first a lone gray over black colored buggy, then another. As they pass, Samuel peers in; he can see a young man with a short beard and a woman with a black bonnet seated in the front, and a little boy standing in between them. John asks, "Bringing back memories, Samuel?" There is no answer.

"Heh buddy!" exclaims John, attempting to get Samuel's attention. He is staring at the buggy as it passes. "Sam!"

"Yo, John, I'm sorry, deep in thought. What's up?"

"I was asking if it brought back memories, but I can see it does." He smiles and looks over inquisitively at his friend.

"I'm sorry, John. I'm sorry for being short earlier and being a little out of it now. I didn't get much sleep last night since you called. And now...well...I have a lot on my mind as you can imagine." Briefly Samuel looks at John, then back out the window. He can be seen lost in thought.

"I understand all that; after all, if I don't understand what might be going on in that mind of yours, then there is nobody who can. No apologies needed, got it?"

Samuel quickly looks back at his friend and shakes his head responding, "Got it, and thanks John."

The rest of the drive is quiet. Samuel, engrossed in the familiar countryside, can be seen moving his head back and forth looking from one side of the street to the other. The Amish farms along the way have their own beauty with a light snow covering the ground as a blanket, signaling a long winter's rest to the earth underneath. There are no wires running onto properties to take away from what is natural and untouched by time for many decades.

Another buggy is in front of them as they continue down Horseshoe Pike. John passes safely at a distance to the buggies left as Samuel looks over his left shoulder to see a young couple huddled in the enclosed buggy. They are bundled against the cold, with a girl child between them, and making good time down the road. Samuel grins as he again looks forward and remembers a time when they too rode as such.

ℰℭ

Mary is walking on this clear, cold day, anxious to reach her destination before the sun tucks behind the horizon. Holding each child's hand, she walks briskly as she crosses Horseshoe Pike from Pleasant View. Looking right again after crossing, she notices two men about her *dat's* age in an unfamiliar black pickup pulling into the driveway of the Hershberger's farm. *English? I wonder who that could be? It's much colder than I thought it was going to be. Maybe it wasn't such a gut idea to bring the kinner on this walk. Ach, the cold!*

Mary picks up the pace a little. As quickly as the children can walk, they make their way down the driveway. Looking down through her own breath, she notices the red cheeks of her young ones. They are breathing so fast as to make each breath appear to be one continuous fog now.

Smiling, she continues to gaze down and clutches tighter to let them know that it is their love which binds them together. As they near the house, they hear other children playing outside. The screams are cheerful as they come into view. Rachel and Caleb tug gently and look up at her, sending a non-verbal cue, *May I play?*

Chapter Two

Inside the fire-fed warmth of the Hersberger's home, Jeremiah sits with his younger brother, Amos. Becky, along with her sister, Emma, is helping their mamma cook and bake. One can smell the bread as it nears removal from the wood burning oven. On the stove simmers a beef stew, just right for a cold day. The table is home for a batch of chocolate chip cookies and two shoe fly pies, still warm from the oven, that are squeezed onto what is left of the counter space.

Katie, now just shy of nine months pregnant, speaks in a low tone as she looks over at her mom, Emma.

"It shouldn't be much longer until Mary is here *mamm*," she says while rubbing the top of her belly.

Pausing, her mamm looks at her grinning, "*Jah* shouldn't be long until your new *boppli* is here, also." Emma pulls the boiling water for tea aside and pours it into the ceramic tea pot to steep.

Becky, standing in the warmth of the kitchen window, is watching the sun begin its final travel as it hides behind some trees outlined in white. While drying a cookie jar, she takes in the beauty of the winter and notices the snow and how it envelopes the scenery. Turning, she lays the cookie jar down, just washed in preparation for the cooling chocolate chip cookies. Looking slightly over her right shoulder, she catches Amos snatching one of them and scolds, "Amos, like a child, must I remind you of supper?"

"But," blurts out Amos, looking sheepish and guilty.

"No, buts! Go now, or I'll shoo you out to play with the *kinner* in the back!"

Grinning, she turns away from her brother, and back towards the scenery of shimmering white trees. She notices John's black pickup nearing the house.

John is careful as he slowly makes his way with children playing outside. They can be seen pulling each other on sleds. Slipping and falling in the snow, they laugh as if not to notice the truck until it reaches its destination near the back porch. Then, just for a moment, the children stop and stare. Then, as quickly as they had stopped, they are back playing.

Refocused, Becky now calls out, "English, English in a black truck, *jah*, nearing the end of the driveway."

Amos walks over to her vantage and spots John. "*Jah*, its John Dietrick."

Becky questions, "Who is the English with him?"

Mamma is there by this time, staring as the men get out of the truck, her eyes fill with tears. "Samuel? Is this my Samuel?" She questions in a near whisper.

Becky, in disbelief herself, whimpers, "Sammy!"

Barely overhearing his mamma and Becky, Jeremiah calls from the other room, "Samuel, where?"

And with that, the two men enter the back kitchen door, Samuel followed by John, as cold air rushes in with them. The sound of children playing and screaming can be heard outside. Then all becomes quiet and warm again when John, smiling, closes the door behind them. He shivers a bit and looks out over the gathering family. Samuel then makes their presence known.

"Mamma," he says affectionately and hesitantly as he reaches out and engulfs her with his muscular arms.

Looking up at him while in his arms and trembling she says, "Samuel, my Samuel, you are here, you are really here."

"Yes, mamma, I'm really here." They hold each other for what seems like a very long time.

When speaking again, she says, "I am going to hold you one minute for every day you were away Samuel."

"It has been a very long time, Mamma, very long," Samuel says in a low voice, as he looks out at the rest of his smiling family. Stepping back, he looks at his mamma while he holds her arms and smiles down at her.

Jeremiah approaches and with his hand stretched out, he takes Samuel's hand, looks down at their hands, and then lunges with his left arm around his youngest bruder. With tears welling his eyes, Amos wraps his arms around both his brothers; no words spoken. One could hear the tears hitting the floor.

A second later, just like little girls, his sisters pull him away. Becky cries out, "Sammy!!!" hugging him, squeezing tightly around his neck.

Emma comes from behind him and, after wiping away her own tears; she rustles his hair and kisses his left cheek. "*Willkum* home *bruder.*"

Katie, standing and holding her not yet born baby with both hands, smiles as she greets her uncle, "*Willkum* home uncle".

Stunned momentarily, Samuel light heartedly questions, "Who is this sandy haired girl who looks as though she is going to pop at any moment?"

She responds, "Katie."

Quickly coming back, he continues, "Katie? It has been a long time."

Just above a whisper, calling out into the house, a raspy voice is heard. It is *Daed's* voice.

"The noise, what is all the noise? Is everything K?" The elderly man with the gray beard, awake now, looking aged beyond his true years, calls out a little louder, "Is everything K?"

At that moment, everything becomes quiet, except for a light wind that can be heard outside as it blows through the trees just outside the windows. The dullness of the sun is now at dusk, and small footsteps can be heard crunching through the snow. Samuel, no longer smiling, looks amongst the family still carrying a faint hint of their smiles. Mamma gives a slight jerk of her head to the right towards the now silenced voice. Jeremiah says in a low voice, "Go ahead *bruder*. *Daed* has been waiting patiently for a long time."

"Go, its *gut*," states Amos.

"We were not expecting you, Samuel. He will be most surprised, jah." Mamma blends in.

Slowly, deliberately, Samuel makes his way down the hall. He spots his father's bed facing the front window and the now setting sun.

"Sam?" John's whispering voice can be heard. "You are staying awhile? How about I take your coat." Jeremiah steps in and takes both of their coats.

"Of course you are both staying for supper, *jah*." Interjects Mamma.

"Yes, of course, thanks," responds Samuel, quietly. Samuel continues to speak in an apologetic quiet voice, "*Daed?*" As he nears his left ear, he says again, "*Daed*, its Samuel." His father gingerly turns his head to the soft voice; he smiles weakly, and lifts up his left hand to the right side of his son's face. Clasping the tips of his fingers behind his neck and pulling him forward, he wipes a tear from his right cheek.

"Samuel, I've missed you so much. I feared never seeing you again."

"I'm here *Daed*, I'm here." Responds Samuel, appearing speechless and pausing before answering, "staying awhile, *sohn?*" His daed asks while smiling weakly. He then turns his head and falls asleep in total exhaustion. Samuel, with a built up lifetime of loneliness, fear, and regret, lowers his head into his father's arm and simply cries.

"I'm sorry *Daed*, I'm sorry. I am staying, yes I am."

Katie, standing behind him, caresses the side of his head, "Uncle, it's ok, *kumme*."

Samuel picks his head up, looks at Katie, then back at his father and pauses before speaking again, "Just to give back any one, any number of days, I would *daed*, I would. I am a good man *daed*. I have lived a good life and I have kept my faith, just as you taught *daed*."

With Katie now holding Samuel's arm, he stands, clears his eyes and face, and follows her into the kitchen. Katie, looking at Mary continues, "Uncle Samuel, this is my *gut* friend, Mary, and her two *kinners*, Rachel and Caleb." With a renewed smile at the children, Samuel stoops down and takes Caleb's hand and shakes it.

"Well Caleb, it's good to meet you." Turning his attention to Rachel, he adds, "And this pretty little girl, you look like your mother." Rachel smiles broadly while clasping her mother's violet dress from behind. After looking up at the tall man in blue jeans and blue plaid shirt, Caleb looks up quickly at his mother.

"He's *Englich*, Mamma." This is followed by his sister's, "Can we play with our cousins outside now, Mamma?" Just as she asks, the children in a clatter come in from the cold darkness.

"*Jah*, upstairs I suppose, but quietly, until you're called to supper." She turns to Samuel who is standing up and turning towards her.

"Mary," says Samuel as he nods, their eyes meeting for the first time, "It is nice to meet you. Are you from nearby?"

Smiling, Mary responds, "*Jah* across the street."

"Wait, the Schrock farm?" questions an astonished Samuel. A look of surprise is now pasted to his face.

"*Jah*, the Schrock farm, Samuel." Responds Mary laughing, while enjoying the surprise.

"Baby Mary; yes, I was sixteen years old and…"

He is cut off with everyone laughing now as Amos chimes in, "*Jah* seems a lot of changes there *bruder*!"

"That was us when you turned down the lane," says Mary, now looking more closely into Samuel's eyes as she continues to ask, "And Samuel, where have you been liven amongst the *Englich*?" Mary laughs at her son's pronunciation.

"North Carolina, I have a horse ranch there."

"Horses," Jeremiah speaks up, "Didn't know that *bruder*. Are there many horses? Who is watching them?"

Samuel, looking back at his brother, states, "I have a ranch manager who lives on and cares for my ranch when I'm not there."

"Well we know nothing about you *bruder*," Emma inquires, "What do you do?"

Looking right at her, avoiding the question, Samuel responds, "That sure does smell good there, Emma. What do you and mamma have cooking?"

"A full meal ain't!" smiles Emma, as she continues speaking.

"Smells like it," says Samuel walking over to the stove and finally answering, "I raise horses."

"Call the kinner for supper; we feed them first," interjects Mamma again, wiping her hands on her apron.

"*Jah* Mammi," as Katie makes her way to the stairs.

$$\mathcal{SO}\mathcal{CR}$$

The children finish their supper and the adults begin to take their seats. Jeremiah sits at the head of the table near the outside entrance to the kitchen. Jeremiah's wife and kinner are at home; the youngest kinner being ill. Amos sits with his wife, Elizabeth, who sits at his oldest brother's left. Mamma now sits to Jeremiah's right.

"Samuel, sit here next to me," Samuel's Mamma says eagerly.

"Yes, mamma," Samuel responds happily, smiling. At the same time, Katie is seating Mary between her and Samuel. The two, Mary and Samuel, look down and over at each other ever so shyly, like school children. John sits across from Samuel and Mary, smiling as he takes it all in.

"The blessing?" Mamma says.

"I would like to say the meal's blessing, mamma... Jeremiah."

"*Jah*, Samuel, *jah*," Amos agrees.

With all heads bowed, Samuel begins to speak. "Thank you, oh Lord, for the food that you have given us to nourish our bodies and our minds. Thank you for all your goodness and mercy. Thank you for friends and the fellowship of this family. And dear Lord, I thank you for bringing me home."

With that, more tears and smiles are experienced around the table as all say a heartfelt, "AMEN."

Looking around the table, Samuel inquisitively tries to catch up. "I am amazed as to how the family has grown, but obviously, not everyone is here. Lil sis, what of your family?" Becky replies with a shy smile.

"I did marry Daniel and we have two *kinner*, Esther and Deborah."

"You married that freckled face; well, he's not a kid anymore." Teases Samuel, Laughing.

"Samuel, *stoppen*. You wouldn't recognize him," retorts Becky quickly.

"No, I'm sure I wouldn't." Samuel, turning serious, smiles at his sister, remembering her as a child. Moving his attention, he addresses his other brother and his brother's wife.

"Amos and Elizabeth, how have you both been?"

Elizabeth responds while looking shyly down at the table, "*Gut, jah, gut*, and we now have five *kinner*."

"And Emma, I remember Solomon. I helped with his father's barn raising. How is he?" She is quick and bold to respond, "*Gut* Samuel; we have six *kinner*, but we would like to know about you Samuel. How many *kinner* do you have? Did you ever marry?"

Silence overcomes the table as everyone now looks at Samuel. He becomes very serious, as he folds his hands in front of his mouth, and looks down before answering, "I was married."

"What happened *bruder*?" asks Jeremiah. Samuel looks up, startled.

"We were married for about five years and one day when I was away again, she just left. Her name was Sandy. A year later, I got the divorce papers." Pausing, Samuel swallows hard.

"I heard this past fall that she was killed in a traffic accident." Samuel, changing the subject again, asks, "Jeremiah, you and Erica are well?"

"*Jah, gut*, except our youngest is on his *rumspringa*. He is a handful, not knowing where he is."

"I'm sorry, but I'm sure it will work out."

"*Jah*, if we have anything to say," interrupts Jeremiah. After thinking for a moment, he continues, "Samuel, did you go to the funeral? Did you have any *kinner*?"

Samuel, now guarded in his privacy, responds, "No Jeremiah, we didn't have any children when she left and I didn't find out about her death until after she was buried."

The dinner was finished when Jeremiah questioned Samuel about his plans. He was serious.....business like.....strained.

"Samuel, there is much going on and we would like to know, mamma and I need to know, what are your plans?"

"I've done enough. I don't sle—" Samuel, catching himself before saying too much, stops then continues, "Well, it's time for me to come home if I'm welcomed. I know I am by my family; but the people, I don't know about."

Mamma interjects for the first time saying, "The people will willkum you Samuel, jah, they will. You will become a member of the church also, *jah*?"

"Yes, mamma, that is my intention."

Jeremiah, with a hint of a smile on his face, speaks up forcefully, "*Gut*, Samuel, *gut*; we need you. You know we all own our own land, which we farm, or businesses. We have all been helping out here, but it still needs help. The barn is in need of repair, as well as this house, and the fences."

Jeremiah continuing to speak skeptically, "Samuel, *Daed* is giving you the farm."

"What!" Samuel exclaims, while staring at his brother...he is frozen in place.

"Samuel, you are the youngest; *Daed* insists. We want you to stay and farm the land." Amos, now in a full-belly laugh, puts in.

"But you will have to do something about…."

"What's that Amos?" interrupts Samuel, still in disbelief.

"You're so English, *bruder*!"

Everyone laughs, especially Mary looking over at Samuel as he continues, "Well, we will have to speak more of this." He then turns, facing Mary still looking at him.

"Mary?" asks Samuel, "Where is your husband?"

Mary shyly puts her head down, "David."

Katie, at this point, interjects, "David died about seven years ago this April; he fell from the loft in a farming accident."

Katie looks over at Mary as Samuel apologetically responds, "Ohh, I am so sorry, Mary, so sorry. It must be very hard on the children and you."

"Danki Samuel, their *Dawdi* is a big help with being there for us, me and the *kinner*. We stay with him now."

Mamma, standing now, instructs, "Well, speaking of the *kinner*, it's getting late and the *boppli's* need their sleep." John and Samuel stand quickly, looking around.

"Mary, you said you walked," says John, looking over at her. "Samuel and I will give you and the children a ride home."

"*Danki*, John, I will get the *kinner*," says Mary.

"Samuel, where are you going?" asks mamma.

"With John," he responds nonchalantly.

Mamma, now very still and concerned, disagrees, "*Nee, nee*, you will stay here." She is holding her apron with her right hand as if she were waving it.

"Ok mamma, but tomorrow, I have to go to the hotel and pick up my stuff."

"*Jah*, that's tomorrow Samuel."

"Heh John, can you help me out tomorrow?" Samuel hands John's coat to him.

"Sure thing," he says. The two men begin putting on their coats. Samuel continues, "I'll ride with you. Mary looks like she can use some help."

"Danki, Samuel. You can hold Caleb. I'll get Rachel."
Samuel takes Caleb, who is bundled against the frigidness of
the winter night, into his well toned but gentle arms. He looks
again into Mary's eyes and just holds them there before looking
down at the young child in his arms.

"Ok, Mary," he tells her while thinking to himself, *you
should see this, Daed.*

Chapter Three

Samuel fell asleep, quietly, as he reflected upon all that went on over the past twelve hours. His sleep did not go restfully. He awoke fitfully, shaking, and covered in a cold sweat twice during the night.

I don't think I screamed. No, no one is stirring. I'm the only one awake. Maybe this was not a good idea. Emma just keeps prying! Am I going to keep all this in my past? This is the second time I've gotten up. Water, where is the water? Mouth is so dry. If only I can sleep the rest of the night. What time is it? Four o'clock. Three more hours are good. Wake up. Get my stuff. Samuel takes a drink. *Three more hours, I need. Lord, help me rest quietly. Just three more hours.*

Mary, she is so beautiful. I love the wisp of sandy blond hair beneath her kapp. How old is she? Those blue eyes. Twenty eight? Couldn't take my eyes off those blue e… Falling off, he sleeps peacefully the rest of the night.

John finds Samuel waiting on the porch when he arrives the next morning. Mamma has fixed him a hardy breakfast of bacon, eggs, and homemade bread with butter and strawberry jam, his favorite since he was a child. Mamma's don't forget! It takes only what seems like a short time to get to the hotel. It takes twice as long to load the truck.

"Samuel, what the heck is in these trunks?"

"My past," says Samuel.

"Weighty," retorts John.

"What?" asks Samuel.

"Your past," quips John again as he's grunting.

"In many ways John," says Samuel. "You have no idea."

31

"Ah, heh, it's me, remember, I have some idea. Did you not sleep well again?"

"Nope, sorry John," says Samuel, as he stops momentarily and yawns.

"It's ok. Let's get you out of here and moved in."

₠⁘

By mid-morning, Samuel has checked out of the hotel, and with John's help, has moved back into his parents' home. The five locked footlockers go into one corner of his room. He chooses a room upstairs at the end of the hall, away from everyone. He finds some plain clothes to wear and wears a new black felt hat.

Daed was awake while he was gone. He ate very little before falling asleep, for a short time. He is awake when Samuel comes in.

"Good morning *daed*."

"*Guder mariye sohn*," responds his daed, turning to Samuel. Samuel notices that his father appears a little spryer. He has a little more energy.

"You seemed a little more tired yesterday, *daed*."

"*Jah*, I feel gut, your back now," says Samuel's *daed*, continuing to talk.

"Yes *daed*, for good. I have some loose ends to take care of, but I'm here to stay."

"You are to move in and stay here Samuel."

"Yes *daed*, Jeremiah already explained last night. He also says I'm to take over the farm. Are you sure about this?"

"*Jah*, I am sure. I am always sure of what I say, Samuel. Now, Jeremiah has told you, this is *gut*! I suppose you can't tell me about where you been these many years?"

"A long story, but *daed* you must know, I have led a good life. I have been a faithful servant to our Lord and I have never lied, cheated, or stolen, *daed*; I have remained a good man."

"I know. I never had any doubt. Your life took you in another direction. The Bishop would not agree, but I know you had a much higher calling by God to something I will not understand until I go home to the Lord. I have missed you though," says *daed* with understanding for his son.

"I have missed you all also, but I'm home now," reassures Samuel.

ℰℭ

Though they are new order, their family having broken away from the old ways and the *ordnung*, one thing has not changed. They cling to the plain life. They have changed their faith, realizing salvation by God's grace and the importance of a personal relationship with Jesus Christ.

Sunday came and with it, worship service. The men sit on one side, the women on the other. Mamma stays at home in order to watch daed as Samuel goes to service and meets with the Bishop.

While there, he lets the Bishop know briefly about his past. He speaks about his ranch in North Carolina and of being married before and losing his wife because his business took him away from her. He also speaks about her death.

He tells the Bishop that he feels uncomfortable about speaking of his business affairs. The Bishop, more concerned about his future, asks if he has come back to place his past behind him. Samuel assures him that it will take some time to finally finish with his past, but it will be done.

As he sits down, he looks up and spots the first of his surprises; Amos standing in front, preparing to begin the service. *Well, I'll be, my brother the preacher.*

At that moment, he turns his head and looks around to spot his sister and Katie sitting with Mary and her two children across the aisle. The women, one in a dark blue dress and the other in gray, both wear white *kapps* and sit on each side of Mary's two children. Mary looks up to catch Samuel's eyes.

33

Oh Samuel, what am I feeling? You are much older, I know. What is it that I am feeling, naer fich, verra naerfich. But these feelings are gut, wunderbaar gut. Let me look at your face one time more; your blue eyes Samuel. What am I feeling? Mary offers a gentle smile and then looks away.

They both look up at Samuel's brother as he begins the service with a prayer. "Lord, we thank thee for bringing us all here in safety, united family and friends, to worship and glorify you. Comfort us with your presence on this day of rest and open our hearts and minds to hear your words. Words that we need to help us heal, to understand, to grow in community and live together in peace and love. We thank you again Lord, for your love for us and for our salvation, Amen."

"Amen," comes from everyone as they stand and begin singing Amazing Grace. It isn't in harmony, but it surely is a joyful noise unto the Lord. The sermon is on forgiveness and the importance of not judging and measuring, as Amos reflects on the words found in Matthew 7:1 and Mark 11: 25-26.

Reflective, Samuel ponders. *There are times I have listened to sermons and felt that the sermon was about me... Today, I know it's about me, with my brother preaching on forgiveness. There are many who may feel compelled to judge, and only for the things they know about me. Would they feel the same way if they truly knew my past? I hope they would offer forgiveness, but more importantly, that they never find out.*

Mary, I feel so close to you, but right now the timing is awful, absolutely awful. But during my courting years, you were but a baby. But you are...Lord give me wisdom...... pay attention to the sermon, Hersberger, pay attention.

The entire Hersberger family goes to their homestead to see dad. Many buggies arrive and the horses are taken to the barn and fed. Sandwiches of ham and cheese are made, relishes and cole- slaw dished out; potato and macaroni salads, which were made earlier, are also opened.

All the while, dad, who is now awake, enjoys a bit of lunch himself. The family takes turns sitting with him. And while he is feeling a bit better, it is also a good time for grandchildren to visit with their grandfather. This Sunday goes well for dad.

Outside, clouds have moved in, the wind begins to blow, and a feel of snow is in the air. Stepping outside, the wind cuts through coats like sharp shards of glass. It's picked up already, laying icy snow as it can be heard from the inside, pelting the kitchen window.

Samuel, coming from his daed's room, finds Katie helping the kinner with their plates. Looking at the wind blowing, she is startled by Samuel as he enters.

"Katie, did Mary come over?" Katie looks up and walks over to Samuel.

"No, I'm sorry Uncle Samuel, she didn't." With a smile on her face and holding her unborn baby with her right hand, she reaches out and clutches her uncle's right arm. Peering at her uncle, Katie is serious as she questions, "Is Mary turning into someone special for you, uncle?"

"I don't know, I can't take my eyes off of her when she's around."

"And she can't you, either." Now raising her eyes and smiling broadly.

"Huh?" Samuel responds stunned.

"Uncle Samuel, tell me you haven't noticed." Katie continues to smile while she shifts.

"Well, I hoped," says Samuel.

"*Jah*, you hoped," Katie teases.

"But, our ages?" asks Samuel, raising his voice in concern.

"Uncle, Mary is no longer a kinner. She is a woman with two of her own."

"Katie, are you playing match maker?" as Samuel gives a nervous laugh. Laughing back, Katie tugs her uncle's arm.

"Uncle Samuel, seems the two of you are already doing that *ain't?*" And with that mamma calls, "It's time for dinner you two. What is all the whispering about?"

"We're not whispering, *grossmammi*, just talking with Uncle Samuel."

With the sun beginning to set, the many Hersberger families go home early. The house is now quiet, except for the wind blowing outside, which could be heard whistling through the not so well sealed windows. Looking out, Samuel can see the cold as it hangs on the trees, spread across the fields in perfect whiteness. Gray hangs in the air over the fields of Honey Brook. Broken cornstalks remind Samuel of many broken homes he has witnessed during his time of being English.

It will snow tomorrow, end Tuesday. That's right, Amanda said a nor'easter was on its way. I wonder how she is doing, Amanda Russo. How long does daed have? He is in very little pain now, but what of the end? Lord, let him pass peacefully. I would not be able to see him suffer; I have seen so much suffering, not my father. Hospice was here earlier in the week. Mamma felt care wasn't needed, but the medicine was accepted as suggested by the doctor. I wonder what the medicine is. I will have to ask mamma.

"Mamma," says Samuel as he turns from the back kitchen window and questions, "How's *daed*?"

"Sleeping, I just changed his bed linens." Mamma can be seen laying a laundry basket down from the front bedroom as she wipes her forehead with the bottom of her apron.

Samuel speaks up, "I could have helped." A look of concern comes over Samuel as he approaches his mamma.

"No, I am his *fraa*, and it is for me to do, I want to do this Samuel, alone, *danki*"

Samuel, stooping, looks into her eyes as he takes her by the shoulders and whispers, "Ok mamma, I understand,"

"*Danki* Samuel," says mamma as Samuel hugs her.

"*Daed* was speaking to me. He was asking if I am going to be ok."

"He was asking everyone Samuel. He needs to know we will be ok when he leaves. Your *daed* spent a lifetime providing and he needs to know that he can leave."

"I understand. This is very difficult mamma?"

"*Jah*, most difficult, *jah*," says mamma.

"Well it's getting late, past couple of days have been very busy. Are you going to bed mamma?" Speaking in German, mamma answers, *"Kein Sohn, will ich hier mit ihnensitzen vater, noch eine weile."*

"Don't sit up with *Daed* too long mamma, you need your rest."

"Ich will nicht, ich danke ihnen Samuel, gute Nacht," she responds.

"Gut mama, *gut nacht."* Samuel's mother, Rebecca, sits next to her husband and looks around at Samuel as he bends over and kisses her left cheek. Then he reaches for his daed and kisses his father's forehead. *"Gut nacht daed."*
Samuel sleeps soundly until he wakes. There are no nightmare or cold sweats. *What's wrong? I cannot place what's wrong. Something is wrong! Daed!*

Quickly putting on his pants, and in a near panic, he runs downstairs, around the corner into his daed's room. He finds his mamma there dabbing his dad's forehead with a damp cloth. He is in obvious pain, wincing, and sweating heavily. Saturated, he is no longer conscious where he should have been because he is in pain, no doubt.

"Mamma, something woke me. I was so afraid of this."

"Samuel, I don't know how to relieve his pain." She speaks with tears in her eyes.

"Where is the medicine the doctor gave you mamma? Do you know what it is for?"

"No," responds mamma. Samuel begins peering at the papers and medicines on the bureau top.

"Let me see." *Papers, lots of papers, here we go instruction, Morphine sulfate 20mg per 1cc give 5mg every 4 hours for pain or labored breathing. It's in a small bottle. How much is 5mg? A quarter of 20 mg? That would make it a quarter of 1cc, .25cc what in the...is a cc? Here's the bottle and the eye dropper. There it is, a quarter of cc. But, he's out. Got to make a call. Phone number. Hospice phone number: 494 200 1200; cell number on call. Phone. No phone. My blackberry.*

"Mamma, I have to run upstairs a minute. I'll be right back."

With a broken voice, she responds, barely audible, "*Jah*, Samuel?"

Samuel sprints up the stairs. *Keys for the trunks. Yes.* He opens the trunk and finds the Blackberry resting on top of his past. It was the last thing to be put away. *The number, 494 200 1200.* Ringing only twice, a man answers.

"Tranquility Hospice, Bill Reilly, may I help you?"

"Mr. Reilly, my name is Sam Hersberger. My father is David Hersberger. He is a patient of yours and I need to speak to a nurse, I suppose."

"Mr. Hersberger, I'm an RN. Just take a moment and catch your breath…Now, sir, what's the problem?"

"My father is having a lot of pain. I have his pain medicine, Morphine Sulfate, but he is not conscious to take it."

"That isn't a problem, sir. Draw up the right amount, and then put the dropper inside of his mouth, putting it under his tongue and squeeze. Or, if that is a problem put it inside of his cheek and squeeze," instructs the nurse.

"Won't he choke?" questions Samuel.

"No sir, is there anything else?"

"No, on my way, thank you," says Samuel.

"Yes sir, call back any time, I personally will be here until 7 a.m."

"Thanks again," says Samuel as he disconnects his blackberry, laying it down on his bed, then sprints back toward his daed.

Samuel, arriving downstairs, finds his mamma now whispering to his daed.

"*Mein Schatz, es wird in Ordnung sein, lassen Sie gehen, ich liebe, aber seine Zeit, nach Hause zu unserem Vater zu gehen.*"

"Mamma, I found out what to do." He gives the morphine to his father inside his cheek.

"Yes mamma, it will be ok. I never thought I would say this, but it is time for daed to go home to our father." *I have seen so much suffering, not my daed. Not my daed. I should have been here to help. It was my responsibility, but I left.*

"No more suffering," says Samuel, as he sits and watch's his daed. It takes about half an hour but daed quiets down and sleeps in silence. After drying off the love of her life once more, Mamma goes to sleep in the second room on the first floor.

Samuel wakes and checks on the heat. Then, checking on the both of them, he finds his Mamma and Daed are still sleeping, which is unusual for Mamma. He looks outside and finds that it is now snowing heavily. A fresh white snow lies on the ground and everything on top is outlined in white.

Samuel prepares, to his mamma's surprise, ham and eggs. She wakes up to the *gut* smells coming from the kitchen. *Let's see, it's Monday, just like Russo said; where is everything at? Put more wood in the kitchen stove. There's gas in the house, but a wood cooking stove?*

"Sit mamma, breakfast is done." With a kitchen towel, he lifts the kitchen skillet over to her plate carefully lifting out the eggs he has just prepared.

"*Danki* Samuel." As the two eat, she looks at all the food that he prepared.

"Samuel, where did you learn to cook like this?" Mamma looks inquisitively at her son. Picking up a piece of bacon with his fingers, he looks over at her and smiles while shaking the bacon.

"I have lived most of my life on my own. If a man wants to eat…and eat well… he has to learn how to cook." His mamma then laughs.

The two eat and mamma insists on cleaning up afterward. Samuel dresses warmly in clothes he has from his time of being English. He goes out and begins to shovel some of the snow from the back porch and makes a path to the barn so he can get to, and care for, the livestock. Monday's shoveling rolls into Tuesday with a total of seven inches coming to rest on the little town of Honey Brook.

Chapter Four

Daed is kept comfortable with the morphine, except now it is being given every two hours. As Samuel steps out onto the back porch filled with snow once again, he can hear a large truck making its way down Horseshoe Pike.

It's a state truck plowing, which is going to make for some interesting work down at the edge of the drive there. He proceeds to shoveling the overwhelming heaps. Completing the porch, he begins on the drive when he is met with a surprise. Coming down the drive with an overpowering sweep is John and his pickup with the plow. John is behind the wheel with a broad grin. Cleanup of the snow takes less than an hour with plowing. John climbs down out of his truck and gestures to his friend.

"Sam, I thought we would make the rounds and clean up some drive ways, family and all, ya know."

"Ok, let's do that. Where do you want to start, John?"

"Well, let's see, where do I think you want to start, Mr. Schrock's place, maybe? Hmm, yep, I think you would like to start there." Samuel, looking forward to this break, smiles as his mind goes straight to Mary.

Bounding up the back porch steps, he sticks his head in the back door, bringing the cold with him, and calls out, "Mamma! I'm gonna help John with some digging family and friends out. Is *daed* Ok?" He spots her with her apron in hand, lifting out a pie from the oven.

She turns to him, "*Jah, jah,* he is gut right now, sleeping, go ahead."

Running back outside, he reaches the truck and settles himself into it. Pointing towards the end of the drive, he directs kiddingly, "Onward buddy!"

A minute later, they are pushing their way into the Schrock's driveway, with an astonished Mr. Schrock looking on with a shovel in his hand.

"You English in the truck there, what are ya doin?"

The truck stops and Samuel steps out into deep snow, "Mr. Schrock, it's me, Samuel Hersberger."

"Samuel!? *jah*, it's you, *jah*. Mary said you were back. What are you doing in that truck?" Mr. Schrock is now leaning on the snow shovel with both hands, winded.

"This is my friend, John. You remember John? He helped as a teenager during the barn raising."

"*Jah, jah*, I remember, *gut buwe* John," Mr. Schrock says as John is out of the truck by now. He approaches Mr. Schrock, shaking his hand for the first time.

John interjects, "Sorry to startle you sir, thought we would give a hand to some friends and family with the snow, hope we aren't intruding?"

"Surprised, *jah*; not intruding. Well, *willkum* the both of you, and *danki*. Lot of snow, ain't so. I'll get Mary to put on some more coffee."

"*Danki*, Mr. Schrock." Samuel takes the shovel while John makes quick work with the truck. Inside of half an hour, the two find themselves walking up the back steps to the kitchen. Mary meets them.

"*Danki* John, *Danki* Samuel." As her eyes meets Samuel's again, she quickly looks away toward her father saying, "It was a lot of snow last night. My *dat* is not a *kinner* anymore, but you can't tell him though."

Defensively, her dad adds quickly, "Daughter, what are you saying? I'm not in my box yet either."

"*Jah dat*, but you must take it easy. I worry about you." Turning now toward Samuel, she inquires as to his *daed*, "Samuel, how is your *dat*?" As they enter the house, he looks at Mary standing and holding the door.

"Without pain at the present. He hasn't been awake for a while now." The men sit around the table. Mary pours cups of coffee for the three. She then places sticky buns on the center of the table. Samuel reaches for the cream as Mary does and their hands meet.

Feeling her warmth, he looks up into her eyes again. This time they linger, only for a second, but for Mary it is a lifetime. As Mary goes to pull away, she is emboldened, and clasps Samuel's fingers for a second, then goes about excusing herself. Samuel pauses after looking down at their fingers, then lifts the creamer and pours cream into his coffee.

"Excuse me, Samuel, you go." *Lord, is this man for me?*

"Thank you, Mary" *By your will Lord, hope it is your will.*

They visit for just less than an hour, Mary and Samuel casually exchanging glances at each other as small talk is made. Then they are off to visit Samuel's brothers and sisters as they open every driveway. By the time they finish, there isn't much shoveling left to do. They head back to Samuel's. It is three o'clock on this Tuesday afternoon of February 6th. Samuel is met at the back door by his mother. "It's your daed, Samuel."

"Is he?" questions Samuel, with panic in his voice.

"No, but his breathing has become irregular," says his mamma. Samuel, without taking off his winter coat and with John following, goes to his father's room. *Daed* is now taking a couple of breaths; he will stop breathing, take a few more breaths, stop, then many rapid breaths, and then stop again.

Mamma is there; she strokes his hair and holds his face. Samuel, as he holds his daed's hand, tells him that all will be well, and it is ok to go. John stands in the background next to the bedroom door.

Daed, opens his eyes, beaming out into space as though looking at someone, smiles, closes his eyes, takes a couple more slow breaths, then passes over to Jesus. No more pain. No more medicine.

"*Bliss, daed, und nun bist du ganz gemacht.*"

"Yes, *sohn*, your *daed* is now made whole," said mamma.

"I am so sorry, Mrs. Hersberger. Samuel, I'm sorry. What can I do to help?" There is a pause. "I will, with your permission. I can gather the family?" John quietly asks his best friend and his mamma.

"Yes John, thanks," says Samuel. After John leaves, dad is cleaned and a clean dry bed shirt is put on him. John goes back and forth notifying and bringing home the Hersberger family. Some come by buggy, as they are already on their way to visit.

Because of the roads, they spend the night, utilizing all the bedrooms they can in the main house, and the now unused *dawdi* house. Samuel's siblings, after visiting, stay at the *dawdi* house.

After nightfall, everyone having had time to visit, the undertaker comes to pick up dad. With care, he is placed into the back of the undertaker's station wagon and taken away. Dad is looked after, and then on Thursday he is returned, where he is placed in a plain pine box.

The viewing is held at the Hersberger's home in the front room. The funeral held that Friday, though solemn, is not outwardly mournful, except for Samuel, who has missed a lot of his father and his family in the many decades.

Mary has a hard time of it also. The last time she was at a funeral was her husband's. In many different ways, it has reminded her of that time. It has also reminded her of her loneliness.

෴

Out on the road Friday, during the funeral, sits a lone white GMC suburban; inside two men look on, "Sir, are you going down to pay your respects?" Tom asks earnestly.

Chris responds somberly, "No, Tom, I promised him a couple of months. Seeing me, he may think I'm pushing. No, I wanted to be here to pay my respects from a distance. I'll send my regrets later on by mail. Listen; keep an ear open for me though. If you hear anything, let me know, ok?"

"Yes, sir, will do," responds a dutiful Tom, as they pull out quietly and drive away.

℘℃

There is a common meal after the funeral at the Hersberger's farm. Samuel appears deep in thought as he stands looking out the kitchen window at the cold on the mid afternoon farm. Jeremiah quietly approaches Samuel.

"Samuel? Mamma, Katie and I would like to speak with you, when you feel you can."

"*Jah, bruder*, when?" responded Samuel, as he quickly turns around.

"Now would be a *gut* time, *jah*," says Jeremiah. Jeremiah, Katie and mamma sit at the kitchen table.

"*Sohn*, I will be leaving here tomorrow," says mamma to Samuel.

"Katie will be having her *boppli* soon and I will be helping her at her home."

"Mamma, I didn't know this. Where will you be staying?"

"They have built a *dawdi* house attached to their home. We have had this planned for quite awhile now, although, I had not planned to move until later."

"Uncle, I am due in a week. If it is a problem though…"

"No, No, oh Katie, no, it isn't a problem. Everything is moving so fast, that's all."

"*Bruder*, if you need any help here, you're other *brieder* and I will be nearby."

"Well, I haven't had time to plan what to do. Let me think on this, ok?"

"Ok *bruder*." Jeremiah goes back into the front room, which now expands out into the front bedroom to make room for the many guests and family members. Samuel stands up and resumes his position at the kitchen window.

44

It is just a moment, a moment to reflect on the past few days, a moment to reflect on his life, a moment to think about and miss his *daed*, a moment when he moves into his *daed's* shadow. As he looks out the window, his mind comes back to…. *Daed*.

Chapter Five

Monday, the twelfth of February, on the ranch in Aberdeen, North Carolina, ranch manager Bill Kramer sits in his office within the confines of the barn. It is a cool and overcast day. It is busy from the standpoint of ranch life when a new foul is born. In the office the phone rings, "SH Ranch Incorporated. This is Bill Kramer."

"Bill, Sam here."

"Sam, how the heck are ya there?"

"Well, good as can be expected. My daed died and now I'm feeling a little like fish in someone else's pond." Samuel is numb, speaking clinically.

"I'm sorry Sam. It looks as though ya got back there just in time."

"Thanks Bill, anyhow, how're things down there?" asks Samuel.

"Ok, the foal was born right afta ya left and we had the vet out the next day to check on him and the mare."

"That's great! Well, I have something for you to ponder with the missus, but I have to know pretty quickly what you want to do, ok?"

"Yes sir, what's up?" asks Bill dutifully.

"Well, I've been given the farm up here," states Samuel.

"The farm! What-r-ya gonna do with a farm now? You're a ranch man!"

"Well, that's where you come in. You ready for this?"

"Yep, go ahead."

"Well, I'm not about to manage two spreads, especially so far apart. So my thinkin is to sell down there, and move the ranch as we know it to Pennsylvania. Now, where you come in, do you feel like relocating to Lancaster, Pennsylvania?" Samuel asks matter-of-factly.

"Stay on as your ranch manager?" Bill questions, enthusiastically.

"Yes, wouldn't have it any other way. Don't want to lose ya there, buddy."

"Well, like ya said, hafta run it past the wife," says Bill.

"Well, speak with her tonight and get back to me as soon as possible, ok?"

"OK boss, call y'all on this number?" asks Bill.

"Yep!" Samuel quickly responds.

"Good talken to ya, Sam."

"Same here, Bill."

Have to bring the family together; get this thing on the road. Let's see… livestock's been fed, cows milked and put out to pasture. There are lots of repairs to do, lots of changes. Well, time to hook up the buggy and do some visiting. Have to get used to riding behind these animals instead of on top. I'm still thinking like I'm in the south. Changes, so many changes, but to Jeremiah's first. Lord, you have seen me through many a tougher spot.

₨₧

Jeremiah lives on an adjoining farm to the rear of what is now Samuel's. Even so, by road it is still a couple of miles away. Arriving at Jeremiah's, Samuel climbs down out of his buggy and lets out a call, "JEREMIAH!"

Jeremiah appears to already be coming out of the barn with a harness in hand. Smiling, he responds in kind, kidding, and yelling back, "SAMUEL! Heard your buggy come in, *jah*. How are you *bruder*?"

"Good, Jeremiah."

"*Gut*." As he shakes his younger *bruder's* hand.

"Can we sit down and talk?" Samuel is now serious.

"*Jah*, inside, get some coffee." Jeremiah waves toward the house. Samuel continues as they climb the stairs toward the back door.

"You have a farm. Jeremiah, but I don't know what everyone else does." Entering the kitchen, Samuel sits down. Jeremiah answers thoughtfully as he pours the cups of coffee and lays out sugar and cream.

"Ahh, let's see, Emma's husband makes memorials, he works with stone in town. Amos has a small farm, besides what he does as a carpenter; it helps sustain him and his family. *Er ist auch ein Zimmermann. Jah, er und Becky ehemann Daniel,*" speaking comfortably, Jeremiah continues to speak in German.

"So Daniel and Amos are carpenters? This is good, Jeremiah." Jeremiah, now sitting, faces his *bruder*. As Samuel prepares his coffee he addresses the hardened farmer sitting opposite him.

"Jeremiah, I am going to continue raising horses. My plan is to sell my ranch in North Carolina and move my assets here to Lancaster." The two men pause and look at each other while holding their individual cups of coffee.

"I want to give you and Amos the livestock and feed. What I would like in return is to help out Emma and Becky with what comes from the livestock, if that is ok with you?" Another thoughtful pause from Jeremiah as he continues to listen in earnest to what his brother has to say.

"*Jah*, Samuel, we can do this. When would you want to start?" agrees Jeremiah. Picking up his cup he takes a sip of his hot, black coffee.

"Right away. I'll hire Daniel and Amos if they're free. I would like to keep the work and money within the family. We can begin to expand corrals and stalls for the animals where we need to. Then I'll have work for them to do at what will be the ranch."

"Ok, Samuel. Its gut to hear you settling down here so quickly, the family will think it *wunderbaar gut,*" Jeremiah states.

"It's a lot of work. They can hire who they might to help out."

"*Gut.*" Jeremiah agrees again.

A week later Bill has agreed to move his family and himself to Lancaster. Initially, the plan is to move from Aberdeen, North Carolina to the *dawdi* house on the ranch. It would keep him close as they essentially begin a new business. There is enough room in the *dawdi* house attached to the rear of the main house now handed down to Samuel. It is clean and still has some furniture from his grandparents who 'passed' a long time ago, while he was still at school.

Samuel talks his brother and brother-in-law into taking money for their labors, convincing them it is his opportunity to give back in some small way.

More stalls are put in place to hold the herd of cows being added to both farms. Barn space is reallocated to make room for the stalls. Two more chicken coops are built, and two more sheds for pigs that the other two farms have very little of.

With the extra livestock come extra responsibilities. Chores amongst the children are divided again. The children, though somewhat burdened, are also excited about their 'new uncle' and all that is going on, bringing excitement to the families.

Being extremely busy, Samuel has little time to socialize. He does, however, make time for some of the women in his life. Katie has her baby a little later than she thought.

Samantha arrives on the nineteenth of February. He visits that following Saturday with Katie, the new baby, and his mother. All are present for a quiet afternoon together. Katie, his niece, is turning out to be a special friend. And with Katie comes a new friend in her husband, Andrew.

Andrew is strong and interested in horses. He helps with trimming hooves and shoeing horses in the community. I'll have to offer Andrew a job when we get going. We can use his talent.

While there, they have an unexpected visitor. As Samuel goes to the back door to see who has arrived, he can see first the outline of a black bonnet in the window of the kitchen door, then what appear to be those familiar wisps of hair.

As he closes in on the door, Mary comes very clearly into sight. *Mary!! Oh how I missed you. You surely are looking good. Get the door Hersberger.*

"Mary, it's wonderful to see you. This really is a pleasant surprise," says Samuel.

"*Guder mariye*! Samuel. It's *gut* to see you also." Mary, looking surprised, smiles at Samuel before attempting to move past him. Because Samuel has not moved out of the doorway right away, Mary begins to brush past, her face within inches of his own. They don't need to, but they pause right there. Mary continuing to smile widely before letting out a nervous giggle. She covers her mouth and looks down and makes her way into the kitchen. *Samuel, if you only knew how you make me feel.*

"Samuel, it's gut to see you," repeats Mary.

"You said that, it's good to see you, too." Samuel is smiling broadly now himself.

"Mary, can we speak some…" Samuel is cut short in his conversation.

"Samuel is that Mary?" calls Katie over the commotion in the kitchen.

"Yes, it's Mary!" He looks once more at Mary and smiles.

"Maybe later Mary, we can talk?"

"*Jah*, ok Samuel, I would like to speak with you also sometime." Mary walks toward the front room looking over her left shoulder as she speaks.

Samuel continues his gaze. "Good, wonderful," he says.

At the end of Mary's visit, Samuel excuses himself before following Mary out the door. As they leave, they bid everyone a good evening. Mamma and Katie with baby in arm, move towards the kitchen to see them out. As the back door closes, Samuel calls from the top step, "Mary!"

He sees his breath in the air as he catches Mary's attention; she turns to him, both of them standing on the snowy driveway.

Responding pleasantly, but not unexpectedly Mary says, "Jah Samuel." Smiling slightly she is visibly cold with her arms crossed in front of her.

Continuing to force the words Samuel says, "I'm not very good at this. It's been a very long time, but Mary…"

Continuing to smile she interrupts, "Jah, Samuel."

"This is not as easy as I thought it was going to be," he comments under his breath. *I feel like an English teenager asking a girl out for the first time.* He rubs his hands together in front of his face as he has so many other times standing in the cold.

Mary, acting like she doesn't know what's going on, continues. "What isn't?" she asks teasingly.

"Mary, I know that we have a lot of years between us, but I really have feelings for you." *There I said it, I really said it. Please feel the same way.*

Mary walks closer to Samuel and looks up deeply into his eyes, as she thinks to herself, *Oh Samuel, how my heart has longed to hear these words.* Struggling, she finally grasps what he has said and responds in kind, "Samuel, I have feelings for you, also." A tear traces down her cheek as both eyes well.

Lifting his left hand he wipes a tear with his thumb while caressing her cheek with his finger tips. Having been a very long time since he has had any contact with a woman, he can now feel the warmth of her face. He is drawn to take her and kiss her right then and there, but just steps closer and says, "Mary."

Feeling the warmth of his breath and catching the scent of mint, she responds, "Jah Samuel." They now feel the longing between the two of them.

"I'm really nervous," he says, as they both laugh.

"I'm *naerfich* also, *jah*," says Mary looking aside.

"Will you go out with me?" asks Samuel, his hands now dropping and taking both of hers as he rubs the back of them with his thumbs. She raises her right hand, with his still in place, to wipe another single tear with the back of his hand.

"Samuel, you want me to be your *aldi*?"

"*Aldi*? Girlfriend? Yes, Mary, Yes! Can I pick you up sometime for a date?"

"A date?" Laughing, she continues to tease as she cries with happiness.

"Samuel, you are so English! Do you wish to court me?"

"Yes. I've never done this before," responds Samuel nervously.

"What, courting, Samuel?" she asks teasingly, and continues to act nonchalant and excited at the same time.

"Yes, courting," responds Samuel again nervously. It is Samuel who is now getting excited.

"Samuel, when would you like to see me?"

"Ahh, next Sunday evening, six o'clock, is this OK?"

"*Gut, dat* can watch the *kinner*."

"OK, next Sunday then." Wanting to take her in his arms and kiss her on the lips, he cautiously leans over slightly and kisses Mary's forehead. Still, holding her hands, he leads her, then helps her into her buggy, pulling the blanket up over her legs to cover her. The two leave in their own separate buggies while Katie and Mamma, unbeknownst to the two of them, watch on from the window, both grinning from ear to ear.

That first Sunday in March could not come fast enough for Mary or Samuel. Samuel wants to do something special for their first date. *Something quiet and intimate, that's what I want to share with Mary. Now where can we go that is quiet and intimate? Good food. Let's see. I haven't been here in so long, John, I must call John. Blackberry. Need my Blackberry. On top of the kitchen table.* Locating his Blackberry, Samuel could not enter the number fast enough.

"Hello, Sam is that you?" John answers his phone, confused.

"Hi John, yes it's me," Says Samuel.

"I recognized your number. Just didn't expect a call from you," responds John.

"John, I have a big favor to ask," says Samuel with growing excitement in his voice.

"What can I do for you? You don't need me to move those foot lockers for you again, right?"

"Ha! No, but I do have a date," says Samuel.

"A date? With Mary!" Excitement can now be heard in John's voice.

"Yes, how did you know?" asks Samuel.

"Samuel, it's me! What do you need?"

"Two things: the first, an intimate place to eat; and the second, a mode of modern transportation."

"You want that intimate, too?" teases John.

"Ok buddy!"

"You're allowed transportation. Small limo, you just can't do a stretch, a smaller sedan. I know someone I use. I'll give him a call. The place: there is an inn in Kimberton, overlooking a water wheel and a small lake I believe. How does all that sound?"

"I'm speechless, John. Thank you very much. You've always been a good friend, John. I owe you!"

"You owe me nothing, Sam, don't mention it ok?"

"Ok, and thanks again." As he ends the call on his Blackberry, he reflects back thinking again of his father. *She is truly a wonderful woman, daed!*

Chapter Six

March fourth comes very slowly for both Mary and Samuel. But it comes, and with it new things for Mary. Courting again, courting with kinner, courting an older man. Courting an older man who knows more of the English than being Amish. It could be a very confusing time if Mary was not looking forward to this evening. As she hurriedly puts the finishing touches on herself, she speaks to her kinner.

"Rachel, Caleb, *kommen jetzt hier, bitte*."

"*Jah mamm*, we're coming," yells Caleb.

"Hurry Rachel, *mamm* wants us."

"Remember, I'm going out tonight, jah."

"*Jah* Mamm, with Mr. Hersberger?"

"*Jah*, Rachel."

"Why?" chimes in a protective Caleb.

"Because, Ach! I didn't know this is going to be this hard! I like Samuel a lot."

"Does he want to be our new *daed*?" questions a hopeful Rachel.

"We are not to speak about this Caleb, Rachel, *verstehen*? We are courting. You will learn about this later, ok?"

"*Jah mamm*, we understand." Caleb smiles, then looks up as footsteps from their grandfather can be heard from above.

"Gut! Be polite," quips Mary while smiling over at her two standing on the bottom step.

"Ok," was heard the two tiny voices in unison.

Looking down at herself, Mary smooth's out her dress, and her apron and makes one last check of all the pins holding

54

everything neatly in place. Then a quick look in the mirror to check her hair, twisted and under her *kapp* properly. *There... now just right. Ach, this is supposed to be so much easier when I'm older ain't? The time, five minutes till six, jah, anytime now.*

"*Dat*! I'll be leaving shortly."

"Ok, be careful out there with the English, daughter."

"*Dat*, Samuel's Amish."

"*Jah*, half pound of feathers worth!"

"*Dat!*" she responds with a smile.

He smiles back at her while coming down the stairs. With headlights coming down the driveway, he says again, "English, *jah*, eat *gut*."

"*Dat!*" Mary is now laughing and shaking her head no. He smiles again at his daughter, then easing on the kidding around he reassures her, "Don't be troubled none about the *kinner* daughter, they'll be fine."

"*Danki, dat!*" Excitement now sounding in her voice. There is a knock at the front door. Mary jumps, then opens the door to a cold breeze and is moved to an overwhelming smile. *Naerfich* she invites him in, "*Kumme, Kumme* in Samuel. *Dat*, Samuel is here!"

"*Willkum* Samuel," he says while smiling. Kiddingly, he then says, "You look plain, *Jah*!"

"*Dat!*" says a rosy faced Mary now nervously laughing as she is embarrassed.

"Eat *gut*, Samuel, Mary," while in a full laugh after teasing his daughter, but again.

"*Danki dat!*" Mary now turns toward the front door and looks at Samuel.

"Mr. Schrock, good evening sir," Samuel says looking over Mary's shoulder before he turns to leave.

"*Gut* evening Samuel," Mr. Schrock responds.

෧෬

Stepping carefully over leftover ice and snow from the last snow storm of the season, they approach the car. The driver opens the car door for Mary and Samuel and then closes it. He drives out of the driveway and proceeds to take a left onto Horseshoe Road, heading for Kimberton. The drive should last about forty-five minutes.

As the drive gets underway, Mary, finally alone with Samuel for the first time begins by saying, "Hello Samuel, it's *gut* to see you," as she turns her head and looks at Samuel's profile, again thinking to herself." *Du bist so schon, Samuel. Jah, so handsome.*

"Hi, Mary," says Samuel as he turns toward her to meet her eyes. "How are you and the children?"

"I'm gut Samuel; the kinner, gut also. Where are we going?" Mary asks inquisitively.

"Dinner, it's a surprise," says Samuel leaning forward now as though telling a secret. Mary continues, "Far away with a driver and no courting buggy, *Jah*?"

"*Jah*," says Samuel as he returns her smile.

෨෬

Samuel and Mary arrive at the Inn in Kimberton. The driver comes around and opens the door for Mary and offers her his hand to assist her out of the car. She hesitates momentarily before giving the well dressed gentleman her hand and smiles at him.

"Danki," says Mary.

"You're welcome, ma'am. Sir, I'll be parked over in that spot. I'll begin to watch for you in an hour and a half," says the driver, now turning his attention to Samuel.

"That will be fine, thank you," says Samuel responding to the driver.

They walked up the broad steps to the wide, main doors of the Inn. As they enter, a harp can be heard playing. Once inside, the harpist can be seen. Mary is looking all around in awe. She is speechless as she takes in the beauty of sight and sound all around her.

"Oh my, this is fancy," says Mary.

"No, this is not fancy, Mary. Very nice but not fancy. Nor is it expensive. Is it ok?"

"Jah, I like the music Samuel," says Mary, as she turns and looks at Samuel with a Smile.

Being shown their seats, Samuel takes Mary's left hand and leads her to the front of him, putting his right hand on her back. She looks over her left shoulder while following the hostess.

"This is *wunderbaar* gut," says Mary still looking around at the other people seated.

"I'm so glad you like it"

The hostess pulls out both chairs where Samuel seats Mary, then himself.

"*Sie verwohnen mich* Samuel."

"You are not spoiled, nor can I ever do enough to spoil you, Mary."

"Your understanding of German is *gut*," says Mary.

"I used it in school and, until recently, I used it for work."

"When would you use German for raising horses?"

"Mary, the food I understand is *wunderbaar gut*." Mary smiles at his avoidance of her question, remembering how he used food to avoid a similar question.

"I'm sorry, Samuel. Is there a time when I will ever know what you did amongst the English?"

"Yes, but only a little. It is important to me that you know that the things I did, I did for the good of man. I care for you, Mary. I haven't known you long, but I can tell you that my feelings for you are real and sincere. I would never do anything deliberately to hurt you. Never."

"I care for you, also, Samuel. My *kinner* wants to know if you want to be their new *daed*. I'm sorry, I should not have said that," throwing both hands up to her mouth.

"It's ok, don't be embarrassed," says Samuel.

"The things they were saying were so funny. What do I say when they ask why I was going out?"

"What did you say?" Smiling now, Samuel had to ask.

"Oh my, I'm about to embarrass myself again. I told them, I like Samuel a lot!" And with that she looks into Samuel's…soul… *I'm falling in liebe Samuel. Can you see this?* The waitress brings their menus and takes their drink orders. Both order tea as Samuel opens his menu.

"I like you also," says Samuel.

"Shall we see what we would like?"

They finally look at their menus, order, and stop long enough for a moment of silent prayer when their meals are brought out. They speak as they eat and enjoy their meal. It does not go without little laughs and giggles.

Mary, not having ever eaten formerly, has not had an appetizer and is astonished at the prices for the 'little teases of food'. But, she chooses the Shrimp Cocktail because she has not had this before. They bring out four shrimps. Laughing, Mary picks up one of the shrimp and brings it up to her face.

"Little shrimp, if only you knew how much you're worth," says Mary, looking with curiosity at her food. Samuel is laughing.

"Mary, do you always talk to your food before you eat it?"

Picking up his own shrimp with his shrimp fork, Mary copies and teases, "they have special forks for you, too!"

As they finish their cocktails, their salads come out. Samuel has ordered the Greek salad and Mary, the house salad with Ranch dressing.

Mary is a little curious and they find themselves feeding each other different foods, beginning with the Greek salad, which she has tried and found that she likes. Samuel insists that they trade salads.

Mary stays with the 'safe' chicken breast and Samuel orders the Maryland Crab Cake. Mary tries this also and finds that she likes it, but continues with her own meal. Dessert is where she wants to experiment with something different, choosing crème Brulee. Samuel orders the Pecan pie with vanilla ice-cream. Lovingly, they feed each other samples.

Mary is laughing as the ice-cream has not quite made it to her mouth and dribbled down her chin.

"You missed, Samuel, you owe me another," says Mary as she leans forward for another bite. This time as she takes the ice cream and pie off the spoon, she looks at Samuel peering into his eyes.

"This is *gut*, *jah*, but we make a better pecan pie though," says Mary, uncharacteristically verbalizing pride in her Amish baking.

As they finish their tea, the conversation never goes back to Samuel's time amongst the English, and he never lets on about his past. At the end of their meal, Samuel pays by placing his plastic inside the folder with the check.

"Sometimes, you are so *verra* Englich, Samuel," says Mary, as she laughs.

"I am," says Samuel. He repeats, "I am, aren't I? Does this trouble you, Mary?" Mary shakes her head no and just looks on in silence.

"I like this in you, Samuel," says Mary.

Samuel shakes his head in affirmation, smiles and says, "*Jah*," and there is more laughter.

Mary is quiet and thoughtful for just a moment before she says with a heartfelt sincerity, "Samuel, I am having such a *gut* time with you. I feel as though I can relax and just enjoy you. Is this ok?"

Samuel standing up goes over to Mary's chair, pulls out the chair with his right hand, and offers his left, as he says in a quiet voice, "Yes, I'm glad because I feel the same way about you."

Mary looks up and remarks, "I suppose amongst the English you were a true gentleman, *jah*, just like now."

"In more ways than you may ever know, Mary," says Samuel. Mary just continues to smile inquisitively.

As they walk out, their car starts up, lights go on, and the driver pulls around. The driver gets out of the car and, while blowing into his hands and rubbing them together; he comes around to open their door. In the darkness of the car,

Samuel looks over at Mary, where he boldly but gently takes Mary's left hand in his. "Is this ok?" he asks.

"*Jah.*" And she places their hands on her lap and then her other hand on the held hands. Not saying a word, they stay this way, just feeling each other's warmth.

The entire drive, they continue to hold onto each other while caressing their thumbs over each other's hands. To each of them, it is a feeling of the longing which exists between them.

They look into each other's eyes, and then lean forward toward each other where Samuel gives a gentle kiss on Mary's cheek. No words are said. Mary continues to look into Samuel's eyes. An hour later, after an extra slow drive, they pull into the driveway. Samuel looks again at Mary, then leans over and kisses her cheek again. Mary, unclasping her hand, touches her cheek where the kiss has just been placed.

"*Gute Nacht, Meine Liebe,*" says Mary as she now traces her cheek down from where her finger tips had been.

"Good night Mary…. Mary, I love you, too."

Mary smiles and doesn't wait for the driver to open her door. She is about to burst, not to mention slip and fall in the snow and ice. The driver calls out after her. "Ma'am, ma'am, allow me, please."

"*Jah* ok," responds Mary, smiling to the driver as Samuel follows her out of the car.

"Mary, I'm going to be very busy, but I'll see you at church and common meals. Ok?" asks Samuel while waiting at the end of the short walkway, leading to the steps.

"*Jah!*" *I feel like a school girl again. I've never felt so wunderbar gut. Jah!*

Mary turns around and waves at Samuel one more time before sliding through the snow in a sprint. Inside the car, Samuel looks on, smiling as he wipes the fog away from the inside of the windows. Once inside, the driver looks back. "Sir?"

"Yes, she is inside, go ahead," says Samuel to his driver. *I wish you could see us together daed.*

Chapter Seven

It was March twenty-sixth when Samuel got a call from Bill. He was sitting at the kitchen table looking at the fire through the cracks of the cast iron kitchen stove, enjoying his sandwich.

"Sam, the ranch has been sold. They were trying to hold out for your herd of horses, but they settled for the land and buildings for three quarter of a million dollars. I think you did well."

"Good, when is settlement?"

"As you requested, I was able to hold them off until late spring when it is a little warmer in Pennsylvania. The date is the sixth of June."

"This is good Bill. All the buildings for the livestock are now completed. Soon we begin moving livestock. I'm beginning work on the houses next. This may add a little more trouble with the community though," Samuel says with concern.

"How so, Sam?" asks Bill.

"I'm having modern amenities put into the house; modern plumbing and electric. The electrician arrives tomorrow. It's good I don't have the Ordnung to worry about."

"Getting a car?"

"No, no, just plumbing and some rudimentary electric. No phone, no vehicles, except for my ole pickup when it gets here. I'll hide that out back."

It was a busy, exciting day at what will be the new SH ranch in Lancaster, Pennsylvania, on Saturday, the seventh of

April. Amos and Jeremiah stay at their farms to manage the arrival of livestock. While the community comes together to help out at all three farms, a common meal is planned at the old Hersberger farm. The women folk all come together to help each other. And the children are found jobs around all three farms.

The electricians from the electric company arrive to run wire from the poles at the roadside to the house and barn. Meanwhile, electricians from a local electric company, with plans in hand, start plotting the layout of the house.

If that weren't enough, the buggies have to be put up on the lawn, away from the house and barn. Then, just in time, come the first of the tractor trailer cattle trucks. *I didn't plan this aspect of the move well! I have the electric company out here at the same time as the trucks. All I can do is hope no one trips over each other. I'm going to have to keep a close management of this whole thing today.*

Samuel's commanding voice goes out. An odd sight of the man now dressed plain with a little longer hair. "Yo driver, what's your name?"

"Andy," the truck driver responds while looking down from the cab of the truck.

"Andy, I need you to hold your rig out here in the street while I have the first maneuvered into place, OK?"

"Yes sir! Got it," responds the driver again.

"You, what's your name, he yells to the first driver?"

"Jim."

"Jim, you have room to pull in and then back up to the gate of the corral. We'll get the cows first."

"Ok!" said the first driver as he begins pulling the tractor trailer in.

"THANKS!" yells Samuel over the din.

The first truck has the first load of cows and the second, the balance of cows going to Amos's farm, where Mr. Schrock is with Amos. Then John arrives with his pickup with a chicken pen in the back. Another two tractor trailers wait on the road. "How'd I draw lots on the chickens?" humored John.

"Thought about loading a herd of cows, but then I thought you needed a tougher job for that truck," quips Samuel, with a smile.

John, now laughing, "Well I guess there were always the pigs."

"Careful now buddy what you wish for," says Samuel now laughing back.

Then there came a shout of a familiar voice. "Samuel. *Hullo! Wie gehts?* It was Mary, standing on the other side of the road, waiting to cross.

Mary, this is dangerous out here. Horseshoe Pike is usually busy enough without all this going on.

"I'm good. Stay there, watch the trucks, ok?"

"Jah!"

The third of the tractor trailers pulled into the drive with force. *That driver was exceptional. He navigated that like a pro race car driver at Daytona.*

"I'll be here throughout the day for meals and drinks" says Mary, now talking in a speaking voice, having crossed the road. She clasps Samuels hand momentarily before proceeding to the house.

"Ok, Mary, Danki" *My Dutch is coming back. Starting to think in it now. I guess it's about time, jah! I get the accent back, and then they'll stop looking at me like I'm 'English'. Except Mary; she doesn't care what I am.*

The livestock and farm implements now being moved to their new homes has left open the entire old Hersberger farm.

ೞ☙

As things quiet down at the Hersberger farm, a white Suburban leaves Carlisle, Pennsylvania. "What's the word, sir?" asks Tom.

"It's time to see what Mr. Hersberger wants to do with his life. I'm going to make him an offer that I hope he takes," says Chris Hutchins.

"And if he doesn't?"

"I guess he'll retire. It'll be a great loss for us." Chris Hutchins sighs. In a couple of hours the Suburban pulls into the farm driveway.

Spotting the white Suburban, Samuel recognizes the kind of car the company has and responds, initially speaking to himself, "Ahh!! Been so busy here hadn't had time to think about these guys. Heh Chris! Is that Tom driving you there?" yells Samuel.

"Hi Sam! Yes it is! He's a good man! And how are you?" asks Chris.

"I'm good, Chris. Still showing folks up with your side arm there Tom?"

"Hi Sam. Yes sir, staying in practice."

"I can only guess what you guys want!"

"That's what we're here for Sam," Says Chris

"Thought so. I've been so busy that I lost all track of time. You have a proposal, I suppose," says Samuel showing the two men to the back door of his house.

"Coffee?"

"Yes, coffee will be good. You never were one for nonsense; straight to the point, straight up and honest. That's why I don't want to lose you. Either way, you know you get a promotion. Retire with one or a second option is to stay on, change your status. That way, if we need you, we give you, well, a holler, if we may. You're an expert we can't afford to lose. I'm certain the next ten years will be critical for us. Sort of stay around until you're needed," says Chris, now bargaining with Samuel.

"Two months ago, I would have said no! But, I agree, things will be critical. I believe what I did was important. I have to step back though and you guys have to be discreet. My community may be new order but, well, I know it won't buy this. I'm a member of the church now. That would complicate my life a lot," says Samuel, continuing.

"Agreed, I'll personally take care of the paperwork. I'll send anything needed for signature by courier," says Chris.

"Thanks Chris. And thanks for dressing casual."

"Well, I figured around here better go for the jean look to blend in. Heh listen, did you get the card from Carol and I? We're real sorry about your dad and especially everything you're going through. How are the nightmares?" Chris asks, as they are shown seats.

"Sit, sit," says Samuel pointing at their seats. He has coffee on already and pours three cups.

"Yes, I did thanks. Nightmares are gone." He puts three freshly made apple fritters on a plate and places them on the table. Chris, taking one of the pastries, takes a bite of his and comments, "Amish food and baked goods, you're going to get fat!" They all laugh. The three men spend a couple of leisurely hours talking and reminiscing about old times. Evening coming on, Chris and Tom get up to leave.

"Listen Chris; send my regards to Carol will ya?"

"Will do, Take it easy there buddy."

"Yes sir," responds Samuel to Chris, then shifting his look to Tom. "Take care, Tom."

"Yes sir, thank you, and do the same," responds Tom. The two men get in their vehicle. As the Suburban makes its way out of the drive, Samuel walks up the steps to his house with a feeling of contentment.

The transformation into a ranch for horses now begins. Contractors arrive to expand out the barn for commercial size stables for horses and a new bunk house is built for the ranch hands.

New corrals for breaking horses, as well as open fields for grazing, are also prepared. Electricity is added to help make the pumping of water easier and for lights, which are safer to use. *I do not use TV and Radio, just doesn't offer anything of value but bad news. Never watched it, never missed it, neither did Bill. Though I think he would miss his country music.*

Finally, Samuel takes care of the bathroom situations also. He takes a bedroom from each floor and turns them into modern baths. Samuel then did the same with the Dawdi house. It takes until the end of May to complete. It is time to move everything and everyone from the ranch in North Carolina.

"Hello Bill! It's Sam,"

"Heh there Sam, how's things progressing in the north?"

"Good, we're ready to begin transporting all our assets north now. How about...wait a minute, someone is walking down the drive. It's Mary. Let me call you right back," say Samuel.

"Ok Sam, I'll be here with my cell," responds Bill.

As Mary makes her way down the now new, but very quiet ranch, she sees Samuel. He is standing out at the end of the driveway and along the corrals fence. Feeling her heart begin to speed up, she loses her breath. She can no longer walk and begins to run, holding her skirt as she bends over slightly.

Not having seen each other in two weeks, Samuel, after a brief pause, matches her stride. There is a breeze blowing on this early non church Sunday morning, the twenty-seventh of May. One can smell an undeniable freshness in the spring air. The longing is palpable between the two as they run toward each other. Mary cries as she closes in on her love.

As she reaches Samuel, she leaps into his arms, coming together in unbridled passion. Mary, kissing Samuel on his lips, then his cheeks and neck, tightens her arms embrace around his neck. The heat of the embrace kindles a fire between the two, which can no longer be extinguished. Samuel meets each kiss with his own while cradling her face. Mary finally comes to rest on Samuel's shoulder with her mouth on Samuels's neck.

"Samuel, this may be wrong, but I need you, and I need to be with you," says Mary, breathlessly.

"I know Mary, I know. I need you too. I need you so badly. I'm so... I just can't be without you any longer." Samuel lifting up Mary's head, and again cradling her face with both hands, kisses her lips once more, gently, firmly, then moves his lips to the tears on her cheeks, kissing them away. "I love you Mary. You believe this, don't you?"

"Yes Samuel, I do believe you. That you love me, yes, yes, and a thousand times yes.

"Mary…" He pauses for what seems like a long time as he looks deep into her eyes.

"Will you marry me? I want to spend the rest of my life with you. I want to love you with all I am and will be. Will you marry me Mary? Grow old with me?"

"Yes Samuel, I will marry you. I also want to spend the rest of my life with you." Mary, pulling back now, cradles Samuel's face.

"I love you very much, Samuel." The two embrace. They hold each other, feeling the warmth between them. Samuel brings his hands up to the back of his beloved's neck, holds her even closer, and kisses the side of her neck once again. Then they kiss each other's lips more slowly, passionately again. More tears are streaming down Mary's cheeks; she can barely talk. "I'm so happy Samuel. I'm so happy," says Mary.

"I'm happy also," says Samuel, whispering into Mary's ear.

"I must tell my dat and my kinner," says Mary.

"Yes, and I must tell my family also. Let's tell your family first. Celebrate, we must celebrate," says Samuel jubilantly.

"Yes Samuel, what shall we do?"

"I will hook up my buggy and we will go to your family first to break the news to them and then we will all go out to breakfast. Then we shall go to each family's home and tell them of this news, jah?" Laughing and sniffling now, Mary follows with.

"Jah Samuel, jah!"

"Mary, I was on the phone with Bill and must call him back. I must tell him the news."

"Jah, Samuel." Pulling the Blackberry from his pocket, he hits the redial button.

"Bill, its Sam, I'm getting married."

"Sam, y'all son of a gun. Helen, Sam's getting married." Helen can be heard screaming in the background.

"Oh my, oh my," her voice can be heard breaking.

"Well, ya got the misses all worked up their boss. Congratulations to ya and Mary, I'm happy for the both of ya. Hear?"

"I'm gonna call ya back later to finalize plans for the move. I'm going to talk to Mary first, ok?"

"Ok and congratulations again," says Bill, hanging up his phone.

"That was my ranch manager. We have a lot to talk about," says Samuel. Once again, holding Samuels face in her hands, Mary looks into his eyes with warmth and says, "Samuel, I know very little of what is happening, but I know you're a gut man and I want to take this journey with you. You have to know that I trust you with all my heart," says Mary kissing his lips once again.

"*Danki*, Mary. Let's hook up the buggy," says Samuel.

"*Jah*, and your *willkum*, Samuel," says Mary.

The two visit many surprised families that Sunday. They share a breakfast with Mary's kinner and dat. Then, after dropping Mary's happy *dat* off at his farm, they continue on to Katie's home to share the news with his mother, his favorite niece, and her husband. Then they visit each of the family members.

The joy is all around. After arriving back at the Schrock farm, Mary prepares the evening meal for the family and Samuel. The meal is enjoyed by all and, as Mary cleans up; her dad goes to finish evening chores. Samuel plays with what, someday soon, will be his children. After cleaning, Mary puts them to bed. They sit on the sofa, Mary lying back against Samuel. Samuel waits for Mary to look up at him, and then he sneaks a kiss, softly.

Plans are made for their publishing and wedding, which, though yet in the planting season, will occur on a non-service Sunday in two weeks. Samuel, in typical command style, goes to work on moving. Arrangements are made first for his furniture, which will arrive on Friday. Before then, the old furniture will be picked up by different members of his family who have needs and memories of certain pieces.

The horses are next, taking many horse trailers to move Samuels herd of 58 horses on the following Monday. The horses are all in the stable by Tuesday. Two ranch hands arrive at the same time. There is a new beauty on Horseshoe Road as many horses now graze the fields along the road.

I will never get over the majesty of these beasts of beauty. This is a great day, a wondrous week. Mary and Samuel walk along the road taking in the beauty of the day. Their favorite thing to do is hold hands and walk, occasionally looking at each other and smiling. Stopping to pet the horse's heads, the horses seem to remember Samuel and come over to the fence.

Mary and Samuel are together that Wednesday, the sixth of June, at the ranch with the children and the rest of the family before the Sunday of their wedding. It is the big day of the arrival of Bill and Helen. The Ranch manager and his wife have wrapped up the work at the old ranch that they called home for a decade and a half and now were beginning a new life with their children. Samuel wants his old friend to feel welcome amongst his Amish brethren. Thus, all the family is here to help move in the furniture and embrace the family. Samuel looks over at Mary, then down the drive and thinks to himself, I've *been sleeping well, no more nightmares and cold sweats. I have the love of a good woman. What a wondrous day.......... Daed!*

Chapter Eight

If Samuel had wondered what had happened to the balance of five horses owned by Bill and Helen, he didn't have to wonder any longer. For rounding the corner and coming down the drive on their horses are Bill and Helen and their three children. Wearing rolled up plaid shirts, jeans and Stetsons in true ranch style. The family has big smiles on their faces. Bill, taking off his hat, waves it at the family.

"Well, I'll be, so that's where his horses went to, in true Bill fashion," Whispers Samuel to himself under his breath.

"Heh buddy, welcome to your new home." He reaches up and shakes Bills hand and pats his horse with his left.

"We couldn't think of a better way to enter the new ranch and our new home, Samuel." They look down at the family of Samuel all quiet and dressed plain. Then, getting down off their horses and holding onto the reins, they move forward and start to introduce each.

"Helen and Bill, this is my Mary," introduces Samuel as Helen moves forward and hugs Mary.

"Well, now surely glad to meet ya, Mary," says Helen, giving Mary a big smile.

"We're going to be great friends. These are our young uns. Roy, Travis and…Mary," continued Helen. The older Mary laughs.

"Another Mary *jah*, *gut* name," says Mary, as she walks over and touches the side of Mary's cheek." She looks back around at Helen.

"I'm looking forward to becoming gut friends, *willkum*, Helen, Bill, and kinner. The other Hersberger family members join with Bill and Helens children and rein the horses. First attempting to tie them to the split rail fence, two are initially spooked by all the activity around them; they whinny then pull back and up as if to want to pull away. Travis, Bill and Helen's middle child, reaches over and brings the one horse under control.

"Whoa there big fella," Travis speaks to the horse. At this moment, Katie's husband, Andrew, joins him. Taking hold of the reins of the second horse and quickly bringing it under control.

"You are *gut* with horses," says Andrew.

"Yes sir," says Travis, with confidence.

"I am Andrew."

"Travis, sir"

"You have *gut* manners, Travis.

"Thank ya." They begin pulling saddles off and finally corral the horses.

Mamma invites everyone to the outside of the barn. As all head over to the barn for the meal, a large horse trailer pulled by a very large crew cab truck enters the drive, followed by another car and Samuel's small pickup truck, driven by another ranch hand. The vehicles are situated, and they are invited to join by Jeremiah. Jeremiah asks his bruder to do the meal's grace. Amos begins, "Can we stand?" With those words everyone stands.

"Heavenly Father, this is a great day. We are all gathered here today to *willkum* our new neighbors and friends into our fold. We are here today, just days before we join two of our own in marriage. We begin a new home here for Bill and Helen and their kinner, and Samuel and Mary and their kinner. All have arrived safely. Dear Lord, for these things and the food that we have here before us, we are truly grateful. Amen!"

"AMEN"

The new guests, children, and men are seated, as the women begin to serve up the dinner meal for the day. Finishing up at near 1 p.m., all could hear the noise of a large tractor trailer truck as it nears the driveway. The driver of the moving truck gets out and walks down the drive, meeting Samuel and Bill. The two men could be seen pointing at the house. Samuel directs the driver as he backs towards the *dawdi* house. Once there, everyone springs into motion.

The Kramer's, after a quick tour, place themselves in rooms to direct where everything will go. By day's end, furniture and all is in place. Bill, Helen, Travis, Roy, and Mary are now in their new home.

The Hersberger women have prepared a supper meal for all to enjoy, including the driver and movers. It is now shortly after seven o'clock. The moving company has left. The rest of the ranch hands are shown the new bunk house and the Kramer's begin settling into their new home. The other Hersberger's, after hitching their horses to their buggies, begin to leave. Mr. Schrock speaks,

"Mary, I will take the kinner home, you follow when ready."

"*Jah dat*" She walks over and takes Samuels hand.

"Samuel, I like what you have done here in such a short period of time. I am looking forward to our life together."

"I'm looking forward to our life together, also," says Samuel. They begin to walk out the drive while holding hands. The days are getting noticeably longer. Flowers are blooming. Trees again have leaves. The air smells clean. It is once again warm out. In the background, horses can be heard whinnying.

"Mary, have you moved all the kinner and your things into the new house?"

"*Jah* Samuel, it is all moved. The *kinner* are looking forward to living in their new rooms," says Mary.

"How are you with the new amenities?"

"What are amenities?" Mary looks at Samuel with curiosity.

"Comfort items in the home; electric, modern bathroom, new gas stove."

"*Jah, jah*, it will take some getting used to, especially the electric lights, but I think it will be gut. The children think the light switch is a toy," says Mary, both of them laughing, picturing the children who have never had electric lights.

"Samuel, I like the new baths. I can use this anytime?"

"*Jah*, everyday and twice a day if you like," says Samuel smiling at her, remembering a time when they took tub baths once a week.

"I'll have to try the shower. I never had this. I shall like not having to wait for a bath," says Mary.

"Ok, *mein schatz*," says Samuel lovingly while smiling. Mary looks over at Samuel and smiles back.

They walk out the drive and down the road. The evening is warm and dry with a slight breeze blowing. As they walk, Samuel leads Mary off the road into the high grass and toward the fence where one of his Quarter Horses stands.

"Heh girl, jah, you made that trip quite well, didn't you now?" Samuel pets the horse's neck as she whinnies and shakes her head up and down. Mary joins him and begins to pet the majestic animal, also.

"You surely like what you do Samuel," says Mary.

"*Jah*, I do. At times in my life, especially as alone as I've been in most of it, the horses have given me company. I would saddle up and just go riding. It was most relaxing *jah, gut*," says Samuel.

"I'm glad." Looking over at Samuel, she smiles. A breeze catches a small wisp of hair from under her *kapp* and blows it. The sun is not quite set yet.

"Mary, I know this is not important to you. You can just blame the English in me. Mary, you're beautiful," says Samuel. Mary smiles and looks up at Samuel, gives a quick look up and down the road, then reaches up and kisses him deeply.

"Thank you for that," says Mary, enjoying the compliment.

"Your *willkum liebe*. Well, while we're out here, I'll walk you home, ok?"

"I would like that, jah," responds Mary. He retakes her hand, and proceeds across the street, toward where Mary lives. *I'm going to enjoy holding this woman's hand forever, as God wills it.*

The next day, Samuel is busy finishing the move of his 'past' to a fourth room, including his footlockers, which will now be in his office on the first floor. He has new clothes for his wedding, a 'plain' black suit, white shirt, and the hat he had gotten in February.

Ok, now for the last time, with the phone shed in place, the blackberry is charged and turned off, and into the desk drawer it goes for emergencies. Becky put a lot of love into these clothes she made for me. I knew she was sewing for me, but this; this is special. Take a walk down to the phone shed. Check for messages.

Samuel goes to the phone shed down near the road and up near another Amish neighbor who shares it. Pushing the button to the answering machine he hears a familiar voice.

"Samuel, it's John. Someone in North Carolina has been trying to reach you. I will see you on Sunday with the information. Heh, you have a phone and an answering machine. Well now!" Beep! And the answering machine turns off.

"Hmmm I wonder what that is about.

℘℃Ↄ

Sunday arrives in an early morning flurry of activity. Samuel's mother and Katie are at Mary's bright and early at five a.m. Becky has the children at Samuel's while all prepare for their wedding day. Breakfast is prepared.

"Guder mariye!" Mamma enters, knocking at the back door of Mary's home.

"And it is *gut*! Isn't it mamma Hersberger?" Mary responds joyfully! With a big smile on her face, she walks over and embraces her soon to be daughter-in-law.

"*Wie gehts* Katie," greets Mary, as Katie comes through the back door.

"*Gut* Mary! This is *wunderbaar*," responds Katie.

"Mary, I have always seen you as a daughter, now it is true. You will be gut for Samuel," says Samuel's mamma.

"And he for me mamma," says Mary. "I like you calling me mamma, jah."

After the morning routine, it is time for Mary to dress for her wedding day. Her original dress is put up. The new dress she made herself is sky blue for this wedding day. Her kapp is now neatly in place after pulling back her hair, grown for many years, twisted tightly, and placed in a bun underneath.

Samuel will see me with my hair down tonight. No man has seen me since David. Lord, let David know I remember him. And though I have gut memories and I remember our love, I now love Samuel. Please help me be a gut wife and may we have many, many boppli's.

Samuel arrives mid-morning to find many of his family already there. Also, there is John, his wife, and their three children and Bill, Helen, and their three children. But especially surprising is Chris Hutchins, his wife, and their older daughter. In a now whispered voice, Samuel approaches his old boss and friend.

"Chris, Carol, this is a surprise, and Elizabeth. I didn't expect to see you."

"Heh, your blackberry must be turned off, otherwise, you might have gotten your RSVP," says Chris with a grin. Samuel taps his forehead.

"I just turned it off, had a phone shed put in. I have a number for you also. I'm really sorry Chris," says Samuel, embarrassed.

"Sam, don't worry about it," says Carol, responding to her husband. John walks up and is introduced by Samuel.

"Chris and Carol Hutchins, their daughter Elizabeth, I would like to introduce you to John and Darlene Dietrick," says Samuel.

"John, you've been the liaison all these years? I have heard a lot about you. You're a good friend. It is nice to meet you," says Chris.

"Thank you. And your...... that's right, Samuels boss," says John.

"Sam, don't worry. I spoke to my family and we all know the drill," says Chris.

"What drill?" Bill questions as he joins the now growing reunion." Samuel ignores the question.

"Chris Hutchins," says Bill, noticing Samuel's boss.

"How are ya doing there, you and the misses? How is North Carolina?"

"Good Bill. How are you and your family?" says Carol.

"Fine, thank ya Carol," says Bill. As the introductions are made, a gray over black buggy is seen coming up the Schrock driveway.

"There's the Bishop, must go get ready now. Good seeing you all," says Samuel as he looks at the Bishop climbing down off his buggy.

The seating is traditional with women on one side and men on the other. The English sit in the back with their families. Amos begins by welcoming everyone and saying a short prayer.

"Lord we thank thee for this blessed day where you bring one man and one woman together as one. This is a special day for my family and I because the man is my brother. He is home with us for the first time in many years. A special day for Mary for she no longer will live life without someone to love and share her life. A special day for her children for they now will have a dat. We also thank thee Lord and remember our Daed though he is not here but enjoys eternal life with you. We thank thee for the safe arrival of our friends who have traveled far and have arrived safe. For all these things, we thank thee in the name of Jesus. Amen."

"AMEN!" The community responds.

The Bishop steps forward and begins with the scripture reading. "The following reading is from Ephesians

5:22-33. Wives, be subject to your own husbands, as to the Lord. For the husband is the head of the wife, and Christ also is the head of the church, being himself the savior of the body. But as the church is subject to Christ, so let the wives also be to their own husbands in everything.

Husbands, love your wives, even as Christ also loved the church, and gave himself up for it; that he might sanctify it, having cleansed it by washing of water with the word, that he might present the church to himself gloriously, not having spot or wrinkle or any such thing; but that it should be holy and without blemish. Even so husbands also ought to love their own wives as their own bodies. He who loves his own wife loves himself. For no man ever hated his own flesh; but nourishes and cherishes it, even as the Lord also does the church. Because we are members of his body, of his flesh and bones. For this cause a man will leave his father and mother, and will be joined to his wife. The two will become one flesh. This mystery is great, but I speak concerning Christ and of the church. Nevertheless each of you must also love his own wife even as himself; and let the wife see that she respects her husband."

The Bishop then calls Samuel and Mary. As they take their vows, Mary's eyes well with tears of happiness. The wedding service takes an hour and a half because it is a rare second marriage for both of them. There are no rings, nor kisses, exchanged. There will be no honeymoon. Usually they would spend weekends visiting family and receiving gifts. In Samuel and Mary's circumstance, they both will begin their life as mother and father, then man and wife, right away.

At the end of the service, the family and the community celebrate at the Schrock farm. Two meals are served during the course of dinner and supper. Many cakes, pies and sweets are also served. After a long day, the children begin to tire. The families begin to hook up their horses and buggies.

"Mary, I have Caleb. I will put him in the buggy first," says Samuel.

"Jah, Samuel. I will go get my dat to say goodbye," says Mary.

"Ok," says Samuel as he lays Caleb into the buggy first. The temperature has dropped to fifty-five degrees this late evening. He pulls the blanket to cover Caleb. Then he goes for Rachel. He carefully places her in the buggy next to her bruder, and brushes back her hair, which has by this time slipped out from under her kapp. Rachel opens her eyes momentarily.

"Hi Rachel, you go ahead and sleep. I'm just putting you in the buggy," says Samuel to his daughter. He then takes the other part of the blanket and covers her. With Mary and her dat now standing behind him, Samuel adjusts the blanket around the two kinners in the buggy. Opening her hazel eyes Rachel looks at Samuel and says, *"Daed."*

Chapter Nine

The horse has been placed in its stall for the night by one of the ranch hands who returned earlier. The children are put to bed, by both Mary and Samuel. Mary now waits for Samuel to come back upstairs to their bedroom. She stands at the top of the stairs wearing a plain, pull over white cotton nightgown. The bottom of her still pulled up hair is wet from the bath she has just taken.

Samuel, in pajama bottoms and no shirt, rounds the corner to the bottom of the stairs. Looking up, he finds Mary waiting. Anxiously, Mary hastens her love.

"*Schnell meine liebe*," says Mary as she waves upwardly with her hands. "*Ich Kumme liebe*" She quickens the motions, smiling broadly and teasing. "*Jah*, I am coming," says Samuel with his first foot on the steps.

"You're not coming fast enough. *Schnell, schnell.*"

"*Jah, jah!*" As Samuel reaches the top of the steps, he takes both of Mary's hands in his. Pulling her close, he kisses her deeply, then holding the sides of her face moves her away and whispers, "I love you very much Mrs. Hersberger, my wife…. I like the sound of that. I thought I would grow old not knowing another love in my life," says Samuel.

"*Jah*, I know, Samuel. I have truly felt the same way many times in my life also. I thought if that is what the Lord wants then so be it," says Mary.

"The Lord had other ideas, don't ya think?"

"*Jah, jah*, I love you my husband. *Kumme*, let's go to bed," says Mary, as she reaches up and kisses her husband again.

"There is something I must do first," Says Samuel, as he takes Mary's hand.

They walk down the hall to the first room. Looking at Mary, he opens the door and peers in at Caleb sleeping quietly. As he now has his hand over Caleb's quiet form, he prays.

"I thank you dear Lord for this son that I now have. Help me be a strong and wise father in raising this child," prays Samuel.

He retakes Mary's hand and walking out the door moves to the third door, opens it quietly, and finds Rachel lying sideways in bed with sheets and blanket strewn all over. The two give a little chuckle. Mary speaking of her little one, "She always has been a restless sleeper, *jah*." Samuel kisses her left cheek.

"She looks like her mother," says Samuel as he looks back over at Mary. Walking over to the bed, Samuel raises his hand over Rachel.

"I thank you dear Lord for this daughter that I now have. Help me be a strong and wise father in raising this child," prays Samuel again.

Turning now to Mary, "Mary, I'm a daed," says Samuel, his eyes welling with tears.

"*Kumme*," says Mary leading Samuel toward their own room at the end of the hall at the top of the stairs. She opens the door and proceeds in to open the windows. A soft breeze is blowing, and the curtains dance to the movement of the night air. A single, dim light from an enclosed candle is flickering. Mary then turns to the man she loves.

"There was a time Samuel when I couldn't wait to do this," as she pulls the pins, undoing the bun, allowing her hair to fall down past her waist. She walks a couple of more steps to Samuel and places her arms around his neck and begins to kiss him softly and tenderly.

Samuel returns her kiss as he caresses the sides of her face and runs his fingers through her hair and down her back. Mary shivers as she looks up into the eyes of her new husband and, opening her mouth, kisses him again, this time lingering.

Mary sits back on the bed and gently pulls Samuel toward her and positions him down next to her. They continue to kiss each other as Samuel pulls Mary to him and the two are one.

₭Ԓ

The sun is already up when Mary and Samuel awaken to two children; one on either side of the bed looking quietly at them. Caleb, at his mother's side of the bed, smiles broadly.

"*Guder mariye, Mamm,*" says Caleb jumping up on the bed, he hugs his *mamm.*

"*Guder mariye,* Caleb," says a surprised Mary as she looks over at her husband and daughter. Samuel rubs the top of Caleb's head. Then without warning, and not wanting to be left out, "*Guder mariye, Daed,*" says Rachel jumping up on the bed and hugging her new *daed.* Rachel appears to have this longing for a dad that up till now was missing.

They both climb to the middle, smiling and looking back and forth at their new family. Mary now bursts in a near panic, "Samuel, I am so sorry. I didn't awaken the children or you, and no breakfast! What kind of wife you must think of me." Samuel sits up in bed and places both hands behind his head and smiles.

"Mary, do you smell that? I don't think it was the quiet of the kinner that woke us."

"*Mamm, daed,* there is a strange man in the kitchen cooking." There is a momentary pause before Samuel continues, "Surprise Mary! We don't do honeymoons, so the least I could do is let you sleep in," says Samuel.

"But Samuel, the chores, the horses," says Mary.

"Bill is handling that," responds Samuel confidently.

"Bill? Samuel, I do not want you to spoil us. Bill is cooking?"

"No, William is cooking; Bill is handling the ranch. Mary, I told you before; I could never spoil you. This is a gift to you, this first day of our marriage.

"Bill sent in the ranch cook, William. He cooked early for the ranch hands and now he is here. He is *verra gut, jah*. Not as *gut* as you *liebe*, but *gut*. *Kinner*, let your mother and I get dressed, and you both get dressed also," instructs the children's new dad.

The children leave the room in a sprint, slamming the door behind them. Samuel turns around in bed to get up. Mary, looking at the back of Samuel, sees several scars on his back. Tracing her fingers over them, she whispers as a tear falls from her eye, "Samuel, you were hurt badly, very badly." She leans into her husband and kisses his scar as she wraps her arms around his waist, placing the side of her head against his back.

"*Jah*, I am better now. You want to know what happened. I will tell you one day. Is that ok?" asks Samuel as he takes her hands and wraps them around him, pressing them against himself.

"*Jah* Samuel, *jah*," says Mary.

"I am very hungry," says Samuel as he turns towards Mary, smiles, and then kisses her once on the lips. Not having enough, he embraces her again, caressing her side and under her arms, he kisses her again.

"Hmm," sounds Samuel. Mary laughs and pushes him away.

"Samuel, who is William," asks Mary.

Samuel laughs back, "Ok, Ok, we will meet William, jah. And we will eat."

They finish dressing and, as they leave the room, they can hear the kinner downstairs speaking with the cook. Something about his skin color. Samuel now laughing questions, "What about your skin color William?"

"Good morning Mister Sam, misses. Apparently the children have never seen a black man before," says William, as Samuel laughs heartily.

"Mary, let me introduce William. He has cooked for us for many years now. Isn't that right William?"

"Yes Sir Mister Sam, many years, and many good years." As William focuses on his work, Mary looks wide-eyed about the kitchen. William, with an excellent attention to detail, has placed settings out for everyone. You could smell the bacon cooking in the cast iron skillet. Eggs lay in the carton and were placed on the stove, ready to be broken and prepared to order. Mary's bread from two days prior was sliced and on the table with fresh butter. A pitcher of orange juice was on the table and a hint of coffee aroma could be picked up besides the bacon.

"*Willkum* William, and good morning," welcomes Mary, as she nods her head.

"Good morning Miss Mary," says William.

"William, you must have gotten in late last night. We have narrowed down a house for you and your family. Are they still down south?"

"Yes sir, they are both excited and nervous about moving here. Between leaving there and moving here; and not only new folks, but different folks," says William, reflecting a nervous family.

"William, are you in the bunk house then?"

"Yes, Sir," says William.

"*Gut*, keep me informed about what is going on, ok? Everything will work out," says Samuel reassuring William.

"Yes sir boss," says William again.

ℰ𝒪ℭℛ

John's black pickup pulls into the SH Ranch driveway. As he nears, a tall man wearing a lightweight canvas cowboy hat meets him.

"John, isn't it?" Bill greets Samuels's friend.

"Yes sir; it's Bill, right?"

"Yep, how ya doin?"

"Ok. Is Sam around?" John asks as he looks around.

"Yep, having breakfast with his new family," says Bill. John looks down at his watch and remarks with a laugh.

"It's eight thirty; we are speaking about the same Hersberger Amish family, aren't we?" Bill, now laughing, agrees.

"Yep, same one. Honeymoon night now, with two kids, think about it. Yep, he wanted to surprise his wife with a late breakfast."

"Knowing the community, she'll think he's spoiling her," says John.

"Well, do you mind if I wait around for him?" John continues.

"No, I was just going to get some horses out of their stalls and turn them out to pasture," says Bill. With that, a couple of more ranch hands ride up.

"Heh boss, ready to move those horses? We'll take the ones from the corral to the far pasture," said the one ranch hand.

ഇർ

Samuel and his family finish with their breakfast.

"*Danki* William. Breakfast was *gut*, *danki*," says Mary.

"Thank you Miss Mary! I'm glad you and the children enjoyed it," says William. The children, one at a time, speak out loud. "*Danki*, Mr. Bill."

"*Danki* William. Do you mind the children calling you Mr. Bill?" asks Samuel.

"No sir, boss. That's how I introduced myself. Good kids you both got there sir, ma'am," says William.

"*Danki* William," says Mary as she smiles again at William.

"*Liebe*, I'm going outside. I believe I saw John's truck pull up," says Samuel, speaking to Mary.

"*Jah* Samuel. I will speak to the children regarding the chores," says Mary.

"*Gut, gut*, see you shortly," responds Samuel.

$\mathcal{EO}\mathcal{CR}$

"Helloo John! Good morning! How are you and the family? What's up?"

"Morning Sam. Family is good, thank you. I was headed for the office and remembered I had a message for you. The Cumberland County Department of Social Services in North Carolina is trying to track you down. I have a number."

As Samuel jots down the number on the hood of John's truck, he's thinking. *What could social services want with me? I wonder if this has something to do with... Sandy?*

After saying goodbye to John and speaking with Bill about the horses, he heads over to the phone shed. Samuel picks up the phone and pulls his phone card for long distance calls.

This would be much easier with my blackberry. Lord, give me patience with all these changes. I'd rather be in with Mary. Phone is ringing.

"You have reached the Cumberland County Department of Social Services. No one is available at the present time to answer your call. At the sound of the tone, please leave your name, phone number, and a brief message as to the reason for your call." Beep!

"Good morning, it is 9 a.m., the eleventh of June, I'm Samuel Hersberger, returning your call. I can be reached at this number. Please leave a message if I am not available to pick up the phone. Thank you."

The next day starts early. Mary is up very early; before sun up. She can hear horses whinnying off in the distance. From the kitchen window, she can see activity in the bunk house. Lights can be seen. As she watches, she gets coffee started.

Even though they have hired help, they both feel it very important for the children to have appointed chores; each of them at the beginning of the day and again at the end of the day. School is out for the summer. She awakens both kinner, feeds them, and then puts them to task. With many horses,

Caleb is sent out to meet the "other Mr. Bill" to help with the feeding. Rachel first helps her mamm out in the kitchen, and then is sent to gather laundry for the day's wash. Many chores have been started as the sun rises on the ranch. And the beginning of the new Hersberger family routine has now started.

ॐ ☊

Samuel, after sitting and having breakfast with Mary and the kinner, is now returning a phone call from the phone shed.

"Mr. Hersberger, it is so good to get in touch with you. I don't know how to tell you this. You know your wife died suddenly in Washington State. Did you know why she was there?"

"No ma'am, I don't. When she left it was sudden and without word. Last I had heard she was in Florida with her folks. That's when I got the divorce papers."

"Mr. Hersberger the nearest I can tell, this is what happened. She was living for a short while in Alaska visiting friends and, while there, she went to Seattle where she had heard of a job prospect. That is when she was killed in an auto accident. Her friends didn't know where she was and how to get in touch with you or her parents."

"Well, why would they need to get hold of me?"

"They have some important things of hers; in particular, one."

"Well, I think I have her parent's phone number. Would you like it?"

"No, Mr. Hersberger, that won't do!" The voice begins to stress.

"Why not?" Samuel responds, dumbfounded.

"Mr. Hersberger, you don't know, do you?"

"Know what?" Samuel can be seen from outside of the shed shrugging his shoulders.

"Mr. Hersberger, sir, you have a daughter!" There was a very long pause.

"Mr. Hersberger, are you there?"

"Huh, yes," says a stunned Samuel.

"Sir, you're a dad."

"*Daed?*"

Chapter Ten

Samuel, as white as flour, enters the kitchen and finds Mary baking pies and preparing lunch. Turning from her pies, Mary's smile quickly turns into a frown.

"Samuel, *liebe*, what's wrong? You look *verhuddelt*; no, you look awful, not confused."

Initially Samuel does not answer right away, looking at Mary, scared himself.

"Mary….." He barely gets out her name.

"Samuel, *SCHNELL*! You are making me *naerfich*, Samuel please."

Samuel is staring, stalling. He continues to start out slowly.

"You remember John had a phone call regarding someone trying to reach me?"

"*Jah*, did you find them, talk to them?" Mary is now turned, holding onto the back of the kitchen chair at the table.

"*Jah*, sit down Mary, this will take awhile. Sandy, before she was killed, had gone to stay with friends in Alaska."

"Far away, *jah*." Mary places two cups of coffee down for her and her husband. "*Jah*, she was killed in Washington State while looking for a job."

Mary sits down next to Samuel and faces him, as Samuel sits himself.

"Anyhow, she had left her friends for a couple of days and they were watching something for her and someone else."

"Someone else? Samuel, who?" Mary clutches Samuel's arm.

"I didn't know, Mary, I just didn't know," as he places his hand on hers.

"What Samuel, what didn't you know?" Mary now leans forward, listening carefully.

"I have a daughter, Mary." Another long pause ensues as Mary takes in what Samuel just said.

"Samuel, a daughter? What does this mean?"

"I have a daughter who has been staying with strangers looking for her family. Well not strangers, apparently friends of Sandy's. They're in Juno, Alaska."

"Oh heavenly father, she did not tell you that you had a child? Who could do such a thing, and why?" Listening to Mary, Samuel is now just staring.

"I don't know, I just don't know." Using his free hand, he drops his head down and just shakes it.

"Samuel, what is her name?" Mary asks in a tender voice.

"Kathryn," responds Samuel, raising his head to speak to her.

"How old is she? How old is your *kinner*? Samuel, look at me, it is ok. Tell me her age. Mary, now very sensitive to her love's feelings, continued to reassure Samuel.

"Five. She must have been pregnant when she left me," says Samuel looking up at Mary.

"No matter Samuel, she is a *kinner*! She will come here. She must be scared, so scared, and alone. I just don't understand why she would not have told you of your daughter."

"Mary, I'm sor…" He is cut off by his new wife as she grasps his arm again.

"*Stoppen* Samuel! Thinking like the English, *jah*! This is your *kinner*. I have two *kinner* from David. Friends are no substitute for family! We are her family."

"Kathryn, *jah*; we will bring her here, she belongs here, *jah*," says Mary now standing and shaking her head affirmatively.

"We will make a home for her here," continues Mary.

Samuel now stands looking at Mary and begins to plan, "We need space for her. I turned two of the bedrooms into bathrooms. I can turn the study into a bedroom and move my office to the barn."

"You'll do no such thing. She can share a room with Rachel. Rachel will now have a little schweschder. God will turn this tragedy into gut," as she stands placing her hands on her hips, and shaking her head yes, again. "Samuel all will be well!"

"*Danki*, Mary," smiles Samuel, ever so slightly at his Mary.

She walks over to him and hugs him whispering, "I love you Samuel, very much. We will have many trials to go through. And together we will see to them. I have waited long to stand by your side."

Samuel looks down into Mary's eyes and smiles, *Dear Lord I do thank you for this woman. How can I ever be as good of a husband as she is a wife? Please help me Lord. Please.*

Sandy's parents are notified that they have a granddaughter. They are, to say the least, surprised and baffled as to why Sandy had kept the secret of their grandchild from them.

Arrangements are made with social services in Juno, Alaska, who are doing the investigating after being notified by the Rainier's with whom Sandy had left Kathryn. Arrangements are then made to pick up Kathryn from the Rainier's in Juno. Kathryn would be put on a plane with a social worker. Samuel insisted that he pay for the flight for both.

The Bishop is notified as well as their family and friends. Their hearts go out to their new kinner as spiritual support is promised from the community as a whole. Another bed is purchased for the other wall. The lamp is placed in the middle on a night stand. Rachel, not fully understanding what is going on, is just excited to have a little schweschder. Caleb is now the 'big brother' to two *schweschders*; an important job.

The big day of Kathryn's arrival comes and the Hersberger's "hire" a driver. John comes to take them to Harrisburg International Airport. The drive to the airport is a quiet one. Samuel sits in the front with John; Mary sits in the back seat. When they arrive, they wait for only fifteen minutes when the plane arrives from Chicago, Illinois, where the flight connected at one p.m. Kathryn, her hand being held by a young woman with brown hair, comes down the hall towards them.

Though the social worker has a smile, Kathryn does not. She has a blank far-away stare on her face. "Samuel, she looks like you. Look at the blond hair and blue eyes. *Was in der welt?* She looks so lost." *Lord, help me be a good mamm to this child of Samuel's, our child.*

"Hi, I'm Samuel Hersberger," introducing himself to Kathryn's escort, he reaches for her hand.

"Mr., Mrs. Hersberger, Hi, I'm Jennifer Raleigh, and this is Kathryn. It's been a long day and I believe Kathryn is tired. We have personal effects packed into two pieces of luggage, which belong to both Kathryn and her mother."

"*Danki*, Miss Raleigh," says Mary as she picks up Kathryn and hugs her very closely. "It's ok Kathryn. This is your *daed, jah,*" as Mary begins to rock her back and forth.

An exhausted Kathryn lays her head down on Mary's shoulder, her face nuzzled in her neck. Locks of long hair are spread down Mary's back.

"*Jah, kinner,* you sleep now," Mary says as she turns toward the kinner's face and kisses her cheek. Kathryn picks her head up and turns away from the kiss then, just as quickly, turns back and nuzzles again but closer this time. They make their way to the baggage pick up area. John is leading the way, followed by Samuel, Mary and Jennifer. Kathryn is sleeping quietly, soundly.

Once there, they gather the two large pieces of luggage that Jennifer identifies. She moves everyone off to the side and formally identifies Samuel. Showing her his identification card, which he has with him, he finally signs some papers. She wishes them well, and heads for her own gate for her return trip to Alaska. John and Samuel load the luggage into the back of John's truck.

ℰᏅℭᎡ

Back at the ranch, William is standing over a very large grill. The family has gathered to greet Kathryn. They had decided to do supper and surprise Mary so that she would not have to cook and be able to spend time with the new kinner and the family.

"Mr. Bill, what are you making?" asks Caleb.

"Steaks, Caleb. Do you like steaks? Hi there Rachel, and how are you?"

"Fine, Mr. Bill. I like steaks," says Rachel.

"Do ya now?" William looks back at Rachel as the two kinner stand looking at 'Mr. Bill' as he cooks for the family.

"I don't," responds Caleb, attempting to regain attention from his sister.

"Ya don't Caleb? How come?" Caleb shrugs his shoulders and just stares.

"Rachel, you're quiet. What's on your mind there now young un?"

"We have a new little *schweschder*. Her name is Kathryn. *Mamm* and daed are picking her up and bringing her home."

"Slow down child. You have a little *schweschder*? Oh! A sister, I know."

"*Jah* Mr. Bill," says Caleb as he looks at Mr. Bill as though he should know what they're talking about. "She is going to sleep with Rachel," chimes in Caleb again.

"Is that right now, Caleb? And how da ya feel about that now?" Mr. Bill responds patiently.

"I don't want her to sleep in my room," Caleb, with a shocked look on his face, looks up at Mr. Bill.

"No, no young un. I mean how da ya feel about havin a sister?"

"A *schweschder*? It's *gut, jah!*" Caleb says, shaking his head yes approvingly.

"I think it's *gut,* too," beams Rachel.

"Now that sounds all real exciten, children," Bill grins.

"We're going to play with our cousins now Mr. Bill," says Caleb.

"Ok, have fun now," says William, smiling after the children as they run towards their cousins.

ᔕᔎ

Samuel looks back at Mary. Kathryn is in a seat belt and lying over on Mary's lap, sleeping. They look into each other's eyes, and Samuel mouths I love you.

Mary smiles broadly and just nods yes, as she caresses Kathryn's cheek. John breaks the silence, "Mary, it won't be long now; five minutes. Samuel, your life has turned a full circle hasn't it?"

"*Jah*, it's *wunderbaar, jah,*" responds Samuel, still looking at his wife.

Samuel is still smiling as they turn into the driveway, now full with gray top buggies and cars.

"What's going on here?" Samuel sits up straight in his seat and stares in bewilderment. With that, Jeremiah and Erica, with smiles, approach the car with Bill and Helen.

"*Wie gehts bruder?*" Jeremiah asks, leaning on the window of the passenger door.

"*Gut* Jeremiah, gut," says Samuel as John gets out of the truck and looks into the back seat at Mary. He looks over to his left and is pleasantly surprised to see his wife Darlene on her way over to greet him.

"Well this is a pleasant surprise! What is going on here?" asks John. Jeremiah speaks up now.

"John, Samuel, we all knew it would be a tiring day for you and decided since it was Saturday to come over and cook a meal for you. Besides, the family wanted to meet your kinner, jah. We let Bill and Helen know and they got *uffgschafft.*"

93

"We got what?" asks Helen.

"Ah *jah*, excited."

"So here we are and decided to turn it into a barbeque," says Bill. Continuing, he asks, "Now where is that special young un?" By this time Mary has the seat belt off of a now very awake little Kathryn. Kathryn looking all around, calls out, frightened,   "Mommy, where's mommy?"

"It's ok Kathryn; this is your *daed*," responds Mary. Everyone stands back and Samuel gets out of the front seat and opens the door to the back seat.

"Hi there *liebe. Kumme* to daed," says Samuel as he lifts Kathryn out into smiling gazes of his family and friends. Kathryn holds both hands on her daed's shoulders and holds him off at a distance and studies him.

"Daddy, are you my daddy?" She takes her right hand and traces his face.

"*Jah, liebe*, I am your *daed*." He bounces her up and down once. At that moment she wraps her arms around him and hugs him tightly. Samuel looks out amongst the family and, with Mary, makes his way to the tables set up outside. As he sits down, Rachel and Caleb come over.

"Is this our new *schweschder*, daed?" asks Rachel as Kathryn looks down suspiciously.

"*Jah*, this is Kathryn," responds their daed. Samuel is looking at all three of the *kinner*. "Can she play with us?" Caleb asks. Again, their daed looks at Kathryn and she holds back onto him.

"Not right now, she doesn't know anyone." And with those words Mary comes over and gently lifts her from him.

"Where is my mommy?" asks Kathryn, looking around and then back at Mary.

"Mommy is gone to heaven Kathryn." Mary kisses her cheek, while carefully looking for approval from Samuel.

Kathryn appearing numb, drops her head down on Mary's shoulder, wrapping her arms and legs around Mary, as Mary whispers to Kathryn, "We will care for you now Kathryn. We will love you and feed you and you have a bedroom now that you share with a new sister, jah! We are not going anywhere. No one is leaving you. You will not be alone."

Sniffling, Kathryn again squeezes her arms around Mary as she shifts her head.

The family, though they get to see Kathryn, keep a respectable distance in fear of scaring her more than she is already.

Supper is indeed a good mix of southern and Amish cooking combined. Amos did the grace and all enjoy each other's company. Around seven o'clock everyone starts home to chores and to prepare for the following days church service.

For Mary and Samuel, they are already settling into a new family life. Kathryn now brings new challenges. Cleanup is completed outside. Rachel and Caleb are anxious to show Kathryn her new home and bedroom and call out, *"Mamm* and *Daed."*

Chapter Eleven

"*Jah kinner*," responds Mary.

"Can we show Kathryn around?" implores Rachel.

"*Jah*, would you like to go see your new room Kathryn?" asks Mary. She shakes her head and, spinning around on her picnic bench seat, is led away by her new brother and sister. The three go up the steps and into the house.

Caleb begins, "This is the kitchen where *mamm* makes our meals."

"I help!" corrects Rachel.

"*Jah* and sometimes Mr. Bill helps too," Caleb counters.

"*Jah* but mostly it's *mamm* and I, Caleb," argues Rachel.

"Ok Rachel. And this is the front room where we sit, talk and pray, right Rachel?"

"*Jah*, *daed* leads the family in prayer every evening and reads the Bible," continues Rachel.

"This is the new laundry room where mamm and I do wash. It used to be the old bathroom, but daed made a new one and made this a laundry room so we did not have to go into the cellar anymore."

Not to be outdone by his sister, Caleb cuts in quickly,

"Kathryn, look over here. This is the new bathroom. And up here is your room!" as he starts to run up the stairs.

"Caleb, that's *baremlich*! You're taking over again! It's my room and I'm going to show her! *Kumme* Kathryn, hold my hand," as she carefully takes Kathryn's hand and leads her one step at a time up the stairs and towards her room.

As they enter their room, Kathryn looks around the room and then walks over to the middle.

"Here, this is your bed," Caleb runs over and pats it.

"*Jah*, right here Kathryn," says Rachel.

Her brother cuts in, "Let me show her my room. I'm her *bruder*, too."

"*Jah* Caleb, you are, and it is a very important job also," says Mary as she is now in the hallway looking in at the three. They move past their *mamm* with Kathryn holding Rachel's hand, and Caleb leading the way. Samuel walks up, kissing Mary on the lips.

"Mrs. Hersberger." He smiles at her. Mary smiles back.

"That was *gut, jah*! Mr. Hersberger." And then she sneaks another kiss. As the children exit Caleb's room spotting their parents in the middle of the kiss, they stop and smile.

"*Mamm* and *Daed* are *liebe*," says Caleb.

"Shhh! Caleb!" exclaims Rachel.

"*Kinner*," Mary now is pulling back and correcting the children's bickering.

"Yes *mamm*," says Rachel and Caleb simultaneously.

"I want you to take Kathryn and go to the parlor for evening prayer."

"Yes *mamm*, *kumme* Rachel and Kathryn," directs Caleb.

෴

"Dear heavenly father, we gather here before you tonight, humble and thankful. Please give us wisdom as we read from your good book so we may learn and grow in your name, Amen. Caleb, Rachel, and Kathryn, the lesson today is quite an important one. It is about God's love and the love he wants us to have for each other. It comes from his word in the Bible, First John, Chapter Four, seventh and eighth verse. Beloved, let us love one another: for love is of God; and everyone that loveth is born of God, and knoweth God. He that loveth not knoweth not God; for God is love. This is important, if you love, you are a child of God and you know God as you would a friend. If you do not love one another you do not know God and you do not have his friendship, as his word says. God is love. Do you understand?" All together they responded, "Yes, *daed!*"

"Very *gut*, go up stairs, get ready for bed, and be kneeling down when we come in your room, ready for prayers. *Schnell!*" Mary now interjects.

"Kathryn, *kumme*, I'll help you, *Schnell* means quickly! Ok?" Rachel takes Kathryn's hand and leads her upstairs.

"*Danki* Rachel," says Mary as she stands. She follows the children with her eyes and as they disappear into their rooms, she turns to Samuel, places her arms around him and whispers, "That was *verra gut* Samuel, new *daed* to now three *kinner*. Would you ever have dreamed this?" Mary kisses him on the lips and Samuel returns her kiss.

Smiling, he whispers, "No, but it is coming naturally. Let's get up there, shall we?" The two reach the top and hear Rachel helping Kathryn.

"This way Kathryn, that's it. Now when you pray just talk to Jesus like your friend. You can ask him for help or to protect people. But it's also important to thank him for things, too. Ok?"

"Ok," a barely audible whispered voice can be heard. Samuel and Mary stand quietly outside of Rachel's room. They just look at each other and smile.

"Rachel and Kathryn, are you ready for your prayers?"

"Yes *mamm*," says Rachel. The two children silently finish saying their prayers.

As they enter Caleb's room, they find him kneeling down and smiling over his left shoulder.

"Can I someday pray like *daed*, *mamm*?" There is silence, which seems to last forever. *David?* Then Mary responds as if awakening, "*Jah*, and you will Caleb, you will."

ℰℛ

"Ok, ya'll now hear this. We haven't been here that long and you're already beginning to act up. You're old enough to know better. On one hand, ya wanna be treated like adults, but then ya go behaving like kids. Now we won't be haven this whining and complaining anymore, got it?" scolds Bill.

"Yes sir," answers Roy, now home from Virginia where he attends school at VMI.

"But dad," Mary answers back.

"No buts; all this over not haven TV. This isn't the first time ya went without TV now! Your mother and I discussed this and there will be no TV programming. We let you have your CD's and you can watch approved movies. That's it, after this, no more discussion."

"Yes sir," answers Travis, agreeing with his older brother.

"To bed now and don't forget your prayers." Their dad says sternly. *Prayer, who cares about prayers? I don't care what happens to people in the world. They don't care about me. Hmmm, I still have my thoughts. Can you read these thoughts? Didn't think so.* Mary is now thinking to herself after being scolded by her father in a family meeting.

"Bill, Mary is really beginning to worry me so. What are we going to do about her?" asks a concerned Helen.

"I know Helen. What has she been doing round the house?" questions Bill.

"Nothing, I know that is part of the problem. Tomorrow is a brand new day for that young lady," says Helen.

$$\infty\omega$$

Upon entering their bedroom, Mary walks up behind Samuel and slides her arms around his waist and places her head against his back. Samuel takes hold of her hands and they just stand for a moment.

"We have *gut kinner* Samuel," whispers Mary.

"*Jah*, we do," agrees Samuel.

"Someday they will go through *rumspringa*," Mary is now thinking aloud to herself.

"NO! I don't believe in it. It is one thing that I will not allow," Samuel uncharacteristically barks aloud.

"Was your time amongst the English so awful Samuel?"

"No, it wasn't the English. It was running from my home. I don't want this. We will love them and raise them straight and honest, and in fear of God and the law of God. And they will know his and our love. They will do what is right in their lives."

Mary just remains where she is, pressed against his back, very still. *What have you been through Samuel? I don't know large parts of your life. When will I learn? Will I learn?*

Mary leaves go, taking hold of his shoulders and, stretching up, kisses his neck. Turning around, he wraps his arms around her waist, lifting her up, and kisses her. She responds by wrapping her arms around his neck, opening her mouth and kissing her husband back. The passion is interrupted by Mary talking while lip to lip, "How do I take a shower Samuel? Will you show me?"

"*Jah, kumme,* I'll show you," says Samuel, smiling.

"*Danki,*" says Mary as they enter the bathroom. Samuel turns the water on and adjusts the water temperature. He then shows Mary how to flip the lever to make the shower functional.

"It's like rain Samuel," she says as she laughs like a school girl.

"*Jah,* you would think you had not seen water before *liebling,*" teases Samuel, taking pleasure in his wife's happiness.

"Go, let me shower," says Mary as she playfully pushes Samuel backwards out of the bathroom door.

"OK," says Samuel, laughing.

Samuel is already in bed when Mary climbs in to the front of him. Samuel wraps his arms around her and pulls her close to 'cuddle', and as he does so, Mary puts her feet between his legs.

"*ACH*!! Your feet are freezing!" exclaims Samuel.

"*Jah*, they are always cold. But you're always warm. *Danki*," teases Mary.

"You're welcome, I suppose," 'suffers' Samuel.

"Samuel!" Mary says looking over her shoulder smiling.

It's three thirty in the morning, Samuel and Mary have been asleep three hours.

"Mommy!!!" is heard; the blood curdling scream.

Rachel jumps and screams herself, "*Maaammm! Daed! Kumme Schnell, Schnell!*" As quickly as Mary followed by Samuel moved, Rachel was already there sitting on Kathryn's bed holding her little schweschder tightly.

"She is scared *mamm*." Mary quickly picks up Kathryn and holds her close.

"Samuel, settle Rachel, I'll care for Kathryn."

"Jah, *kumme* Rachel, back to your bed now, *mamm* will take care of Kathryn."

Samuel tucks Rachel into her sheets for the night. As he brushes her hair with his fingers he tells her, "You were a gut *schweschder*, Rachel. *Danki* and *gut nacht*."

"*Gut nacht daed*," says Rachel.

ෆ ೦૨

After Mary carries Kathryn downstairs and to the front parlor, she sits in the rocking chair that her dat made her. After making Kathryn's bed, Samuel goes downstairs to find Mary now rocking Kathryn like a boppli and humming quietly. Kathryn sniffles occasionally and then finally falls asleep. As she stands with her new kinner, Samuel reaches the bottom of the stairs.

"*Wie geht's?*" Samuel asks.

"*Gut liebling*. The *boppli* is asleep," reassures Mary appearing tired.

"*Gut*, shall I carry her?" asks Samuel, reaching for Kathryn. Mary looks up from the warmth in her arms, smiles, and shakes her head no.

When Mary and Samuel awaken the next morning, they go to check on the two kinners and they find Rachel sideways in her bed holding onto Kathryn's hand.

"*Ach* Samuel, look; they are so precious," says a doting Mary.

"It was a *gut* idea for them to be together in the same room Mary," says Samuel reflecting on their original conversation.

"*Danki* Samuel," says Mary, as she lays her head on Samuel's arm.

ℰℭ

The sun is just beginning to peak over the eastern horizon of trees and the Kramer's are already at the breakfast table.

Helen looks up at Mary and lays out the new chores for her, "Mary, when we are done with breakfast, you will gather up the laundry and start it?"

Mary, rebellious, quickly retorts, "mom why?"

Not to be giving any room to Mary, Helen quickly asks her son if he will help, "Travis, will you help me in the house?"

"Yes ma'am," is his quick and respectful response.

Helen follows up by asking, "What have you been doing since we arrived?"

Travis, smiling, responds, "mucking and cleaning the horse stalls and putting down a new bed of straw."

Helen, getting her answer, looks back towards Mary and says "good, then for today Mary, you will muck out the horse stalls and put new straw down."

Shocked, Mary retorts again, "What?"

"You heard me!" If you want to do this every day, you sass me every day."

"If that is not enough, then I'm certain your father will find something as suitable to add to this work."

Bill, shaking his head, quickly agrees with his wife and speaks up, "Yep, lots of horse manure to move. A little shoveling will help build a little muscle and respect for both your mamma and yourself. Now, what do you say about that?"

Mary doesn't say anything and stands up. A little taken back, she says solemnly, "I'll be gettin my jeans on then. I'm sorry I sassed ya mom."

ℰℭ

The whole family is sleepy today. Samuel and Mary decide it is wise to allow the kinner to sleep in. Mary begins breakfast. As she lights the stove, she leans forward and the cloth she is holding catches fire. Samuel turns as it flares up. Bounding to it, he pulls it from Mary's hand throwing it to the floor and stomps it.

"*Ach*, Mary! *Wie gehts?*"

"Ok, just tired Samuel, and I have another headache."

"Go lie down. I will make breakfast. Go while I get ice for your head." Mary stands, looking at what has just happened.

"*Schnell liebe!* I will take care of things."

"*Danki*, Samuel." Samuel gets ice out of the freezer, puts it in a cloth, crushes it, and then places it in a bag and goes upstairs to their room, placing the bag gently on Mary's head. He gets some medicine from his night stand, water from the bathroom sink, and has her take it. After going downstairs, he cleans up the mess.

Preparing breakfast for the family, he awakens the children. Caleb is the first down the stairs asking, "*Daed*, where is *mamm?*"

"Resting in bed, you and your sisters need to be quiet this morning so she may rest, ok?" They nod their heads yes as the two sisters reach the kitchen. After they eat, he has them change.

"Rachel, can you find some plain clothes for Kathryn?"

"*Jah daed.*"

"*Gut, Danki.*" He is putting together a meal for Mary.

"Mary have some of this. I put together some toast, eggs, bacon, apple juice, and tea. I know you like tea and the caffeine might help the headache."

"*Danki* Samuel." Samuel then kisses her forehead and returns downstairs.

Samuel gets something to eat himself as activity out in the yard begins. He watches horses being moved and Bill and Helens children outside working. *Is that Mary with a pitch fork? Hmmm. Wonder what that is all about. I have paperwork to go over today. Empty out footlockers. Then I'll meet with Bill.* Pouring himself another cup of coffee, he heads for his office as Caleb comes running down the stairs.

"*Stoppin* the running Caleb." Caleb with a shocked look on his face slows his pace. The girls soon follow behind with Kathryn dressed in plain. Samuel smiles at her and takes a sip of coffee. The girls walk slowly down the stairs as if to make an entrance to a formal.

"*Jah*, Kathryn, you look plain. Rachel, teach Kathryn your chores today, she will help you. Caleb, you know your chores sohn?"

"Jah daed?"

"Mamm helped us with the pinning's daed."

"Ok, well considering I have no idea of what that is all about, I guess that is gut, Danki Rachel." Both girls smile up at him. *It isn't that, it's enough to steal my heart away. They have stolen my heart away. Dear Lord, thank you for these kinner. Now how's Mary?*

Samuel makes his way upstairs to find Mary lying down with her eyes closed. He sits down next to her, takes her kapp off, and unpins her hair. Stroking her hair with his fingers he lets down all her hair. Mary turns to him and smiles.

"I'm feeling much better Samuel, *Danki.*"

"Your *willkum, liebe.* You sleep a while longer. When you're ready, you get up. I'm headed out after some paperwork."

"*Danki* Samuel," Mary thanks Samuel again, as he kisses her forehead and now standing, smiles down at her.

Once in his office, Samuel locks the door and proceeds to take down the footlockers and open them up.

Make sure these things are locked in a fire-resistant safe. If we had a fire, there could be some very unhappy firefighters. Get a count. Two thousand. Spot on! Into the new safe, this footlocker empty. Next, two side and two shoulder, into the safe and secured. Clothes from the third footlocker can go in there also. Lord please, I don't ever want to use these things ever again, but if it be your will. It was gut you had not known these things daed, it was gut.

Samuel pulls the three footlockers together, unlocks and opens the door, and there stands Caleb.

"*Daed*, Mr. Kramer is looking for you."

"Tell Mr. Kramer I'll be out in about an hour, ok? *Danki.*"

"*Jah daed.*" Samuel rubs his head and Caleb turns, placing his straw hat on, and proceeds down the hall until Samuel hears the kitchen door close.

Get locked back up again. Samuel opens the fourth footlocker.

Electronics. Into the desk drawers under key. Where do I secure the keys? Place the keys in the safe. Combination in my head. Not safe for Mary to have the combination. Give it to Hutchins. Phone book, circle the page numbers to remind me of the combination, just in case I forget. Another footlocker empty now. All the electronics with their appropriate electrical cords are secured. Let's see, hardened sat uplinks and computers, no room in the desk. Guess I'll have to squeeze these in the safe also, pull the clothes, no squeezing, plenty of room. Clothes in on top. No, put these in the fifth footlocker with the rest of my clothes. Last footlocker on top of safe and locked. Glad I checked out the flooring underneath. Daed would have been pretty angry if this room ended up in the cellar. Now outside.

ဆၣ

The business of managing horses continues. Bill Kramer is putting in a full day as another foal is being born today. Then he is contending with his seventeen year old daughter in rebellion. All the horses are corralled. Mary, working slowly, is now on her third stall.

The hardest part she would have thought is the mucking of the stalls. It turns out that the hard part is the weight of the bails. Even though she asks for help, she gets none. Everyone has their own work to do on the busy ranch. It is hard, but she gets it done, learning a little about perseverance.

"Dad, when I'm done can I take Armistead out for a ride," Mary asks politely.

"Yep! Good idea," her father says, noting a quick change in attitude and good work.

"Thanks!" A now excited Mary works more earnestly and before she knows it she is saddling up her horse, Armistead, and heading out into what used to be Hersberger farmland. Wearing clean jeans and a t-shirt with her white canvass Stetson, she has Armistead head out in a trot.

ಬಿಂದ

Samuel reaches the corral as Mary is leaving. Bill, leaning on the corral's fence rail, is watching his daughter head out. Laughing, Samuel asks, "So Bill, what's with Mary and the pitchfork today?"

Bill, responding to his friend and boss, joins in the laughter as he says, "Misbehavin."

"Hmmm, mucking stalls?" asks Samuel.

"Yep," responds Bill, with a piece of straw in his mouth as he looks over at Samuel.

Samuel then asks Bill, "Kinner learn anything?"

"Hope so." Bill is looking serious now. Samuel continues to inquire, "Where's Travis?" Bill, without flinching, answers, "Doin laundry." Samuel quickly counters, "Wonder who was punished more?" Both men begin to laugh as they turn and lean with elbows hunched up against the rail.

"So, what's up?" Samuel asks catching up with why he was called out.

"New foal born, vets been called, on the way over now."

"Gut!"

"William looked into that house that you suggested. David Stutzman's old place. Nice place. He couldn't believe it. Close enough to get to work. His family will like it a lot. He'll be thankin ya."

"Will he be movin his family up?"

"He notified them already. Heh Sam, Helen and I been talken, we like the Dawdi house. Any need for us to move?"

"No Bill, not at all."

"We're settling in quite nicely. Roy is getting used to a long distance relationship. He'll be headin back down south to finish school, then I think he'll be getting married and starten out on his own. Let's take a look at what Mary did. She had twelve stalls to do," Bill says, as they near the old barn where the personal horses are kept.

"*Gut*, she really misbehaved, twelve stalls *jah*?"
Kidding, Bill says, "*jah*." Both men begin to laugh again as they enter the stables.

"Mary did a gut job Bill. Real *Gut*, *jah*! Helen is a gut *mamm* and you're a gut *daed*!"

Chapter Twelve

Somewhere along the way, Mary and Armistead cross over into Jeremiah's farm where tobacco is growing. As Mary rides, she comes across a young Amish man. Standing up, Daniel catches site of Mary. He has soil in his hands, letting it drop down through his fingers after smelling it. As the last of the dirt hits the ground, Mary reaches Daniel, who is now staring at her.

"Hi, I'm Mary, Mary Kramer." Mary's long auburn hair is blows in the wind as she pulls it out of her face. She gives the stranger a smile.

"Good morning Mary, Mary Kramer. Strange name Mary, Mary Kramer," as he smiles back at her.

"No my name is….." Now laughing the young man interrupts, "I know, Mary, like my Aunt Mary, *jah*?"

"You're related to Mary Hersberger?" Mary looks down at Daniel.

"*Jah*, I'm Daniel Hersberger. We met briefly at your homecoming, Mary."

"I don't remember you," a confused Mary continues to look down.

"Many of us!" as he laughs some more.

"Yes," Mary answers as she begins to feel warm inside as her heart speeds up.

"Nice horse, Mary," he says as he walks up to Mary's horse, taking his bridle and rubbing his ear.

"Thank you. This is Armistead." At that moment Armistead whinnies.

"*Gut buwe*, Armistead. My daed is Jeremiah; my Uncle Samuel's oldest brother."

"So, Mary, what brings you to our tobacco?" Daniel looks Mary over from her long sassy auburn hair, her body curves, past her form fitting jeans and down to her brown boots. Not one inch of her is missed.

He too begins to feel giddy inside as he realizes his attraction to this English girl. He begins to take in her features. Dimple on her right cheek when she smiles, couple of freckles on each side of her cheeks. Full lips. No makeup. *She is beautiful. I can't help being attracted to this girl. How old is she? The wind, the way it blows through her hair. Her lips, the way they look as she talks. Green eyes, playful…..a little mischievous…..*

Mary looks around, smiles, and looks down at the ground. *He is so handsome…strong….and funny in his own silly way. His eyes are determined, a man who knows what he is doing. How old are you Daniel?*

"Could you help me down?" Mary asks.

"*Jah*," Daniel smiles up at Mary. He takes her reins with his right hand and with his left, takes hold and steadies her right stirrup. As Mary comes down off her horse, Daniel reaches up under her right arm. Mary stumbles forward a little and ends up against Daniel face to face.

Her hair dances from the wind again, this time in Daniels face. He thinks to himself, *her hair smells so good, like apples. Her warmth, her body is against me. Her lips so close to mine, I could just kiss her right now….Ach!!! Temptations…*

"Thank you, Daniel," Mary says as she feels his closeness. *He is so strong… blue eyes like the rest of his family. And gentle…he is so gentle… he is Amish. What am I thinking? I am so attracted to him!*

"*Jah*, would you like to walk?" Daniel asks.

"Yeah, yes, I would enjoy that," Mary responds emboldened by her attraction to Daniel. They begin to walk down between the rows of tobacco with Armistead in tow.

∽◯◠

Back at the Ranch, Mary is feeling better and is up and completing dinner. Something light. Ham, potato salad and coleslaw and fresh bread for sandwiches. The *kinner* is helping now with dinner. Kathryn and Rachel go to get their daed.

"*Daed!*" Rachel calls out.

Samuel comes out of the stables and questions, "Time for lunch, *kinner*?"

Smiling Rachel corrects, "Dinner, *jah daed.*"

As he reaches the girls, he removes his work gloves laying them on the porch table. He reaches out and takes each of the girl's faces in each hand. They both look up and smile at him and take his hands.

"*Mamm, daed's* here." The girls lead him into the house, practically pulling him in.

"*Kumme*, dinner is set."

"*Danki, liebe.*" Samuel walks up and caresses the left side of Mary's face with his right hand, kissing her softly at the same time. When they look, all three children are looking at them and smiling. Caleb says grace today, simple.

"Thank you oh Lord for these gifts for which we are about to receive, Amen."

All respond "AMEN!"

₨₧

Bill and Helen are having lunch with their two boys. Having said grace, they begin to converse.

"How did Mary make out, Bill?" Helen asks her husband just as he raises his sandwich to his mouth, "Good, good! Especially after she found out she could go riding."

"Where is she now, do we know?" asks Helen.

"No, but I'm sure she's ok; only been gone an hour," Bill says, anxious to take his first bite.

"She's missen lunch," Helen has her hands folded under her chin and leans on the table in front of her. The boys look on.

"Helen, she'll eat when she gets here. She'll be fine. Don't fret so."

"Just bein a mamma, can't help that none, ya know that."

"Yes ma'am." Speaking for the first time, the boys look up and smile at their mom."

"When you boys get done, we'll start bringing Mr. Hersberger's horses in, then ours. Put them in their stalls. OK?'

"Yes sir." Roy looks directly at his father.

❧❦

Daniel and Mary, having reached Daniels home, climb the short way up the back porch steps.

"Just in time for dinner, let's get something to eat. Ok?" says Daniel.

"Is it ok?" Mary asks as she ties Armistead to the hitching rail.

"Jah," Daniel says, looking at Mary strangely.

"Why would it not be ok?"

"Bringing a strange girl into the house, the way I'm dressed." Mary answers, looking down at herself. Realizing she is not dressed as she knows anyone else would be.

"You're English; maybe that's strange, *jah*?" Daniel starts to laugh at his own sense of humor.

"I'm not strange!" Mary picks up quickly on Daniel's sense of humor, smiling at him.

"That's what I've been trying to tell you." Daniel opens the door to his house and directs Mary in before him.

"Mamm, Daed, I brought a guest." They both stop and look. Waiting, his daed directs Daniel in to sit.

"Daniel, will you be introducing us?" asks his mamm.

"*Jah*, I'm sorry, *dummkopp!*" Daniel smacks himself across the head.

"This is Mary Kramer. She lives over on Uncle Samuel's farm."

"Hello Mary, I remember now, *willkum*."

"Thank you, Ma'am," Mary is looking over at Daniels mother.

Mary finishes having dinner and it is getting onto one o'clock. She is also afraid she will be missed.

"Thank you for lunch. I appreciate it. Daniel, I have to be going. Do you know how I can get back to the ranch from here?"

"*Jah*, I'll show you....wait, I have a better idea. It's quiet at this time of the day. I'll hook up the buggy and take you back to the ranch. We'll tie Armistead to the back of the buggy."

"Daniel, you be careful now," his father says.

"Yes *daed*, I will."

"Thank you Daniel," adds a relieved Mary.

Daniel hooks up his horse to the buggy which is pointing out of the driveway. Then he ties Armistead to the back of the buggy. Daniel offers a hand to Mary and she comes face to face with Daniel again as she smiles and places her hand in his. *I am so attracted to this guy, Oh my gosh, his warmth.*

"Erica, did you notice what buggy he hooked up?"

"No, which?"

"The courting, do you think she knows?"

"She's English, no Jeremiah. What are you thinking?"

ॐ

"I hear horses approaching there Bill."

"Oh yeh, where?"

"There!" as the buggy enters the driveway.

"She's with my nephew." *On the courting buggy. Daniel....and nahh...*

"Hi sweetie, how ya doin?" Mary's dad quickly engages her.

112

"Ok dad, just got a little lost after I got to Daniel's and his family's farm."

"Are ya hungry?" Bill, being the concerned dad, asks.

"No sir, had lunch there, thank you." A relieved dad now turns to Daniel.

"Thanks a lot, Daniel, for bringing Mary home." Then thinks to himself, *No sir?" What a change in attitude.*

"Your welcome, Mr. Kramer." As he hitches Armistead to the rail.

"Mary, can I speak with you a moment?"

"Sure. Excuse me dad." He leads her away from the ears of the 'adults' and, in a whispered voice, "Can I see you again?" Mary looks at him and smiles.

"I would like that, yes, I would like that a lot." Daniel turns all giddy and bouncing.

"*Wunderbaar,* I have an *aldi*. I'll see you later then, *jah.*"

"Yes ok." She watches as the buggy leaves. *Must ask Uncle Samuel what these words are.* She has been referring to her dad's boss as uncle since she could speak.

"Uncle Samuel," a smiling Mary approaches Samuel.

"*Jah.*"

"I understand what *jah* is, but what is *wunderbaar* and *aldi*?"

"Huh, *aldi*?" Samuel reaches up under his straw hat and scratches his head.

"Jah, aldi and *wunderbaar.*" kiddingly she responds.

"Mary *wunderbaar* is wonderful, and *aldi* is….Well, *aldi* is girlfriend." Smiling broadly, she looks up at her uncle's eyes and says, "Girlfriend huh?" Looking away and down the drive she continues, "Yesssss!!!!"

৪৩৫

Bill and Samuel enter their respective homes after a long day on the ranch.

"Mary, guess who our Daniel is seeing?" asks Samuel.
"Who?"

"Mary," responds Samuel, as Mary looks at him, grinning.

"It is a complicated life you have brought with you Samuel Hersberger, *jah*" Samuel just smiles. Mary giggles and finishes.

"*Jah*, complicated, nothing our dear Lord can't handle."

The routine begins to set in at the Hersberger's. The end of June comes quickly and with that comes changes. Every other Sunday, Daniel comes by with his courting buggy and picks up Mary and they go off to town. In between, they walk in the fields. At times, they are seen holding hands. Summer becomes very pleasant. The Kramer's, as well as her brothers, enjoy the new attitude in Mary. She enjoys her chores. But something remains missing in her life. And what troubles both the Kramer's and Hersberger's about their children is that they are unequally yoked, or are they? Is Mary an unbeliever and Daniel a believer? Or maybe they are both unbelievers. If they are both believers, one is English and the other Amish.

&)(&

It is July nineteenth and the Thursday before a non church weekend, coming to the end of a long week. The children are in bed, and Samuel and Mary are sitting in the love seat swing they have hanging from the front porch. Mary lays her head over and rests on Samuel's shoulder.

"Samuel, how tall are you?"

"Six feet, why?"

"I'm five inches shorter than you."

"Jah, and...."

"Nothing. Do you love me? I mean, am I everything you ever wanted in your life?"

"Yes...... yes many times yes and more. You and the *kinner* are my life Mary."

"Because of the kinner. Do you love me because of the *kinner*?" Mary begins to cry.

"Mary, what is this about? You'll never know how much I love you with or without the *kinner*."

"You don't want the *kinner*?"

"No, I never said that. Look at me now, right here," says Samuel, gently taking Mary with one finger under her chin.

"I love you with all that the good Lord has given me to love you with. I am not now or ever going anywhere. I look forward to growing old with you. Do you understand all of that?"

"*Jah*," reaching up and kissing Samuel deeply and passionately, she crawls over on top of him, sitting on his lap.

"Mary, I think we should take this inside."

"Uh…huh? Hmm… whatever you say *liebe*." Samuel picks Mary up as they are still kissing. Carrying her upstairs, he is thinking, *putting on a little weight*. As they get upstairs, Samuel does something he has never done before.

"*Ach*, pin stuck me!" yells Samuel. Mary is now playfully laughing and just not acting herself.

"I'll do this," she says as she removes her apron, then her skirt and blouse. She sits on the chair and removes her shoes and stockings. She then stands and removes the pins from her hair. It falls and she shakes her head. She smiles at her love. By this time he is sitting on the bed. She goes over to the front of him and falls on top of him kissing him passionately.

Next morning, Mary is up first and in the bathroom. She is throwing up.

"Mary, are you Ok?" Samuel holds back her hair.

"Ahh no, not at the moment, danki Samuel. *Sis mer iwwel*. And I have an awful headache again."

"I can see that. Maybe we should start thinking about a doctor, Mary."

"We'll see, Samuel. Ok? I think the doctor can't help with part of what is going on here, Samuel."

"What do you mean?"

"Samuel, I am with *boppli*." Not getting the idea right away, he responds, "Huh?"

"Samuel, you are a *daed*."

"Jah, I know."

"Samuel, again. You are going to be a daed again, Samuel. I'm pregnant!" Samuel is now beaming as everything begins to sink in.

"A *daed*."

Chapter Thirteen

Mary and Samuel return from the doctors. The date is Friday, the twentieth of July. The baby's due date is the seventeenth of March. Mary is healthy. The two took the buggy to the doctor's office in Honey Brook. After returning, they get out of the buggy. Andrew, Katie's husband, and another one of the ranch hands come out of the corral and walk over taking hold of the horse.

"Samuel, I'll take care of Luke here."

"Thank You, Andrew and how are Katie and the *boppli*?"

"Samantha, *gut*! *Jah*, *gut*! And also my Katie, they are both *gut*."

"I understand you are doing a very gut job here Andrew, *danki*. Are you enjoying the work?" asks Samuel now coming around to help Mary down from the buggy.

"You're *willkum* Samuel. *Jah*, I am enjoying the work *verra* much. You should see Samantha. She is pushing herself up now. And sometimes, when she is all excited, she looks like she is swimming real fast. It's funny to watch, *jah*," says the beaming new father.

"*Jah*, I can just picture that," Samuel says looking over at Andrew.

Being helped down from the buggy, Mary is now at Samuels's side, takes his arm and, looking at Andrew, begins talking. "Andrew, please tell Katie that I am with *boppli*."

"You are!? That's *wunderbaar*! She will be so excited!"

"You are the first to know, so don't spread the word to fast. Give us a chance to tell the rest of the family, ok? Tell Mamma though." Mary continued.

"*Jah*, I will!" Andrew is beaming in the hot sun while he covers his eyes. He bolts over and shakes Samuel's hand and then, looking for a moment, hugs Mary. "This is *wunderbaar, gut!*" Everyone laughs. Andrew walks away taking Luke with him. Mary holds Samuel's arm again and walks toward the house. Climbing the steps, Samuel, takes her left hand and helps her.

"Samuel, I am ok *liebe*. I will not break. I have had *boppli's* before."

"*Jah*, be patient with me, I'm new at this," as they both laugh. He continues to help her up the steps.

"*Danki* Samuel," she says looking at him with a smile.

"I love you very much, Samuel Hersberger."

Reaching the inside of the house, they find Helen who was watching the children.

"Well, did you find out why you were sick, Mary?"

"I am with *boppli*," says Mary, smiling at Helen.

"*Boppli*? What in the world is ......you're pregnant!? Good Lord, I knew it! I surely did! I can't wait to tell Bill! Well, you two have a lot to do I'm sure. Kathryn and Rachel are still working on the chores you gave them this morning. And Caleb is out watching and learning from one of the ranch hands how to shoe horses."

"*Gut* Helen, *danki*," Samuel says with his Pennsylvania Dutch accent all but completely back now.

"*Danki* Helen!" Mary follows Helen to the back door. Helen turns and hugs Mary. Excited Helen continues, "This is such great news!"

"*Jah*, we are both very excited and thankful to the Lord." One more smile from Helen and she is out the door.

Mary goes about working in the kitchen preparing dinner. Samuel retreats to his office to go about the daily business of horses. *Let's see, four fouls born total. That brings the total to sixty horses. There is a pending sale of seven of them, four mares for Ten-Thousand each, three geldings for six -thousand each. That is a total of Fifty eight-thousand dollars. Business is picking up. Delivery of these will be completed in one week. Gut. Who is working? Bill is managing and Andrew is assisting him. William's the cook. Then there are seven ranch hands at minimal wage plus room and board. I must have Bill look into bonuses for these men and themselves. This will help keep everyone on board. We are already going to lose two of them to the National Guard when they go for two weeks training. We should be able to manage.*

Samuel is in his office for another hour when he hears a knock on the door. He gets up, opens the door, and before Mary says anything, he smiles at her and simply gives her a quick kiss. "I take it dinner is ready, *jah?*"

"*Jah*, Samuel, it is," as she looks past him into the office.

"You want a tour Mary? Let me show you. This is my desk. It is *gut*, I have electric for light." He then flips on the switch again. I have a filing cabinet for our workers and taxes and another for the horses and the daily running of the business." Mary then looks over at the six foot tall, six foot wide steel safe.

"And that? That holds my past. Time to eat, I'm hungry."

"*Danki* Samuel," *your past again, it keeps coming back, but never to the surface.*

"You're *willkum*. I'll call the *kinner*," says Samuel until interrupted by Mary. "No, first, I know my place Samuel, but I know nothing of your past which is ok. You told me that you couldn't speak to me about this, but I also know nothing of our finances. I know nothing of what keeps our life here going. Is this not for me to know also?"

Mary crosses her arms. Samuel is quieted as he looks deeply at his wife then answers her, "this is truly no excuse, but you are right Mary. *Kumme*, I will show you." Walking over to his desk he pulls a chair around for Mary to sit down next to him. Out of the top drawer he pulls out their two checkbooks and opens them.

"We have two accounts. One is our business account. Out of this we pay those who work for us. This is our personal account. This we pay our own personal bills from, which we do not have many. I will start with this." He moves it in front of her.

"Our checking account balance is $14,000. There is a balance of $533,000 in savings, which is attached to the checking. There is just a little over $6,000 which is deposited into the account every month. This comes from my other business which I have not left completely. They have me on a standby status. If they are in need of help, they come to me." Mary is just staring, basically in disbelief, and keeps looking. "Samuel, this is a lot of money. I did not know we had so much."

"Mary, the large sum is mostly from the selling of the ranch in the south; after taxes $250,000 went into our personal accounts. The other part of that money $400,000, went into the business, it is over in this checkbook." Mary cuts in, "there is more?" Mary asks with her hands over her heart.

"*Jah* but let us finish over here. If something should happen to me, then this amount, more or less, will continue to come in as part of my retirement pay. You and the children will never be without."

"Samuel, I thought you left the past behind you?"

"I have, as you can see I work with horses, but there is a part which, if I am needed, is still available. Is this ok, Mary?"

"Jah, one day you will have to let me know of your past," responds Mary.

"*Jah*, I will, not yet, I can't yet. Please try to understand."

"You are my husband, I trust you Samuel."

Samuel relieved continues, "*Gut*, this is the business account, The checking has $61,000 to operate the business. The savings has that balance of $407,000 in reserve."

As Mary gasps, Samuel laughs, "Horses, this is a big business Mary."

"I just didn't know how big Samuel."

After dinner, Samuel approaches Mary as she does dishes, placing them to dry. Samuel picks up a cloth and begins drying and putting dishes in the closet.

"Mary, you have not seen the horses we personally own outside of the business. I would like to show you them."

"*Jah*, I would like that. I have not been outside very much. Samuel, I didn't know we owned horses outside of the business."

"*Ach*, it would be gut for the *boppli* and for you to be outside, *jah*? There is much you don't know. Our time together happened so quickly, Mary. I should have spent more time explaining. I'll start now."

"*Jah*," as she looks excitedly to her left at Samuel.

"Gut, we can go now after we finish this."

"Now?" Mary glances over, looking curiously at her husband.

"*Jah*, now," says Samuel as though he has something going on.

"Samuel, I must prepare supper," says Mary, begging to differ.

"We can go out for supper to the Smorgasbord."

"No, I will cook. We will save the restaurant for later."

"No, time to celebrate Mary, *Kumme*, please."

"Ok," says Mary, wiping her hands on her apron as she smiles at Samuel.

He looks back into the house and calls for the girls, "We'll call the kinner. Rachel! Kathryn! *Kumme, schnell*," calls out Samuel.

Two barefoot little girls come down the steps, one with *kapp*, and one without. Mary, noticing right away, stops the two in their place.

"Kathryn, where is your *kapp*?"

Rachel answers for her sister quickly, "I have it *mamm*. Here Kathryn, I'll help you put it on. It fell off *mamm*."

"*Gut, danki* Rachel!"

While walking outside, Samuel sees Bill and shouts down to him, "Bill!"

"Yes sir," responds Bill to his friend.

Samuel asks Bill, "Can you send Caleb up to the personal stables?"

"Yes sir!"

"*Danki.*"

Caleb, running, arrives at the stables. When he arrives, they all go in to see the horses of both families together. The kinner are wide-eyed as they begin looking all around the stables. Horses are whinnying everywhere as though in chorus. Beginning on Bill's side, Samuel begins to show his family the horses.

"These are Bill's, Helen's and their family's horses. This is Bill's horse, Jeb." The name JEB can be seen in print on the front of the stall of the horse as he whinnies.

"And this is Helen's horse. Hi there Pemberton, good buwe," speaking to the horse, he pats his neck. Looking at the next three horses, he points them out as they are walking. "Roy has Gordon, Travis has Polk, and Mary, of course, has Armistead. And Armistead, jah, Armistead likes to run. Armistead, like Mary, has a lot of energy. He is spirited." They walk over to the other side where the other horses can be seen.

"This is my horse. We haven't gone riding in quite awhile, have we Traveler? And this is Lee. This is the horse I want you to have. This is my gift to you," says Samuel in a low tone and patting the horse's neck while smiling at Mary.

"Mine? Whatever for Samuel?"

"He is to ride, Mary. Not now, while you are pregnant, but afterwards. It will be *verra gut* for you, *jah.*"

"*Danki* Samuel" As she pets Lee between the ears. "*Danki*," she repeats as Lee whinnies. "Lee, gut name, *jah.*"

"Caleb!", Samuel turns and looks down at his son.

"*Jah daed!*" Caleb is excited and steps up promptly.

"Caleb, this is Pickett. Now you will have to help care for him if you want him."

A broadly smiling Caleb nods his head up and down and is initially speechless.

"*Jah daed, Danki!* Can I pet him?"

"You can ride him! Would you like that?" Again, wide eyed and shaking his head even harder. No words this time.

"Go get Mister Kramer then, Ok?" A silent Caleb doesn't even speak or shake his head, he just starts running. It couldn't have been one minute before Bill shows up with one of the ranch hands.

"Bill, can we saddle up some horses and get a couple more riders?" Samuel is smiling like he's up to something.

Bill, with a smile as if in on what's going on, responds,

"Yes sir. Chuck go on down and git a couple of the fellas to see who wants to ride with a couple of young uns, Ok?"

"Yes sir" Chuck goes down and gets two more riders. They come back and saddle Pickett initially. Samuel reaches down and picks up Rachel.

"Rachel, your mamm and I want you to have this horse. His name is Hood. Do you want to go riding also?" Rachel, stunned silent, also just nods her head.

"Pull out Hood and saddle him. Kathryn, *kumme* here to *daed*," says Samuel quietly. He picks her up, now holding both girls.

"This is Hill. If you have a lot of help, will you care for her?"

Kathryn just stares. Then slowly, as if in a dream, both girls nod their heads. The horses are saddled and the kinner are handed up one at a time to the respective riders for their horse. Once all are on, they are shown the reins and then begin their education in riding. All in a row they head out.

"Take them for a nice ride out into the high meadow boys," orders Samuel, smiling.

The ranch hands nod affirmatively as one answer's, "yes sir."

Mary remains quiet and smiling the whole time. Before she can say anything, Samuel looks at her and quips, "they won't be spoiled Mary. They will work hard for what they have, jah." "They were like in a dream, Samuel. They were so excited."

123

"*Jah*, I liked watching that also."

೮ಂಶ

Out in the woods, Daniel and Mary, walk hand in hand, out of site and mind of the world they know and that knows them. Daniel, dressed in jeans and t-shirt and Mary in the same.

"You never did tell me what you are doing in jeans, Dan?"

"I can. I'm on my *rumspringa*. I just don't wear these in front of my *mamm* and *daed*."

"Daniel Hersberger, we have been going out for one month now and during this time, not once have you tried to kiss. Mm." At that moment, Daniel kisses Mary. Running his fingers through her hair, he quickly kisses her mouth, then her face.

Mary, caught up in the passion, responds by kissing Daniel back. Then stopping abruptly, Daniel steps back and apologizes,   "I'm sorry Mary, I just wanted to kiss you once, I got carried away."

"I'm not sorry Daniel... That was nice... What took you so long?"

"Being respectful?" Mary a little bolder now steps into Daniel, and with mouth open slightly kisses him again. This time Daniel responds, "I can't...breathe."

೮ಂಶ

The children, full of laughter, return to a waiting Bill in the yard next to the back porch. Hearing the laughter and commotion, Mary comes out wiping her hands on her kitchen apron followed closely by Samuel.

"Well, looks to me as though the kinner had a gut time of it Bill," says Samuel.

"Yep, I'll show them what we do with the horses after a hard ride."

"*Jah*, you do that Bill, *danki*." The children are lifted down off their horses and allowed to hold the reins with the ranch hand as they each lead their own horse into the stable. Bridle reins and saddles are taken off and the horses are brushed down.

"Ok, you young uns, git to your parents now, Ok?"

"Yes sir, Mister Kramer," says Caleb as all three excited children run across the drive, through the yard, up the wooden steps, and into the house.

෨෬

The Friday has been a full one. They arrive at Shady Maple for dinner. Bill and Helen are invited to go with their family. They take two cars for the trip. Once arriving, they head for and stand in a short line. Behind them step up three service men and one service woman and their dates or spouses. They stand in stark contrast to everyone while wearing their Battle Dress Uniforms. Samuel notices them. *All enlisted jah... Mary*. He finds Mary looking at him.

"Mary, go ahead, I'll catch up."

"Ok Samuel. Is everything alright?"

"*Jah*, go ahead." As they leave following the hostess, and before another couple can step up, Samuel turns to the cashier. Handing her his card again, he whispers to her, "The four soldiers and the four other people with them, right there, I'm paying for their night. Let's see that's eight for supper, *jah*?"

"Yes sir," says the woman smiling. She looks out at the soldiers who are looking back. They appear to wonder what may be wrong. Samuel signs the check and leaves a message.

"Tell them thank you and keep up the good work, thank you."

Then, as the four soldiers step up, Samuel is gone to be with his family, walking quickly to catch up. The receptionist questions the first soldier in uniform, "There are eight of you?"

The soldier looking back answers quickly, "Yes Ma'am, but we're paying separately."

The cashier smiles and simply states, "It has been taken care of. All eight of your meals are with the compliments of the Amish gentleman that was standing here a few minutes ago. He left a message. Thank you and keep up the good work."

Bewildered, he humbly says, "Thank you, ma'am." He turns and explains what has just occurred.

The other two service men and one woman all in turn say, "Thank You, Ma'am."

"No need to thank me, thank you."

As they are seated, the service woman heads for the buffet tables. Spotting Samuel, she walks up to him with a smile.

"Thank you very much sir, from all of us." She reaches out and shakes his hand. Samuel responds with a smile and a nod. The young soldier walks away to rejoin the others.

Dinner for all the Hersberger's and Kramer's has been a new experience. None of them have ever been there. There is so much to eat and there appears to be a 'mile' of food.

The children's attention is obviously on the desert table where they have spotted whoopee pies. They are on their mom's ear. It starts with, of all people, the quiet one. She gets down off her chair, comes over to Mary in front of everyone and for the first time Kathryn says,   "*Mamm*, may I get a cookie or whoopee pie?"

Mary, with tears in her eyes, reaches over and picks up Kathryn, and squeezing her tightly says, "I love you Kathryn."

Kathryn pushes her mom away, looking at her and smiles, "I love you, too, *mamm*."

Caleb, not to be left out, "*Mamm*, will you love me, too, if I want a whoopee pie?"

Everyone, laughing now, stands up with Bill stating, "Looks like it's time for desert."

"We'll take them" Travis says, still laughing. The other Kramer children take the hands of the Hersberger kinner and quickly walk off toward the desert tables.

৪৩৫৫

The night, being a memorable one for all, comes to an end. Before going to bed, the *kinner* at the Kramer house sit through their *daed's* bible lessons. They say their prayers while kneeling next to their beds and the fall asleep.

"*Kumme liebe*," Mary says as she takes Samuel's hand. She walks down the steps, out the front door, and onto the porch to the swing.

"Hmm!" Samuel says, kiddingly, with a smile.

"Samuel!"

"What Mary?"

"You know very well what," exclaims Mary, as she begins to bite her bottom lip with a smile.

"I remember that night very well, let's see who...?" Samuel is teasing his wife.

"Never mind," she says as she playfully pushes Samuel onto the swing then quickly jumps on herself.

Lightly swinging, Samuel begins to reminisce. "The whoopee pies reminded me of a time when I was a young teen before *rumspringa*. Becky and mamma would make all kinds of pies, cakes, and whoopee pies and wrap them. Daed, Becky, and I would take the wagon with the cabinet loaded with those baked items and firewood that daed would cut and bundle from the woods. We would take them to a local campground and sell them. It was a hard ride. We would feel every bump under the steel wheels. The campers would love to come out and buy things from us. I think they were curious about us also. I remember one German girl in particular. She must have been visiting this family. She came over and spoke to *daed* in German. They spoke for a short while. *Daed*, I think he enjoyed it."

The night was warm. In the distance orange flashes can be seen. A slight breeze can be felt. Mary sat quietly taking it all in and then she asked, "Samuel, what did you study in school?"

"College?" asks Samuel, after pausing.

"*Jah*," says Mary smiling at him as he answers.

"Business Administration."

"*Ach*, that is why you have your own business," Mary now understands another part of her husband's life. A rumble is heard in the distance and another flash of orange light is seen.

"*Jah*," says Samuel, looking over and smiling.

"*Danki* Samuel for sharing this with me."

"I missed a lot of years here. If my life had happened any other way, if I did not leave, we may not have met the way we did. My life has been one circumstance, leading to another circumstance, to another, to now. Oh what did the good Lord have planned for me?"

"But we have met Samuel."

"I know, I still miss…"

"Who Samuel?"

"My *Daed*."

Chapter Fourteen

Monday morning, the first week of August, starts out very hot and humid. Mary finishes helping her mother with chores that she readily does now.

"Mom, if it's ok with dad, may I go riding on my horse with Daniel?"

"Yes, where would ya be headin out ta now?"

"Don't know mom, just riden."

"Where is this relationship with Daniel going, Mary?"

"Mom, we're just friends."

"How close Mary? Heh, I've been there and I remember what it's like. Talk to me Mary. It may surprise you to know that I may be more understanding than you think."

Mary, sitting down at the kitchen table with a little perspiration, yet smiling, pats the table opposite her. She looks up at her mother with some tears starting to well in her eyes.

Her mother, not wanting to miss this invitation and appearing anxious, pulls a chair out quickly and sits down next to her.

Mary reaches out and takes her mother's hand and begins, "Mom, I really care for Daniel. He is so very different from all the other boys I have dated. He is more mature and caring. He kissed me mom and then he apologized. He backed away from me and apologized. It was so sweet and considerate. He makes me want to be a better person."

"I truly can see that; I can. But you must remember he is Amish."

"Mom, I believe that is what makes him, them, so special. He is forthright and, even though he is on his *rumspringa*, he looks forward to farming. He enjoys his family. *Rumspringa* to him is just a time to take a break and wear jeans. He is especially faithful and talks about his being Amish. Do I know where this relationship is going? No, but I, we, have time to find that out. For now it is enough to know that I care for him very much and enjoy his company." Mary is looking directly into her mother eyes.

"Thank You, Mary. It was very mature of you to sit down and speak of your feelings like this with me."

"May I go riding now mom?"

"Yes, go have fun!"

"Thanks!"

Mary, grabbing her Stetson, is off and out the back kitchen door and toward the stables. As she reaches the stables, she hears a horse and buggy coming down the drive. Sure enough. *Daniel, I missed you. I'm not gone from you for more than a day and I miss you.* Daniel pulls up to the corral looking over to his right at Mary, and smiles.

"It is a hot day, jah?" As he takes off his straw hat and fans himself.

"Hi Mary."

"Hi Daniel, I have a surprise for you. We're going riding, my way."

"We are?" Asks Daniel, excitedly.

"Yep! Help me get the horses, ok?"

"Jah, but first I must put this one in the corral and rest it,"
says Daniel.

Mary smiles, "Ok, I'll meet you in the stables." A short time later Daniel is in the stall. He is watching Mary pull out Travis's horse Polk. Armistead is out of his stable and cross-tied.

Daniel walks up to Mary from behind and, taking her arms, he leans over and kisses her neck through her hair.

Mary, looking over her left shoulder, smiles and whispers, "That was nice." She turns around.

"Hmmm, do it again then?" This time he kisses her lips ever so softly and tenderly. He does what he knows he cannot do with an Amish girl; run his fingers through Mary's long hair. He traces it down her back then brings his hands back to her forehead and strokes her hair again. He leans back a bit to study her features. Mary places her arms around Daniel and meets the tender touch of his lips with her own. She pulls away giggling.

"Come on, let's get saddled up." They saddle the horses and, as they do, Daniel starts to ask about the horses.

"Where did the names come from?"

"They are names of famous Southern Generals from the war of northern aggression."

"Ach! Names of who? And from what war?"

"I think ya'll know it as the Civil War.

"My dad and Uncle Samuel named them. They said that they were brave and faithful men who gave up much for freedom. Does this bother you, Daniel?"

"My Uncle Samuel helped name the horses after military generals. This is not Amish."

"Ahh, he wasn't Amish at the time, Daniel. Don't be so judgmental. Many a different people love Jesus, Daniel. Those southern soldiers were people of faith and they also loved Jesus."

"*Jah*, I suppose so. It's just not our way, that is all. I didn't know this. I didn't know this about my uncle. But then, there is so much we don't know about him. I do not understand this; what is it? A western saddle? I don't know how to put it on. Can you help me?"

"*Jah*," Mary says teasingly, breaking up the obvious tension. It works as Daniel now smiles again and pays attention as Mary throws the saddle up.

"You handle that like a man, Mary."

"Are you amazed, Daniel?" She smiles at him and giggles.

"Now what's next?" An inquisitive Daniel asks.

"Git in the saddle, so we can git! Here, this way." She steadies a stirrup.

"Put your left foot in here." Daniel is a little clumsy but manages to get into his saddle.

ഇൟ

The two are seen riding off through the meadow by Mary and Samuel.

"*Ach* young *liebe, jah*!" As Mary pushes up to Samuel's side and holds onto his arm.

"*Jah*, young, gut kinner, but growing fast," Samuel surmises.

"They are growing fast, aren't they Samuel? They will face many challenges if they remain together."

Mary continues her distant gaze. The wind begins to pick up and the sky is cloudless. Roses planted by Samuel for Mary in the spring give off their intoxicating fragrances. They are a beautiful deep crimson red. They can be seen from the porch as they reach above the third step. Off in the distance, a siren can be heard. *Lord let whoever is at the receiving end of this emergency vehicle know your presence and peace.* Mary prays to herself.

As the siren disappears, they look out at a balloon passing in the distance. It is colorful. Colors of the rainbow in diamonds fill the entire balloon. Two ranch hands can be seen moving horses out of a corral.

Mary turns toward Samuel and, with her left foot, steps between his, and into him. She reaches up with her right hand, caressing his face, which now has a short, dark, sandy-blond beard. She caresses back his hair with her other hand. Stretching up slightly on her toes, she reaches and brushes his lips with her own, then again. Then opens her mouth slightly and presses her lips onto his. Samuel holds her face gently in his strong hands and returns her kiss fully. He moves his hands down her back and pulls her into him, and they both can feel nothing between them but each other's warmth.

"Samuel," calls Mary quietly…and again, "Samuel."

132

"*Jah liebe,*" Samuel whispers back. Mary kisses him more. The passion grows.

"Samuel. I love you." As she tilts her head back and looks longingly into his eyes.

"I love you, too, Mary." Samuel looks down at Mary, her *kapp* disheveled, wisps of her blond hair blowing in the wind. Samuel removes her kapp then begins to let down her hair when she stops him.

"Not here," she whispers. They move to the inside of the house, Samuel following with his hand clutched tightly to hers.

"Where are the *kinner*?" asks Samuel.

"The girls are at the Kramer's. Caleb is with Bill."

"Hmm." He says as he is kissing her again. Letting down her hair, he runs his fingers through it.

"It is in the early afternoon, what are we doing?" whispers Samuel.

"Why are we whispering Samuel, and do you really care?"

"Uh uh," he whispers back as he continues to kiss her.

‟‣‣

Mary, looking over her right shoulder, calls to Daniel.

"How are you doing, Daniel?" Bouncing up and down quickly with the horse, he appears to be getting comfortable. He looks as though he has been riding for years as he holds the reigns with one hand and waves with his left. He smiles almost smugly. Mary giggles.

"Be careful how comfortable you get up their Daniel."

"This is *gut, jah*?"

Teasingly she responds, "*Jah, gut.*"

"Are you poking fun at my Pennsylvania Dutch there English girl?"

"*Jah,* careful yourself there little Amish boy."

"I'm not little, nor a *buwe.*" He heels Polk to catch up to Mary.

"A what?" Mary looks back again inquisitively.

"A *buwe*, a boy." Daniel retorts quickly.

"Oh, a man, are you?" She slaps Armistead and gallops towards the tree line. Arriving amongst the trees, she quickly comes to a stop and jumps off, tying Armistead to one of the nearby oak trees. As Polk arrives carrying her 'man,' Mary takes Polk by the bridle and steadies him.

"Well, ya comin down off there?"

"*Jah*, I am," says Daniel as he awkwardly climbs down. Mary ties the horse to another tree. Ignoring Daniel, she walks off.

"Mary! Mary! please wait," he calls out to her.

Looking over her shoulder she teases, "catch me if you can!" Flirting with him, she takes off running. They run between trees, ducking under branches as they breathe heavily. Mary hides and plays 'hard to get'. Neither says anything. They just laugh and giggle.

Finally, a winded Mary halts and says, "Uncle!"

Daniel, unaware of these sayings, responds in a panic, "Where!?"

Mary, now confused, questions, "Who Daniel?"

"My Uncle," responds Daniel, still panicked.

"Your uncle?" Mary, still winded, laughs.

"Uncle means I give up, It's a saying. And Daniel, I don't anymore!" And with that, Mary is off and running again, laughing and still winded, until Daniel comes around some brush that she couldn't see through and she runs right into his arms. Daniel has his hands at the back of her hair pulling her head back ever so gently, but firmly. They look at each other, expressionless, breathing hard as Mary holds his arms.

Daniel kisses her deeply and passionately, this time there is no apology. It stops only by Mary, still winded and out of breath, wrapping her arms around Daniel's neck.

"I'm falling in love with you, Daniel." Daniel holds her tighter.

"I, too, am falling in love with you, Mary. Come, we should go now." The two hold hands and walk toward their horses.

"Daniel, you told me you love me."

"Jah, Mary, I do. But I think we should not speak of this, our parents will worry."

"Ok," says Mary, looking seriously at Daniel.

"Mary, by next year, I have to make decisions regarding joining the church and becoming part of the community."

"And?" Mary asks while pulling his arm.

"And if we continue seeing each other, we must ask ourselves where this relationship fits into this. We will have to talk regarding this."

"Yes Daniel, I understand. Do you still want to see me?"

"*Jah*, I do. I truly do love you, Mary. But difficult decisions have to be made by us both, if not now, then after the holidays, early next year."

"Yes Daniel, you really are a man," as she trails off to a whisper.

"I'm sorry, what was that Mary?"

"Nothing, Daniel!" *Lord, I am having so much fun, but is this moving too fast? Please send me a sign. Anything. I'm praying, I've gone from doubting to praying and believing. This is a sign. What has this man done to me? We are so young, yet I want to be with him constantly. And it isn't anything bad. He hasn't even touched me in a wrong way, but the passion is there. We could do something more physical. I know I could, but he won't. I am glad. He is so good to me. There are the horses. This could be so confusing. I'm glad I can speak to mom, I wish I could speak to Dad.*

Chapter Fifteen

It is in the middle of a warm August, a church Sunday of the twenty sixth. The community meets at church. It is this day that Mary comes with her 'Uncle' Samuel and his family. Amos starts the sermon off with his prayer after the hymns. Then he starts with the Gospel to begin the lesson.

"I read from the word of the Lord. The gospel according to Luke, chapter eleven, the first through the thirteenth verse.

And it came to pass, that, as he was praying in a certain place, when he ceased, one of his disciples said unto him, Lord, teach us to pray, as John also taught his disciples.

And he said unto them, when ye pray, say, Our Father which art in heaven, Hallowed be thy name. Thy kingdom come. Thy will be done, as in heaven, so in earth.

Give us day by day our daily bread. And forgive us our sins; for we also forgive every one that is indebted to us. And lead us not into temptation; but deliver us from evil.

And he said unto them, Which of you shall have a friend, and shall go unto him at midnight, and say unto him, Friend, lend me three loaves;

For a friend of mine in his journey is come to me, and I have nothing to set before him?

And he from within shall answer and say, Trouble me not: the door is now shut, and my children are with me in bed; I cannot rise and give thee.

I say unto you, Though he will not rise and give him, because he is his friend, yet because of his importunity he will rise and give him as many as he needeth.

And I say unto you, Ask, and it shall be given you; seek, and ye shall find; knock, and it shall be opened unto you.

For every one that asketh receiveth; and he that seeketh findeth; and to him that knocketh it shall be opened.

If a son shall ask bread of any of you that is a father, will he give him a stone? or if he ask a fish, will he for a fish give him a serpent?

Or if he shall ask an egg, will he offer him a scorpion?

If ye then, being evil, know how to give good gifts unto your children: how much more shall your heavenly Father give the Holy Spirit to them that ask him?" Finishing with the gospel, the Bishop comes to the front to deliver the sermon. Everyone's attention is drawn to him.

"A few months back, I heard a story about a young *buwe* who was spending the day with his daed on the farm. About mid afternoon, while his *daed* was caring for the chickens, the buwe had done something to get in trouble and so his *daed* decided to send the buwe to the barn to clean the stables and think about what he had done.

It wasn't long before the buwe returned. Before his *daed* had an opportunity to say anything, the *buwe* said. 'You know *daed*, I have been praying about why you sent me to the stables.' His *daed's* eyes widened and then he said without hesitation, that's *wunderbaar*, gut sohn! You know if you ask God to help you, you will do better.' The *buwe's* face suddenly turned sad, when he said, I'm sorry *daed*, I didn't ask God to help me do better, I asked God to help you put up with me.

This funny story, like many funny stories, has some truth to it: we pray for what we want. It is easy, though entirely wrong, to think about prayer as if we are rubbing a cow in the hopes of getting milk

We often find ourselves trying to make deals with God during the times of sadness in our lives. 'God if you just do this one thing for me, if you will save my relative from this bout of cancer, then I will never doubt you again', Or one of my personal favorites: 'God, please let me have rain for a good harvest.' We are often guilty of turning a prayer into something that focuses solely on ourselves and our wants.

This creates a bad situation when our prayers are not answered the way that we want them to be answered. When our harvest is not gut, we blame God for not answering our prayers... If someone passes away who we wished would not, we may become angry with God because our prayers can't save that person. And some may give up easily and lose faith feeling that perhaps God isn't real.

While some may misuse prayer in our community, the disciples in today's gospel lesson from Luke don't know how to pray at all. It is gut, though, they are eager to learn and ask Jesus to teach them. Their eagerness to learn isn't surprising in the context of the gospel of Luke, as Luke frequently emphasizes the importance of prayer-- in fact, Luke talks about prayer more than any other gospel writer. Our text for today is Luke's version of the Lord's Prayer, a shorter version of Matthew's account, which is basically the version that we say each Sunday.

But Jesus doesn't just tell them how to pray, but also what to expect in return. At the end of our text today, in verse 13, Jesus tells his disciples that God will respond to prayers through the Holy Spirit. The 'answers' to prayers don't come simply as fulfilled wishes, with the praying disciples always getting what they want. They aren't the result of the farmer rubbing his cow to get milk. No... in Jesus' remark about how much the Holy Spirit will be given to those who pray, he means that the answers to prayer are gifts of the Holy Spirit.

These gifts of the Spirit will help the disciples be joyful and thankful in those times when things do work out in the way they desire and in those times when they don't, however, the Holy Spirit will help the disciples persevere despite their disappointment and suffering.

Later in the story, Jesus' teachings will apply to his own prayers. On the Mount of Olives in Luke 22, just before he is handed over to the authorities, Jesus prays that his Father may take away his imminent suffering. The answer to this prayer, however, is a lot like a *mamm* or *daed* might say to their kinner eager for an answer: 'We'll see.' It may have been possible for Jesus to avoid the suffering and death if all the leaders suddenly converted, repented of sins and believed in him... As we know, that didn't happen, but Jesus nonetheless receives the necessary strength and perseverance that carries him through his crucifixion.

Similarly, we often pray for healing and the answer is, 'We'll see.' There are times when healing does happen--many times, it comes through the knowledge and skills of the doctors and nurses, and through the effects of medications and technology of the English. Other times, the healing seems to be a miracle. But sometimes, even the best efforts of medicine aren't enough and the 'we'll see' becomes a 'no.'

But by answering prayer through the Holy Spirit, God keeps us in a close relationship. It's like the presence of daed or mamm or a husband or wife or gut friend, and although they do not always say or do things to change the situation, their simple presence can often change you as they bring their comfort and love to a difficult situation -- and perhaps... because of that comfort you are better able to accept what lies in the future with their help. It makes it easier to live with the uncertainty of the 'we'll see' answer. Patiently waiting together to see what will happen.

With prayer, we experience the comfort of knowing that GOD IS PRESENT, not that God will always change a situation, but we know that God is with us and God is going through a tragedy or suffering or depression or even a death with YOU AND WITH ME; God isn't a farmer rubbing the cow, but instead, God is with us through the Holy Spirit, close by to comfort us, as any loving daed would.

Prayer is not about what we want, but about God keeping us in a close relationship. When we say the Lord's Prayer, and every prayer, we acknowledge that we are undeserving of God's Grace, love, and salvation. And knowing that these gifts have been offered to us freely, we give thanks for all of these things, with the trust and confidence that God through the Holy spirit will ALWAYS AND UNCEASINGLY help us know the unfailing love that God has for us."

After the church service, the large Hersberger family gathers with the other families of the community for a common meal outside amongst the trees in a covered pavilion. Mary, with Daniel, is quiet and full of thought.

"Daniel, I feel as though that sermon was for me."

"Ah, it is that way sometimes, jah? I think it means the most when it does."

"It meant a lot to me today. I feel very strongly that my life is in the midst of many changes. Good changes." A glow comes upon her face. No smile, a glow which reflects a new peace comes over Mary that day. And as she stands there in her own presence before God she silently prays. *Lord Jesus, I truly have not been everything that you would have me be. I have not been a good daughter to my parents. I have not been a good sister. I believe in all my heart that you did die for my sins and for this, Jesus, I am truly thankful. I will not ask that you come into my heart. I believe you have come into my heart and again I am thankful. I feel drawn to you and called by you for something special though I do not know what. I am prepared to do my best to live up to your expectations of me. Thank you again, Jesus.* And as she finishes, she turns to Daniel as he is staring at her in her moment and just simply smiles at him.

"You prayed just now that is gut, Mary," says Daniel, softly smiling. Mary surprised, responds, "How did you know?"

"Your eyes!" At that moment her eyes well with tears. *I do love this man, he looks into my eyes and sees the prayers of my soul.* Looking around and seeing no one around, Mary whispers to Daniel.

"I do love you, Daniel Hersberger." Daniel simply smiles and responds in return. "I love you too, Mary Kramer."

ഹരു

"Something is new, Bill," says Helen while standing over their brunch table.

"What do you mean, Helen?"

"She went to church with the Hersberger's."

"Is that where she is?"

"Yes!"

"Well that's good. What are you worried about?"

"Do you think she will turn Amish?"

"Helen, would that be so bad? Think about it."

"No, I suppose not, but it would be difficult, very difficult."

"Yes Helen, but this is Mary we're talking about and she is a strong-willed young woman." Both of them laugh and look at each other.

Helen responds, "Kids, huh?"

Bill, looking lovingly at his wife, simply responds, "Yep!"

℘℧

"*Daed*, I'm going to take Mary for a ride in the courting buggy, then take her home. Is this Ok?"

"*Jah* Daniel, does your *mamm* know?"

"*Jah!*"

"*Gut*, enjoy your time with Mary, Daniel."

"*Danki, daed!*" He helps Mary up into the courting buggy.

"Thank you, Daniel!" Daniel, looks at Mary and smiles. The sun is high in the sky now. A small plane out of Lancaster airport can be seen circling for a landing as on many other days. The town of Honey Brook is quiet in the farming community. A few cars with tourists are on the roads. Onlookers of curious English, gawking at gray over-black buggies can be seen. And in the case of Daniel and his English girlfriend, cars actually slow down, curious about the plain dressed 'boy' and the not so plain dressed 'girl' within the open buggy.

ಬಂಜ

At the close of the evening, Samuel and Mary, becoming a tradition in the Hersberger home, are now out on the porch swing. Birds can still be heard chirping. A breeze is blowing up past the horse stables and the 'fresh' scent of 'farm' is noticed in the distance.

Mary and Samuel sit quietly swinging and holding hands rubbing their thumbs over each other's hands as in a not so long ago limo ride they shared. They watch the red glow of the setting sun.

Off to the right, in the distance, can be seen a couple of riders bringing in the few horses which remain out. They look at each other and, as they kiss they can hear in the distance the clip clop of a single horse making its way down the road from Honey Brook. They snuggle close and watch the road as the courting buggy carrying Mary and Daniel nears the drive.

ಬಂಜ

The open buggy turns into the drive, passing Mary and Samuel, the young loves wave excitedly.

Daniel calls out, "*Wie gehts* Uncle Samuel and Aunt Mary?"

Then Mary calls out cheerfully, "Hi Uncle Samuel! Hi Aunt Mary!"

They pass by and as they come to a stop, Mary jumps from the buggy. She begins hitching the horse to the rail before Daniel can get out of the buggy.

Acting from instinct, he scolds, "Mary, this is not our way!"

"Oh Daniel, quit worrying so. I am not helpless, just simply helping the one that I love." As Daniel stares at her, she gives in, "Ok Daniel, just don't be angry."

Calming down, Daniel speaks quietly, "I'm not angry, it's just not our way. I have responsibilities." Bounding out of the buggy, Daniel walks over to Mary. Looking around he asks, "Is there somewhere we can say goodbye?"

"Up on the porch silly." Leading Daniel by the hand they go up onto the porch.

"Good night and I love you very much," says Mary.

"I love you, also." Daniel kisses her on the lips, softly and slowly.

"Hmmmmm." sounds Mary.

"Good night," she says. As they leave each other, they continue to hold each other's hand until only fingertips are touching, then Daniel is in his buggy and riding away. Just then, as Mary is turning around, a voice catches her off guard and she responds.

"DAD!"

Chapter Sixteen

"Sweet pea, you two getten pretty close there? Come on inside, let's have a little ice-cream, huh?" Mary's dad holds the door open for her as they go inside.

"Hmm, let's see, what do we have up here now? Chocolate, then there's cookie dough, whada ya think there now sweat pea, chocolate or cookie…"

"Chocolate daddy, thanks," says Mary with a bit of a concerned look on her face, she adds, "I'll get the bowls and spoons."

Her dad begins, "so, tell me, how da ya feel bout Daniel?"

There is a long pause as Mary slowly gets the spoons and bowls, almost slow and mechanical. Stalling, wanting to avoid the conversation coming on her like a rushing river. Or high winds. Laying the bowls and spoons on the table she looks up and over at her daddy.

"Daddy." Her father's attention now hers, she softly says,   "Daddy, I'm in love with him." *That felt so natural to say. The words came out so easy. I'm in love with him. I am.*

"I can see that sweat pea. Really I can. Are ya plannin to marry?"

"We haven't spoken bout it yet, but I want to marry him. We have time though."

Smiling, Bill says with a smile, "yep, sure do. Thanks for speaken with me, now where is that Hershey's syrup?" The two of them take their seats and look at each other as her father holds up the syrup and says. "Great stuff, this Hershey's!"

"Oh Daddy," says Mary, now smiling again. *The men in my life that I love very much, Daniel, my brothers, my Uncle Samuel, and always, always, my Daddy.*

ℰℭℜℭ

It is a peaceful evening this Sunday, the ninth of September. It is another church weekend. Harvest is well underway in this small Amish community of Honey Brook. Samuel's extended family has brought over fresh produce and fruits from their gardens to add to the small garden supplies of Mary's. Mary prepares to get canning underway.

The days begin to get a little shorter. It is quiet outside except for the horse's whinnies and crickets chirping. Inside the Hersberger home, Caleb plays checkers with his daed. Kathryn and Rachel are cutting patterns for a star quilt.

This will be Kathryn's for the cool weather coming upon them. They are bright rainbow colors which Kathryn picked out. Reds, yellows, blues, oranges, and her favorite color, purple, are being cut from the fat squares. They are giggling together and Rachel is very patient with her little sister.

"*Ach, daed,* I beat you, jah I beat you," Caleb enthuses.

"*Jah, gut* game Caleb. I think it is time for our bible reading and bed. Mary, are you in a place to stop?" Samuel looks over at Mary, hopeful.

"*Jah,* Samuel, we are in a gut place. Rachel and Kathryn prepare for bed and come join us for our nightly bible lesson." The two with Caleb scurry up the stairs. Mary follows closely behind, Samuel, left behind, is putting away the checker set. He walks over to the back door and opens it just in time to hear one of the horse's whinnies.

It is a quarter after seven in the evening. The sun is giving one final show for the evening as it gives off a bright red with orange hues on the horizon. It has been a warm 82 degrees today and is now cooling off. The wind is picking up in short, warm gusts. One of the gusts almost lifts Samuel's straw hat from his head. *I'm ready for a ride tomorrow. It has been a long time. It is so peaceful out tonight.*

"Samuel, we are ready!" Mary calls out into the kitchen. Samuel returns to his kinner all in their pajamas or night gowns. As is common, Samuel turns open the bible to where 'the Lord would have him turn it'. It turns open to Mark, Chapter 13. He reads to himself initially, *but when you hear of* …He stops, looking over at his children and his wife.

"Lord, allow angels to look over our *kinner* and ourselves as we sleep tonight. Let them go to sleep knowing our love for them and your love for them Lord, Amen. Sleep *kinner*," says Samuel solemnly, as he stands and walks over to Caleb first, picking him up and kissing his cheek, "I love you *sohn*."

Then he repeated this two more time with his daughters, "All of you have a *gut nacht*." Looking at Mary, he says, "Mary, I think I will see you on the front porch when the *kinner* are settled." Mary looks at Samuel, smiles, and shakes her head.

"*Kumme kinner*." Samuel walks over to and opens the front door to another warm breeze meeting him as he steps out onto the porch.

ॐ

As Mary settles onto the swing with Samuel, she looks over at him, not saying a word. She leans against his left shoulder as he cradles her with his left arm, brushing down her side with the back of his fingers. He looks over her head and as he stares into his past, he bends his head down kissing the top of her head.

"I am so very much in love with you *liebe*." Mary looks up to her right and, with her hand, she brings Samuel's head down toward her and very lightly kisses his lips, then lays her head back down to his chest.

ℰℭ

"Bill, our children are growing, can you believe it? Roy is now in his third year at school and Travis, in his first year of college. I overheard him tell a girl he met, who is from Texas, that he is in love with her."

Startled and curious he looks up, "oh?"

Smiling Helen continues, "They met as seniors last fall. He had her over several times, but you were very busy when she was here. Do you remember Kelley? Well, she has started at Albright to be close to him," says Helen.

"Well, can't say I'm surprised," responds Bill as he looks straight ahead and ads, "hmm, good for him."

Helen walking over to the stairs and, looking up, comments, "Then there is Mary, what change the Good Lord is taking her through, it is wonderment."

ℰℭ

"Samuel, what are you doing today?" asks Mary while wiping her hands on her apron. She smiles at her husband and walks over to him from behind and leans over wrapping her arms around his neck. Placing her cheek next to his she continues, "Do you have a busy day today?"

"No, I don't. I thought I would like to go riding today, look at the woodline, *jah*, go riding." Samuel retreats to his office. When he comes out, he is in blue jeans and a plaid shirt, with his brown Durango boots and Stetson. He exits his office and enters the kitchen as the children all turn toward him. They just stare at their daed as he is pulling on his tan, goat skin gloves.

"I'm going out for a ride. Give me a hug."

Mary now gives a look of concern, "Samuel, *Wie gehts*, dressed like the English," whispering, Mary looks down at Kathryn who is holding onto her skirt.

"I want to ride, Mary, everything is ok; I need time with the Lord."

ℴↃↄ

"He-ahh, Traveller, come on boy." Samuel heals his horse into a gallop into the fields of his ranch. Once in the open fields, he points Traveller toward the tree line a half mile off in the distance. He doesn't go far before pulling back on the reins and bringing his horse to a walk.

"Don't want to get you too lathered up there now, huh boy?" As he makes his way, he gazes down at the left over wild flowers and some butterflies.

In the distance he can see the tree line closing. *Leaves are still green. Won't be long now until they begin to turn color. I remember this about my Pennsylvania falls. The color display. Lord, this is my time with you. I don't know why, just felt as though I needed to come back out and make contact with you, quietly, just you and I, up close and personal. We have been through a lot together. You have brought me home. You have given me rest. You have given me the love of a gut woman. You have given me kinner. And Mary and I now have another on the way. I am blessed Lord. We are blessed Lord. For this I am truly thankful. Lord, you know that I work hard at our relationship, you and I. For whatever I may have let you down in, well, I'd be asking your forgiveness.*

Samuel reaches the tree line spotting hoof prints on the ground. *Mary and Daniel have been here.* Grinning he continues to think to himself, *Jah, this must be their spot. I have become distracted again. What is going on Lord. I feel your calling. I know not why. I know something is amiss. I am needed but don't know why. Well Lord, your will be done.* Samuel climbs down off Traveller and ties him off to a tree. He notices some bark worn from the same spot where he is tying off. *They must come out here more often than I know.*

He steps through the undergrowth crunching under his feet. Off to his right a squirrel scurries up a tree, then just in front of him, a doe and its fawn.

Samuel comes to a stop, holding perfectly still, he looks back. Then, just like that, they are off running out into the fields he just came from. Walking off a little further he comes across a fallen log.

Holding onto the branch sticking up, he steps over and continues on his way. His senses pick up a noise, not a yard away on the ground. As he looks, he sees a black snake about four feet long slithering away. He hears chirping in the trees above him.

As he looks up he can feel a warm breeze cooling his moist face. Some clouds can be seen above the green of the tall oaks and maples.

Stooping down, he takes in the smell of the freshness of earth underfoot. Old leaves lay from the previous winter. As he moves the leaves, an earthworm ducks into its protective covering beneath the surface.

Then off to his right, hidden on a branch, a praying mantis. He is reminded of the scripture and thinks to himself, *A daisy, a flower, birds, God cares for you all so very much. How much more important are we to him to think that we lose faith and think otherwise. And you live amongst each other in peace...God is gut!*

As he finishes his trek through the woods, he comes across his brother's tobacco fields. Looking down, he sees wash hanging from a clothes line. A courting buggy is out and parked without its horse in front of the barn.

The familiar gray over black buggy with a horse can also be seen tied to a rail. The leaves of the tobacco shimmer in the glow and bask of the sun.

Samuel takes a deep breath, turns, and begins his walk back. He nears the end of his journey when he comes across Traveller who is happy to see him as he whinnies and shakes his head up and down.

"Heh boy," talking to his horse he pats him on the side of his neck. He unties him, takes up the reins in his left gloved hand, and takes hold of the saddles horn.

He places his left foot in the left stirrup and with his right hand on the back of his saddle pulls himself up and onto

Traveler. Traveler whinnies once again, shaking his head up and down. He is ready to take his owner and friend back down to his known surroundings of the ranch.

Pulling hard with his right hand, he turns Traveller into the field and, with a quick heel, he is off and galloping through the fields again. Samuel is a hundred yards into the run when he looks up, smiles, and feels God's peace with him and thinks, *God is gut, Jah.*

He slows to a stop and dismounts. He walks Traveller the rest of the way leading him by the reins, stopping momentarily to pat his horse on the neck and rub him between the eyes.

Arriving at the gate to the corral, he is met by his wife with her skirt blowing softly from that same breeze which cooled his face not too long before. A wisp of her hair not secured under her *kapp* also escapes. It crosses her face, kissing her lips. She moves it away with her hand and approaches her husband.

Without a word, she encircles his neck with her arms and tiptoeing up, slightly opens her mouth and places it on Samuel's and kisses him ever so softly. She runs her fingers through his hair. Then brings her hands down and cups his bearded face in her hands. She looks at him and kisses him again, gently, just touching his lips as if teasing him.

"I love you Samuel, I can never tell you enough." She kisses him again.

"I am truly blessed to have you in my life. I have never been happier," responds Samuel, leaning over and returning her kiss.

Traveller whinnies. Samuel's attention is brought back to the task at hand, cooling down Traveller and putting him in the stable. As he walks with the reins in his right hand and his wife to his left, he reflects, *Life is gut daed.*

Chapter Seventeen

Wednesday, September 12th, another quiet morning at the Hersberger ranch. Mary, Samuel, and their three kinner finish breakfast and clean up. The two older children are preparing for school. The ranch hands are up, off in the distance in the bunkhouse. As Mary turns, she sees a shadow at the kitchen door. Then the silence is broken with a rude banging at the door.

Samuel quickly answers it to find his ranch boss, Bill, Bill's wife Helen, and William, the cook, at the back door, panic stricken. Helen is crying. The other two appear ghost like. Before Samuel can ask what is going on. They all begin to talk very loud and fast. Samuel puts his hands up, "One at a time, Helen, what is going on with you?"

"They're all dead, Sam, all dead. It's awful. How can they…" Helen is cut off by her husband.

"Sam, we were attacked yesterday in New York, Washington, and my God, right here in Pennsylvania. There are thousands dead." Tears well in an otherwise emotionless ranch manager. Bill, the cook, cuts in.

"Late last night, I caught it all on TV, Mister Sam. They used planes. They moved the president to a secure location. They crashed the…" Mary comes out of the house with horror on her face and the children clinging to her apron.

ಶಿ ೧೪

At that moment, a siren is heard approaching the front of the Hersberger property. Two Chevy Suburban's with United States government plates, one white and one black are seen approaching at high speeds. The white one enters the driveway of the ranch. The other pulls over in front, alongside the road, cutting off the entrance to the driveway.

A state trooper tells the men to remain in the car. They don't listen. The unshaven and weary looking driver of the black suburban, armed with a side arm on his hip, holding his ID in front of him, approaches the trooper's car behind him. He is dressed in tan slacks and white dress shirt without a tie. The trooper exits the car. The two talk.

Quickly, and at the same time, another three men exit the car, also armed with semi-automatic pistols on their hips. They quickly take positions guarding the Hersberger driveway. All are dressed in slacks and polo shirts.

ഇൻൿ

As all of this unfolds out front, a very scared group of people watch as the white suburban, which slowed little, screeches around onto the Hersberger driveway. As it speeds down the drive, Samuel steps forward. *That's Chris. My dear God in heaven what has happened that all of this is occurring now!? What is going on?* Four more men jump out of the vehicle.

By this time, a once quiet Amish ranch has been transformed into a surrealistic nightmare, especially for the women and children. As quickly as they are out of the vehicle, one of the men takes up his position in front of the barn, the other at the bottom of the steps.

Ranch hands begin to gather at a distance to watch all unfold. A very serious Chris Hutchins steps forward. Looking at Sam, he calls out, "Sam, there's trouble and we have a sit rep. Where is a good place?"

"Let me settle my family and neighbors, Chris. We can speak in my office. It's through the doors, down the hall to the left, in front of the house."

Chris Hutchins and another man, both dressed in suits, both carrying two soft sided bags and briefcases walk past the crowd. As they pass Mary, they both nod their heads.

"Ma'am."

"Ma'am," Both men show their respect to Mary as they pass. Samuel begins to bring order to an otherwise no order morning.

"Mary, the *kinner* should all go to Helen's. Helen, do you mind? Bill, I'm going to need your help. Can we get the men back to work? I don't want anyone around that doesn't need to be. William, I need you here to help Mary out."

℘℘℘

Back out on the street, a young state trooper calls for another car. A sergeant arrives and puts on his hat as he exits the car. He is approached by the agent.

"Sergeant, I'm Tom Hastings. I'm with the United States government."

"Well, it seems you were traveling at a very high rate of..." the state trooper is cut off by a now very irritated Tom.

"Sergeant, this country is at war. Though I respect you and what your job entails, I quite frankly don't give a dang what you might have to say about speeding. I have a mission and I won't let you or the governor of this state stand in my way," says Tom Hastings firmly before continuing.

"The way I see it, you can write me a ticket and be on your way, help provide security for what is going on down here, or you can carry on with this charade and we'll be on the phone with justice. Then we'll see who is charged with obstruction!"

The state police sergeant and the trooper standing behind him look at Tom, momentarily deep in thought before responding,   "No need to get upset Mr. Hastings. I can see you're busy. I wasn't and am not going to give you a citation. Just trying to get an idea of what is going on. By the way, what could be going on at an Amish farm?"

A very serious Tom Hastings looks at the trooper and simply says, "buying horses." The sergeant, shaking his head, moves away and stays with the other trooper on the road. Nothing else is said.

ℰᏯ

The kinner are whimpering as Mary takes Samuel's arm and whispers to him, "Samuel, I am very scared. What does all of this mean?"

"I'll explain the best I can when I'm done inside with Chris.
Meanwhile, pray. Many have apparently died yesterday. I don't know all that is going on, but when I do, I will let you know. Please be patient with us."

Us, they are an us. Is this part of his past, come back to visit in this way. Oh Samuel, what is going on? There are many men here. They will be hungry and thirsty, thinks Mary.

She turns to the man standing guard on the step questioning, "You all look as though you haven't slept. Have you eaten?"

The man on the step responds politely, "No Ma'am, I haven't."

Samuel speaks up. "I'll check with Chris if we can tend to his men's needs."

"*Danki*, Samuel." Samuel returns a short time later.

"Chris says he would appreciate whatever you can do. The men have been up for over twenty-four hours and have eaten little," reports Samuel.

"William, can you help me?" asks Mary.

"Yes Ma'am, Miss Mary, you just tell me what you need and I'll do it," responds William eagerly.

Mary begins to busy herself. "Let us start with coffee. We are going to need a lot of it."

Helen gets into the mode now and volunteers, "I'm bringing the children over to the house. I'll get Mary to watch them. Doesn't appear they will be going to school today. I'll get my coffeemaker. That should help. Do you need anything else, Mary?"

"Coffee, Helen, if you have it."

"Surely do. Be right back."

"Sam, I don't rightly know what's going on, but If ya need anything, I'll be tenden to keepin everyone busy."

"*Danki* Bill. Pray."

"Have been! Yep, y'all take care in there now, hear?"

Mary gets out bread, eggs, and bacon. She also brings out a fresh jar of blackberry preserves and then all of her fry pans. Bill has a pot of coffee on.

"William, we will start by feeding the men in here. At the same time, we will get coffee out to the rest of the men."

"Yes ma'am, Miss Mary, couple of minutes it'll be done."

"William, how is your family?"

"Pretty upset with what happened yesterday."

"I don't understand what happened. We were speaking when all of this happened."

"Some very bad men flew jet liners into many buildings. Do you know the World Trade Center, those tall buildings in New York City?"

"Jah, I've seen pictures."

"Those, one in Washington and one of the Airliners crashed here in Pennsylvania."

"All those people killed, who could do such a thing? And what does this have to do with Samuel?"

"Don't know, Miss Mary. I know he used to be gone a lot when he was in North Carolina. Coffee is done."

"I have a cookie sheet here. I'll put a cloth on it and we can put the coffee with the cups on it. Here is a thermos, to put the coffee in."

"That should work just fine. Here is a cup of sugar and some cream."

"I'll bring it up," insists Mary.

As Mary leaves the house with the tray, Helen comes in. She holds the door for Mary.

"*Danki* Helen, I'll be right back." Helen, with a slight smile, nods her head. Mary approaches the end of the drive and is met by Tom.

"Ma'am, you must be Mrs. Hersberger, allow me to help you." Tom takes the tray.

"The men will be thankful for this. I'm Tom Hastings. I work for Chris Hutchins; well we all do sort of."

"Tom, *danki*," says Mary, her eyes welling.

"Mrs. Hersberger, I know they didn't have time to talk to you down there.

"Tom, please call me Mary," says Mary.

"Mary, I assure you that you and your family are safe and well, ma'am. I am truly sorry for all of this. Your peace has been disturbed. It's just not right, but at the moment, it surely can't be helped. I'm truly sorry ma'am."

"*Danki* again Tom, what does this have to do with Samuel?"

"I'm sorry, ma'am. I'm not at liberty to speak about us. Mr. Hersberger, ma'am, he is a good man. I never met a more faithful man."

"Are you a believer, Tom?"

"Yes ma'am! I'm from the south, Tennessee, that's the Bible belt. Hard to find anyone down there who isn't? At least that's from my way of seeing things anyhow. About Samuel and knowing your background, he will let you know everything he can. There will come a time."

"I am reassured by your faith Tom, *danki*. We understand the men haven't eaten, breakfast is coming soon."

"Thank you and anytime ma'am. Sergeant, trooper, ya'll want some coffee? Mrs. Hersberger brought some," offers Tom.

"Thank you, appreciate it. I'm sorry for all that went on before. It's a terrible time now, things do get skewed. I think we're all upset," says the state police sergeant.

"Have some coffee sergeant; I'll get my men," As Tom gets one of his men and has some coffee, the other two remain out of sight. Helen is on her way with food.

&⁓&⅌

As Samuel enters the room, Chris and the other gentlemen have communication equipment set up with satellite links. Two computers are up.

"Chris, I was getting a little of what was going on when someone opened the coral gates and started a stampede. It surely is bad to my understanding, what happened and where?"

"Come here, I'll show you. This is a picture of the first tower being hit. The second picture is the second tower being hit. They thought it was a horrible accident until the second tower was hit. And now the third picture, this is the pentagon."

"The Pentagon and the World Trade Center. How bad is the damage?"

"You really missed it all haven't ya?" questions Chris.

"Samuel, the World Trade Center is…well, look for yourself."

"Where is it? Just smoke," asks Samuel, staring at the carnage on the computer screen. Chris continues, "They're gone, collapsed, along with other buildings in the area."

"My God, the Pentagon?" continues Samuel, asking.

Chris continues with his sit-rep, "A whole wing, and all floors. There was another plane, it didn't make it. The passengers may have interrupted the plan. That airliner crashed west of here in Pennsylvania. We are surmising it was meant for the White House or Capital," continued Chris, solemnly.

Samuel responds, "I thought I have witnessed horror before. I hadn't. What is needed?"

"We haven't gone public with this, but we think its Osama bin Laden, al Qaida in Afghanistan. We have no eyes there. There may be friendlies in the north, amongst the rebels." Chris pauses momentarily as he brings up pictures on one of the secured computer screens, and an intelligence map of the area. He then proceeds with what he needs from Samuel.

"We need a team on the ground initially to gather info, establish an OP, and establish relations with the locals. Then we need to start pinpointing targets, so we can bring the military at large to bear." Chris goes on with the sit rep (situation report).

"Do you have a team in mind?" quizzes Samuel.

"I have a team in mind, but we could use your help with the operation. You know the terrain and are familiar with the people," continues Chris.

"Done, from where? Washington or North Carolina," asks Samuel.

"North Carolina."

"Hard sell with the wife and the community, but I'll get it done. When?"

"The day before yesterday if I knew who it was then."

"Understand. Tomorrow?"

"Yes."

"Transportation."

"We'll spirit you out of here, Reading Airport, Biz Jet to Pope, O-six-hundred."

"Done." Samuel states, now his mind in the zone.

"Outstanding. See you down there. Be thinking about it."

"It's already done." states a decisive Samuel.

"Sam, the President wants this guy, real bad."

"At least we don't have to worry about support from him." Samuel looks clinically at Chris.

"No, put a plan together, prep a team, put them on the ground." A somber Chris looks back.

"Chris, I already have ideas surfacing. Have that team ready. I'll have them in-country in twenty four hours from finalization of plans."

"Consider it done," responds Chris.

"*Danki*, Chris." Chris Hutchins smiles when there is a quiet knock on the door.

"I'll get it," says Samuel, gesturing towards and opening the door. He finds Mary, holding plates of food.

"*Danki liebe.*"

"Mary, on behalf of my men and I, I thank you very much."

"Tom has thanked me already, Chris, though you're *willkum.*"

"It is a very trying time for our country. I understand this is not your way nor of your communities and I respect that. We will be leaving in about an hour and leave you to your peace, again, with our apologies."

"*Danki* Chris, may I ask how many have lost their lives?" Chris looking at Samuel for approval gets a nod.

"There were four planes full of souls used as missiles to fly into high value targets. Two planes hit each of the buildings of the World Trade Center; they and other buildings in the area are no longer there as they were. One plane hit the Pentagon. One plane we think was stopped by the passengers just west of here and crashed in western Pennsylvania. The number of dead is unknown, but it is in the thousands. The survivors are many more, and they who have lost loved ones are even more than that. They need our prayers."

Mary, with tears again, "we will pray, *Danki* for your kindness."

"Thank you for your husband, Mary"

கை

Two hours later, a third police car is seen up the street a little ways. A horse and buggy attempt to enter but is politely asked to come back and the young man is reassured that everything is ok by Tom himself.

A short time later, two men from the security detail inside of the perimeter walk out, double checking along side of the drive and checking deep into the fields. They wait until the white suburban comes out. They are picked up. The other men enter the black suburban and within minutes after he shakes hands with the sergeant and trooper, Tom enters his vehicle and they are gone. Quiet returns to the ranch.

ॐ

Samuel, now in his office alone, sips at a cold cup of coffee thinking of all that has happened and will happen. He goes to the door and calls his wife.

"Mary, I promised you I would speak to you." *I left this life behind; I have made promises, dear Lord. Please understand and I implore your help. I know the job. Please help me find justice for all those who have suffered. I know what I have promised, but there is no other way. I am truly sorry, Daed.*

Chapter Eighteen

"Mary, there is something we must talk about," states Samuel, gesturing for her to come in.

"*Jah liebe*," answers a very nervous Mary standing in the doorway of Samuels's office. It has only been 15 minutes from the time Chris left. Mary appears ill.

"I have sent William back to the bunk house. I thought you wouldn't mind. Helen has gone to get our children and bring them back. Samuel, what has just happened here? I know that I may not have any right to ask but this, men with guns on our ranch, this is not our way. Many are going to ask questions. What am I to tell them?"

Samuel is staring as though he is looking thousands of miles away. Sweat rolls down his face. He bows his head, looking at his desk, and then looks up again at his wife. Though still neatly dressed, she appears aged beyond recognition. It is as though the stress of the day has taken what youth she had right out of her.

Being married to someone who is all but English in his nature has given her some degree of freedom not known by other women in her community and she enjoys it and her husband. But now, it feels as though it is slipping away. And she still doesn't know who her husband really was, his past, or what he has to do with what is going on in the world. And why they are not separate from the world. After all it is their way to be separate.

As Mary is speaking, little feet are heard coming up the steps. Three kinner are heard entering the house. Entering through the back the door, the three are staring, scared, as they slowly approach with young Mary in tow.

"Uncle Samuel, here are the young-uns." Mary appears to be treading very lightly, not knowing what to expect, continuing she asks, "Everything ok here?"

Samuel, looking up again at Bill and Helen's child, answers guardedly, "Mary, *danki* for watching the *kinner*. No, they're not, but I promise they will be ok.

"Ok, Uncle Samuel. I have to get back over to my mom and dad." She leaves quickly.

Samuel stands and looks over at Mary and gives a small reassuring smile as he comes from around his desk and approaches her.

"We should go to the front room for prayer and I will do my best to explain what is going on." As he passes Mary, he stops long enough to give her one longing look into her eyes, smiles, and kisses her gently as though it may be for the last time.

"I love you dearly, you are my life." Looking down at the kinner, he runs his fingers across the girls' cheeks, caressing them and their tears with his thumbs, and then he runs his fingers over and across Caleb's hair, as he whispers again, hoarse.

"You and the *kinner*," smiles Samuel, while looking at his wife and cradling her face.

"Heavenly father, you know the heart of all of us. You know my heart. At this time, I pray that you give me wisdom and strength of heart and mind to do what is needed of me, as the time of David, when you gave him the strength and wisdom to destroy those who would hurt your people." *Help me explain this to my family Lord Jesus, so they may understand. The hard times are yet to come. They are not English and know nothing of this world and of violence. Give them rest and peace of heart. Forgive me for bringing this to them.*

"Lord Jesus, many have lost their lives yesterday. We ask that you come into the hearts of those that survived, and those who lost their families. Give them rest and peace in a time that peace seems very distant. We pray for those who have lost mothers and fathers, sister and brothers. We pray for all in this country who are affected in any way by this tragedy and devastation. Amen." And at that time three young kinner and their mother say together in a heartfelt manner,

"AMEN"

"Mary, you must believe that there is nothing that I wouldn't do to keep peace in this community and especially in our home. You have asked me many questions, which I will try to answer.

I work for a group of people who work tirelessly to see justice is done in the world. We reach those who would do and have done evil when and where others cannot reach them. Evil has come to this country, just as it did during the time of David as we read here in 1 Samuel, Chapter 17, Verse 45. Then said David to the Philistine, Thou comest to me with a sword, and with a spear, and with a shield: but I come to thee in the name of the LORD of hosts, the God of the armies of Israel, whom thou hast defied.

We live in peace and there are those who would not. They have harmed us and the children of this peaceful nation. I am called to bring justice and I have a responsibility and a duty.

The work I have to do should not bring me in harm's way, but I must leave. I will be back as soon as I have done what I am tasked to do. I realize I am not of the English anymore, but I feel strongly that as God tasked David, he has as well tasked me."

Mary, with tears in her eyes, is now shaking her head back and forth. "It is not our way Samuel, you know this. What will the elders say?"

"Mary, I obey the elders and disobey God. We have our calling, all of us. We as children of God are called of God to do things which we may not always like or agree. We call them jobs or labor. But if we choose to follow God then we must follow! God chooses our calling, not our community. Thus, it was when I left the community. God had my calling and it was not within the community. It hurts me looking back on it because my life would have been much easier remaining within the community, but it was not my plan." Mary is crying uncontrollably now, as well as the children who do not understand.

"Daed, are you leaving us?" Question's Caleb.

"Yes *sohn*, I am, but I will return. And we will return our life here to the way it was. But I will need your help. Can you, will you help?" Caleb is now nodding his head yes as his *schweschder* is now nodding her head also.

"I can help, *Daed*. How can I help?"

"You can help by helping your mother. Be *gut kinner*, do your chores without being asked many times. Do you understand?"

With sniffles they all say, "yes *daed*".

Mary looks down at them momentarily with a small smile. She sniffs back more tears and looks up at her husband asking, "When must you leave?"

"First thing in the morning, my transportation leaves at 6:00 AM. I must leave here at 5:00 AM." Mary, still with tears in her eyes, puts on a brave face and smiles.

"It is so soon, so early. I and the *kinner* will miss you *liebe*. I will miss you. It is so not right. We were just married. Everything in our life has moved so fast. I want to enjoy the life we have. It is just not right... I will care for all those we hold dear while you are gone. I will do my best." She wipes away at her eyes. Looking down at the children, she brings them in close to her and hugs them. Kathryn, with a lost look, still and silent, is picked up. Mary kisses her cheek while she is on her lap.

"Should I help you pack Samuel?"

"There is very little to pack, *danki* Mary. We must let the rest of the ranch know. Our families will find out the next Sunday of service."

"We can have supper outside this evening. I will ask Helen and Bill if we can all eat together with our two families and the other workers also. We shall ask William if he can help and have his family join us."

"*Jah*, this would be gut Mary, *danki*." Samuel stands and walks over to Mary and bends over and kisses her cheek with the remaining tears. She raises her head and smiles, trying very hard to be brave.

ℰᏜ

Picnic tables are pulled that evening, as so many times in the past, for the supper. Samuel makes his announcement and all wish him well. As they are eating, the familiar clip clop of a horse is heard as it **nears** the drive. All look up and coming into view is Daniel and his mother and father. The horse pulls up. Daniel climbs out of the buggy and ties the horse to the coral fence. Jeremiah helps Erica down from the buggy and the three walk down toward the barn, joining the group, which has formed for supper.

"*Bruder wie gehts,* Supper? What is the occasion?"

Samuel stands and greets his brother. "We are all fine, Jeremiah. How are you Erica, Daniel?" Samuel, for the first time, begins to wonder of the visit.

"What brings you here Jeremiah?" questions Samuel, suspiciously.

"Can't a *bruder* visit?"

"*Jah*, it's just been an unusual day and I can't help but feel that it has something to do with it."

"Well, Daniel came to visit earlier and was turned away by police. You can understand that we may be concerned. Is everything alright?"

Mary, a little annoyed, quickly cuts in, "Jeremiah, Erica, Daniel, everything is ok. Would you like something to eat? We have gathered here because Daniel has business which is taking him out of town for a short while," says Mary, very uncharacteristically.

All look at her fully in charge of the conversation. Jeremiah, with a shocked look on his face, speaks up, "I was speaking with my *bruder*, Mary," annoyed that a woman is speaking out of turn.

"And she is doing fine answering *bruder*, *Jah!*" says Samuel supporting his wife. With that, everyone around both tables smiles and begins to shake their head in agreement.

"Well, I guess that leaves us nothing else but to sit and eat," states Jeremiah abruptly. As room is made for the smaller Hersberger family, young Mary stands and shifts over, making room for Daniel.

"Daniel, please join us over here," as she gives him a warm and inviting smile. Daniel joins her, their eyes meeting as he sits. Jeremiah with his wife joins his bruder. Prayers, having already been said, the three briefly bow their heads in thanks and begin to put food on their plates.

Daniel begins to speak with his aldi, Mary, on the day's events, when he is quickly, but politely, cut off by Helen.

"So Daniel, how was your first horseback ride?" This question brought laughter from the rest of the table. Mary coughed and quickly put her hand to her mouth and excused herself.

"*Gut, Jah.*" He looks to Mary for help. Mary shyly shrugs her shoulders.

"He did well for his first time riding," says Mary, embarrassed. Mary's father, with a huge grin, quickly cuts in, "So Daniel, you were seen disappearing into the wood line a yonder. How is the sassafras doing?" More laughter and Daniel is staring like a 'deer caught in headlights'.

"Sir?" Daniel begins to respond nervously. Then saved by his ever vigilant Mary,

"Daddy!" Clearly, the subject is being changed, but the eyes of the table are on them.

The rest of the evening, the conversation stays light. Everyone who was there that day wants quiet and to speak of anything but the day's events. Jeremiah attempts to speak with Samuel once more and pulls him aside.

"Samuel, Mary spoke out of turn. She did not show respect to either one of us." Samuel, responding with a firm tone, sets his older bruder straight.

"Considering all that she has to tend with bruder, I don't blame her. Besides, she is my wife and if I felt that she spoke out of turn, it is for me to say. She spoke for me and has done quite well spelling out all that needed to be said. *Danki bruder*, for your understanding and concern for us."

Samuel looks into Jeremiahs eyes, locking them there, making sure that his *bruder* understands who was in charge of his household.

"While we are speaking *bruder*, Bill will be in charge of the ranch. If Mary has needs, I'm sure she will send for them. You can do one thing for me. Let the rest of the family know of my travels and ask for their prayers. My work will keep me very busy. I will need God's help in all that I do while away, danki."

"As you say it *bruder*, I will let the family know and we will keep you and your family in our prayers. You will, in your time, talk of what is going on, *jah*?"

"*Jah*," Samuel now smiles, as the two *brieder*, having come to an understanding, part ways. Mary and Daniel come down the drive as the rest of the family and friends are breaking up and cleaning.

Jeremiah, with Erica and Daniel, get into the buggy and leave. Night falls quickly on the Hersberger home. Evening prayer is skipped; the children kneel and pray next to their own beds and go to sleep right away.

The next morning, all are up even before Samuel, if that is possible. They were about to sit down for their last breakfast together when the black suburban pulls into the driveway and parks. Tom Hastings climbs out of the passenger side and stretches.

"I'll get that," Samuel says and opens the door, "Tom, is that you?"

"Yes sir!" An alert Tom states briskly.

"Have you eaten?"

"Yes sir, thank you."

"Want some coffee for the two of you?"

"I would appreciate it, yes sir."

"Come on in then."

"Beg your pardon sir, but we'll be glad to have our coffee out here, being this is your time with your family and all. Thank You."

"*Jah*, you're a *gut* man, Tom. Come in and get a couple of cups."

The family finishes their breakfast and all kiss and hug Samuel goodbye. Tom and the driver help Samuel with his bag and two footlockers into the back of the large truck. With his family looking on in tears, Samuel holds back his. *Dear father in heaven, be with them all. Forgive me for what I am about to do. Though I feel I am in your calling, I do not take what I do lightly. I tried to keep my promise to you, forgive me… Daed.*

Chapter Nineteen

The Biz jet with a security detail is already on the tarmac of
Reading Airport waiting for Tom and Samuel when they arrive at the airport. They show their ID's to the security official when they enter the entrance ramp. Samuel gets a quizzical look from security. Still dressed plain, he certainly does not match his ID and what is printed on it. The driver and the steward load the luggage into the belly of the jet. Its turbines are already whining and warming up.

Standing at the top of the jet's short stairway, Samuel takes in the scene around the airport, airport lights give off what little light there is. The sun just begins to give a hint of its intentions for the day as a glow in the distance. He takes one more look around the area, shakes his head no, and boards. The two men sit across from each other. The steward approaches the men carrying two cups of coffee.

"We'll be at Pope in a few hours. Mr. Hutchins will be awaiting you on the tarmac when we arrive."

Samuel, still thinking in his Pennsylvania Dutch, responds without thinking.

"*Danki, gut*"

"Pardon me, sir?" asks the confused steward.

"I'm sorry, thank you, good."

"Thank you" responds Tom with a smile.

ℰℭ

"*Mamm*, is *daed* going to heaven like our other *daed?*" An upset Rachel asks.

"What?! No *kinner*, he is not, he will be home. It will be awhile, but he will be home. He loves you all very much you know."

"*Jah*, I know *mamm*," responds a relieved Rachel.

"How long *mamm?*" Now asks Kathryn.

"We don't know *boppli*." Kathryn just looks at Mary a little misty eyed. Caleb again not to be outdone chimes in.

"Am I the man of the house?" Mary just smiles at first.

"Not yet, Caleb, you have time *jah*. Now go and get dressed, *schnell!*"

The two older *kinner* scurry away from the kitchen. Kathryn remains, still looking up when Mary bends over and picks her up.

"*Kumme boppli. Mamm* will help you, *jah*." She carries Kathryn up to her room and sets her down on her bed. It is still dark outside. Mary looks down towards her unborn *boppli*, holds her belly, and smiles again at Kathryn to begin the day.

ॐ

The leer lands mid morning. A suburban picks up Samuel and Tom, and as quickly as they had landed, they are whisked away. Both Samuel and Tom make one more, quick phone call on their respective blackberries to let their families know they have arrived safely. Samuel gets hold of Bill on his cell phone, who then runs over to Mary and their kinner, allowing them to speak with their father.

The two men then turn off their blackberry's and disappear. They will not be heard from again, at least not until the mission is on the ground.

ॐ

The two older *kinner* are off to school. Mary begins, this September day canning as she has for many years before, but this time with the help of Kathryn. She begins to retrieve supplies, then there is the familiar sound of the horse and buggy.

"Kathryn, who could that be?" She looks out the kitchen window as she has gotten used to doing.

"Don't know *mamm*," As an inquisitive Kathryn now is standing on top of a chair next to her *mamm*.

"Careful now, Kathryn. Oh look, it's Katie and Andrew and your cousin, Samantha." *I hope this doesn't have anything to do with yesterday. Mamma is here also! Oh my!*

Mamma comes in first followed by Katie holding three month old Samantha.

"*Guder mariye* Mary." Andrew quickly greets Mary.

"I must be going to work now."

"*Wie gehts* Mary, Mamma and I are here."

"*Jah*, Katie, but why?"

"Mary, have you forgotten? Every year for the past four years we have come to help you can on this very day. Have you forgotten?"

Katie is now smiling and approaching Mary with her *boppli*. "*Ach*, you haven't forgotten about canning. Kathryn, *ach* you have grown tall." Kathryn begins to laugh as she peers down at the *boppli* from atop the perch of the chair.

"Do you want to see your cousin?" Nodding her head up and down, Kathryn climbs down off the chair.

"*Kumme*, sit in the front room. Would you like to hold her?"

"*Jah*! I would like to hold her," says Kathryn as she is given Samantha. She cradles her carefully with one arm while reaching with the other and brushing her hair with her hand, then holding her fingers.

"You're Dutch is *gut*, Kathryn." Katie stoops down next to Kathryn.

"*Danki*, Aunt Katie, where is *grossmudder*?" Kathryn looks over at Katie.

"I'm here, Kathryn, *jah* your Dutch is *gut*." Kathryn looks up over her shoulder.

"Here let me take Samantha and put her down to sleep. You can see your *grossmudder*." Kathryn bounds up as soon as the baby is taken, runs and leaps into her arms. *Grandmother* squeezes Kathryn as she lays her head down on her shoulder.

"Have you missed me *kinner*?" Not saying a word Kathryn nods her head up and down.

"Mary, what are we canning this season?" Asks Katie as she hugs Mary.

"You are a *gut* friend. They are out on the front porch. Peaches. Tomatoes for today."

"*Gut*, we'll get started," responds Katie as she looks at her grandmother walking in holding a now sleeping Kathryn.

"My *sohn* making you *naerfich* Mary?" she asks, as Mary looks over at her. She is smiling at the same time her eyes well.

"Nervous, *jah*, *verhuddelt*, more. He told me some of what is going on but he will explain more when he returns."

"*Gut*, we must trust in the Lord, all will be well."

"*Danki*, mamma."

"*Kumme*, I will put Kathryn on the sofa so she can sleep."

"Mamma, Katie, is Jeremiah still angry?"

"You don't worry about him. He spent a long time being in charge of everything while his *daed* was alive. Now it is no longer that way."

"*Danki*, mamma," says Mary. With Kathryn sleeping on the sofa, Mary walks over and hugs her again.

"Uncle Jeremiah will be OK Mary," reassures Katie, now smiling at her.

"*Kumme*, we must start. I see the baskets are full, *jah*!" interjects Samuel's mamma as she holds her apron. All the women laugh.

The canning took the rest of the day. Kathryn woke up in time to smell the peaches cooking. Katie looks over at Mary and offers, "We should catch up on your quilt, Mary, if it's ok? We can all come together. It will be *gut*. How is next Wednesday?"

"*Gut, jah*, I will like this." Mary, nodding her head, looks over at her friend Katie and nods her head. The two remain until Andrew finishes his day on the ranch.

ഇൗരു

Young Mary arrives home from school and her mother sees that she is 'down in the dumps'. It is Friday and since Wednesday she has not heard from Daniel. No explanation, no Daniel.

"I don't know why I haven't heard from him mom, nothing!"

"Well, it's been busy with school and all."

"He's not in school anymore, that's just it. He can't be angry."

"Mary, I have an idea. Sunday, go to church with Aunt Mary. She could use some help with her children, ok?"

"That's a great idea. I'll do that. Wait, the next service isn't until the Sunday after next, mom!"

"Well, seems to me then that it won't wait for ya now. Why don't ya take a ride over?

ഇൗരു

In the quiet, very small southern Virginia town of Rural Retreat, a now calm Roy Kramer sits on a rail of his girlfriend's porch. Lindsay comes out of the house on this cool Friday night carrying sweet iced tea.

"When will ya be going back Roy?"

"Sunday evening. I have all ins at 1900 hours."

"Going to church with me?" asks Lindsay.

"Yes of course, now more than ever, are we going to Corinth Lutheran, Lindsay?"

"Yep, I like it there; it's small and personal." A smiling Lindsay says to him.

"I like it there, also. My folks called yesterday to make sure I was ok. They were asking about ya."

"Were they? Thanks. How are they doing?" asks Lindsay.

"My dad is working a little more, nothing too different from when we were in North Carolina. Uncle Samuel is gone again. I think I figured out what he does. If I'm right, then I can't talk about it anyways." A now very curious Lindsay turns to him.

"So, what do you think he does?"

"Well, he travels the world and, in one of this country's greatest crisis, he has to leave and without a word. I would rather not say yet."

"Roy?"

"Not yet Lindsay! My mom is doing well. You'll never guess who my sister is dating."

"Who?" asks an inquisitive Lindsay.

"His name is Daniel, Daniel Hersberger. He's my 'Uncle Sam's nephew. He's Amish.

"Really!? You're Lutheran. How does your family feel about it?"

"They seem to be alright about it actually. He has really changed her a lot. My brother is cool about it, too. He gets along real well with Dan. So do I."

"Want some more sweet tea?" Lindsay offers graciously.

"Thanks." Roy hands his near empty glass to Lindsay.

ॐ

Daniel is again walking amongst what was his family's tobacco field; they had spent the past couple of days harvesting the crop. Deep in thought he is unaware of anything going on around him. It is a little cooler this day. There is no wind blowing. The air is still and a relief from the hot summer days, which are now passing.

It is after dinner time. His parents have put a lot of pressure on him about his future. He looks out over the wood line separating the farm he lives on and his uncle's ranch.

The leaves are just beginning to turn; spots of yellow and orange can be seen. In his mind's eye, he sees a pretty girl with flowing dark red hair, which at times smells like apples and other times smells like lavender.

Closing his eyes for a moment, he pictures her and her hair blowing in the wind. He sees her in jeans and a t-shirt. She is atop her horse. Then there is the sound of a young woman's voice. He opens his eyes.

Around the left side of the wood line he sees in the distance a lone rider. The rider takes her time and does not appear to have noticed Daniel. As he watches, the horse closes in on him. There is a sudden change as the horse begins to gallop towards him.

This is Mary, jah! There is calling out, just not audible yet. Then, as she nears, Daniel hears his name getting louder. He can hear anger in the tone.

"Daniel! Daniel Hersberger! Why haven't I heard from you? Not one word from you!"

She jumps from the horse just as it comes to a stop. Mary charges Daniel and goes right up to his face.

"I want to know. Don't you love me anymore?" Mary's face is now as red as her deep auburn hair, her eyes misty, doing all she can to hold in her tears.

Daniel simply looks around his empty field as he begins to explain, "tobacco brought a gut price." Daniel follows the simplicity of it all with a slight smile.

Mary looks around and responds, "Your tobacco is gone." Bewildered, Mary looks around.

"*Jah*, brought the family a *gut* price. We finished the harvest yesterday."

"Oh my, Daniel. I did not know."

"*Jah*, you did not. You also don't know how I feel about you?"

"I am so, so sorry Daniel," responds Mary, scared.

Daniel smiles a little more. He walks over and kisses her firmly on the lips. Hugging her tightly, he whispers in her ear, "I missed you, too."

Mary stands back momentarily then leaps up hugging Daniel and just holds him. The sun shines a little brighter this day. Resolve has settled into a hurt people of a peaceful nation and amongst the citizens of a small town, life continues.

∞⊰

A non church weekend comes and goes. All settle into new routines. It is quick. Yes, but also needed. The children need to see normalcy return.

Monday, starts out early for the Hersberger family. Mary needs to fight another headache, put on a brave face, and go on with chores, early as usual.

The children are up and do their chores. Afterward, the older two children prepare for school. They attend at the small school house, which houses up to eighth grade. After the children go to school, Kathryn remains with her mamm, helping with laundry. Mary and Kathryn hang the first of the laundry, as the sun is coming up. It is still cool out.

William is seen walking towards the bunkhouse to start his day. As Mary looks over toward William, Bill comes out of the house to start the day.

"Good morning Miss Mary. How are ya doing?" He walks over towards her.

"*Gut* Bill, *danki*. How is your family?"

"Good, thank you. Is there anything you need?"

"No *danki*,"

"If you need anything just let me know. We can give you a ride if you like. You just say when." Smiling, Mary shakes her head. God has blessed me with gut friends.

"Bill, you and Helen are gut friends. God has surely blessed us."

"Don't ya mention it now. You have a good day."

"*Danki* Bill," says Mary again. Briefly, she feels life in her womb and lowers her hand to her belly just for a moment.

Late in the morning a letter arrives addressed to both Samuel and Mary. The return address is from Florida. Kathryn's grandfather. I wonder what is going on. Mary opens the letter.

September 13, 2001

Dear Samuel and Mary,

We are sorry it has taken so long to write. We have been very busy. We have not forgotten about what has happened and feel that you must have gone through a lot in regards to Kathryn and her losing her mother; not to mention her beginning a new life.

We would like to visit and are hoping it will be convenient for all of you for us to meet our granddaughter this fall. We hope all of you are well. We hope to hear from you soon.

Sincerely,
Lou and Kathy.

Samuel is not even home. What am I to do regarding this?

෩෬

Roy wakes to reveille early at the beginning of his third year at Virginia Military Institute. Because of the surrounding mountains, the campus and the area have gotten cool early in the fall season. Looking out the window, a heavy fog is lifting off the trees. The trees are turning a beautiful crimson. Young men and woman in blue gray are seen through the Sally ports of the Quads.

These are buildings with history going back to after a nation was born. Facing these buildings is a street with houses just as old. These now hold offices of the renowned military school. Amongst all of this, in blue gray, is Second Classman, Cadet Sergeant, Roy Kramer. Army contracted, Reserve Officer Training Course, Engineering major. Roy's world has changed within a week since the country has gone to war. On his mind is a girl he loves; a girl a couple of hours away.

Lindsay has finished college this year with a two year degree in nursing and is now working at the hospital in Wytheville, Virginia. Lindsay will see her boyfriend on his open weekends, which were few. The open weekends are used by the Army for training. When they do see each other, it is meaningful and precious. Lindsay helps keep it faithful and special.

෨෬

Standing on the empty tarmac of an airfield in North Carolina, Samuel stands alone deep in thought. *Now it begins. CIA lifted off tonight under the cover of darkness. God go with them. Next we move. Cool evening this evening. Breezy. I miss Mary and the kinner. I hope the boppli is ok. This is where I was a year ago and many other years prior. I missed a lot. I missed Daed.*

Chapter Twenty

Returning to his office after leaving the airfield at pope,
Samuel is met by Chris Hutchins. "You have done outstanding work Samuel, but the word is, fifth group will take the lead. They are to be on the ground in early October."

"It's being done, right?" responds a determined Samuel.

"That's right. We now have an operational base on an old Soviet airbase in Uzbekistan. Some teams and SOAR are already on the ground there. It's your plan. We don't know if you will have to go. I know you want to."

ꕤ

I wish Samuel were here. What am I to do about Kathryn's grandparents visiting? *Since I do not know when Samuel is returning I will treat this as if he will not be here. I will write Kathrin's grandparents back, but first I must plan, when is a gut time for them to visit.*

September 18, 2001

Dear Lou and Kathy,

I will start by introducing myself. My name is Mary Hersberger and I am Samuel's wife. I am writing this to let you know that Samuel is away on business. We do not know when to expect him back. Kathryn is doing well. When she first got here, she had nightmares. It was very hard on her, missing her mom. Our other children have helped her settle into our life very well. The routine in the day starts early. The day is long, but Kathryn is always so eager to please. She is bright and cheerful and brings laughter and smiles when we least expect it.

It would be gut for you to come and visit. I think and hope for Samuel to be back soon to help plan for your arrival. With that being said, a gut time for you to visit would be Thanksgiving. We will have you stay here with us and celebrate this holiday with us. Please let me know if this is a gut time.

Christ's peace be with you,
Mary

℘⟩⟨℘

Another early day at the Hersberger home and this day the women of the family settle in together to quilt. First to arrive is Katie with her boppli. Mamma is holding Samantha as they come through the door. She is wrapped in a light blanket of white cotton. The temperature is in the low sixties, a slight breeze blowing with some gusts just starting this morning.

The leaves in the distance continue to turn as they show a golden color in the maple trees with a green backdrop of evergreen. Some of the horses in a distant corral are heard whinnying.

As the women arrive, a ranch hand led by Andrew tends to the horses and buggies. Normally, they would have left them with the buggies, but since the women will be awhile, they decide to place the horses in the near corral that borders the end of the driveway.

As Andrew finishes with their horse, he hears the familiar clip clops of other buggies entering the drive. Looking up, he sees Becky, Samuels's younger sister.

"*Guder mariye,* Aunt Becky!" Andrew greets Becky as he takes hold of the horses bridle and initially ties him off to the fence of the corral.

"*Wei gehts,* Andrew?" responds Becky, climbing down from the buggy. Smiling over, she asks.

"Is Mamma inside?"

"*Jah,* and Katie and Samantha also." Andrew is prepares her horse for the corral.

As Becky enters, she finds Mary preparing coffee and placing apple strudels on a plate. Katie and Mamma are preparing the quilting frame, which has been placed on end while not in use during the past couple of months, since Mary's marriage. Chairs are also set up all around.

Kathryn finds her place on the sofa, watching as all goes on. She stares at the diamond in square patterns in pastel colors of blues, reds, yellows, and oranges. Perfect colors for the fall and the quilt will be done before the day has ended.

After what seems like ten minutes, the back door opens to Katie's Mamma, Emma, and Jeremiah's wife, Erica, and Amos's wife, Elizabeth. They have arrived by driver, having a greater distance to arrive from.

After all have cheerfully greeted each other, they sit down for coffee and the freshly prepared apple strudels. Kathryn, barely reaching the table, eagerly, but in small bites, devours the tasty morsels before her with milk.

"I haven't seen the *kinner* in such a long time Mary, I bought your *boppli's* a small treat. Is it ok?" Emma stands for a moment and brings the basket up to the kitchen table.

"*Jah* Emma, they will like this. What did you bring?"
Emma pulls out six whoopee pies. Kathryn's eyes grow to the size of small peaches and as bright looking.

"*Ach* Kathryn, what do you see?!" mamma notices her eyes.

"Whoopee pies, *grossmudder!*" And before anyone can say anything else, Mary smiles and says, "Yes you may have one, Kathryn."

Emma takes one out and places it with the rest of the strudel on the plate in front of her. She continues to talk about her.

"You would think this *kinner* never had a meal *Jah*! Where do you put all your food Kathryn?"

Pointing to her toes she tells them, "*Daed* say they go to my toes, *Mamm*" as everyone laughs.

Everyone gathers and begins the quilting process, which also involves chatting about everything. Curiously, they speak about everything but Samuel, who has been left out of the conversation. As the quilt progresses and nears completion toward the middle of the day, the Hersberger women pack up and leave.

Mary, not wanting to eat alone, invites Mamma, Katie, and Andrew to stay for supper. They happily agree. For the meal that evening, they prepare pork sauerkraut, fresh bread, and mashed potatoes.

As Wednesday comes to a close, Andrew hitches the horse to the gray over black buggy. He comes back in to get everyone and they leave. The sun has not yet gone down and they leave amongst the coolness of the coming fall.

ॐ

"Mom, I do not see education beyond this year. My plans do not include college." Mary respectfully begins sharing her plans with her mother.

"Mary, I am disappointed that you don't have college planned, though I do understand why. Have you and Daniel shared your plans with his parents? Do you have any worries?"

"I do have fears. I fear I will not be able to live up to the expectations of Daniel's Amish community. The language I believe I can handle. I am starting my third school year of German and this year I feel like it's more meaningful." Mary appears serious, but also bright with the ideas of her future.

"When do you plan to see Daniel next?" Mary's mother continues in a very matter-of-fact way.

"Tomorrow is Friday. I want to do something different for him."

"What did ya have in mind?" Inquisitively Helen continues.

"Pizza and then the movies. He has never been to the movies. 'Legally Blond' looks to be funny, followed by ice-cream to finish the night. What do you think mom?"

"Sounds like fun, but do you think it'll be ok with him?"

"What do you mean. He's still on his *rumspringa*!"

"Noooo, you buying." Helen says as she looks up at Mary from her glass of lemonade.

"It'll have to be, because I am." And with that, Helen smirks and Mary giggles as she throws her long hair back and over her shoulder.

ℰ⚭ℛ

Friday morning comes quickly at the ranch, but not quickly enough for the sometimes inpatient Mary. After doing her chores, she joins her dad at the corral for the sale of some more horses. Another mare has gone for ten thousand dollars. Another gelding sells for five thousand dollars. Mary helps her father move the horses from the stable to the trailer. Afterward, it is off to school.

This day she drives. The vehicles that are kept at the ranch are all kept behind the bunkhouse where garages were built for the vehicles to be kept out of sight and mind until needed. Samuel still owns a small Ford Ranger, a four cylinder truck, which he chooses not to use.

With Friday comes another cool evening. The cool air smells fresh on the ranch. Leaves on the tree line begin to show more vibrant colors.

The day is ending for a couple of the ranch hands as they head out together in their car. They wear battle dress camouflage uniforms as they leave for two and a half days of

National Guard duty. In the air wafts the smell of steak cooking from outside the bunkhouse.

Samuel, in support of his extended family's farms, continues to buy whole cows and pigs in order to support their efforts and their farms. They argue about family buying from family, but he argues that it is his business buying for his hands.

Young Mary, with Rachel and Kathryn in hand, come up from the stables. The two kinner look up and smile at Mary as they near the house. They wear dark maroon-colored dresses and their white kapps are pinned neatly to the tops of their heads. Just as they reach the bottom of the porch steps, their mother comes out, meeting them at the top.

"*Kinner*, go wash for supper *schnell*. *Danki* Mary for your time with them."

"*Jah mamm!*" she hears from the slight but excited voice of Kathryn.

"*Kumme* Rachel." Kathryn says, picking up some of the words and phrases of the 'Pennsylvania Dutch'.

Young Mary, letting go of the *kinners* hands, looks up at Mary and speaks up carefully, "You're welcome. Aunt Mary, may I speak with you?" she asks as she follows the children with her eyes.

"*Jah* Mary, *kumme*, sit with me in the kitchen." The two go into the kitchen. Young Mary sits at the table while Mary puts a tea kettle under the faucet and begins to fill it and asks, "would you like some tea? I seldom have someone who I can sit with," she says with a smile.

"Yes, thank you. I would like that and to also sit with you."

Mary calls out after her kinner, "go wash up for supper now," as she opens a jar containing sugar cookies and takes out one cookie for each of them.

"We should not be doing this, but we must have something with our tea, *jah!*" The tea kettle begins to whistle. Using her apron she reaches for the old tea pot passed down from her own mother.

She pours the tea onto the bags in two mugs. A faint hint of mint is immediately picked up by the two of them.

Running water can be heard upstairs as the kinner are cleaning up. Caleb's voice, young and demanding, makes its way downstairs, "Rachel, *schnell*, you are taking too long."

As Mary lifts the bag and begins to dunk up and down, she hesitantly begins.

"Aunt Mary, you know how I feel about Daniel. It is possible that we may someday get married. Well, because of this, I have a deep respect and growing love for your faith and people. Did I say that all right?" Mary looks and smiles deeply at her.

"*Jah*, Mary, you said that *gut*. What are you thinking?"

"I need to learn. I am so afraid of failing at being a good Amish wife and I want this so much. I don't sound stupid, do I?" Young Mary at this point looks very serious and panicked.

"Relax Mary, you don't sound *mupsich*, stupid, nor *dumm*. You want to learn our way *jah*? Two words you learn now, Ok? What do you need from me?"

"Is it possible to not move in, but be around sometime to learn how to be a good wife in the Amish way?"

"*Jah*, it is possible, but we must speak to your mother and father first. And we will have to speak with Samuel."

"Thanks, Aunt Mary!" Mary nearly shouts in excitement and jumps up. The quick clip clop of hoofs and scratching of wheels on the black top of the drive can be heard outside as a horse drawn buggy nears the back porch.

"That's Daniel, Aunt Mary! We have a date tonight. But he is going to be surprised. I'm taking him out."

"You are?! That is very bold Mary, very English! I suppose."

"Is it OK? Do you think it will anger him?" questions young Mary hesitantly.

Smiling, Mary simply says, "have a *gut* time!"

৪০‍৫৪

"What do you want to do again, Mary?" asks a surprised Daniel.

"I know it is not your way, Daniel, but I want to share with you. I want to give something to you, please," pleads Mary.

"Ok, what is your plan again?" reiterates Daniel, still holding the same confused look.

"I'm already dressed and you look great as always. I have my dad's permission to use his truck. First we are going to get pizza, and then I'm taking you to a movie."

"*Wunderbaar, gut*! Sounds like fun!"

"Really!? Thanks so much! In the excitement of the moment, Mary jumps over and kisses Daniel.

Daniel holds his cheek, "And a kiss also! When do we leave?"

"Now!" Mary is beaming and heading for the back door of the *dawdi* house to tell her mom.

ജ‌ന‌ര

The sun has not set yet and sitting in the pizza restaurant is Mary in blue jeans and Daniel dressed plain. Others in the somewhat crowded restaurant try not to stare, but they do look at the 'odd couple'. Mary orders a medium size pizza, half mushroom and half Canadian bacon, which Daniel has never heard of. They wash it down with a couple of sodas.

"Mary, I love looking at you. When I fall asleep, I dream of your face," whispers Daniel.

"I dream about you, too, Daniel. I need to ask you, do you think I could ever fit in?"

Daniel, smiling now, becomes a little louder, "Do you want to Mary?"

"Yes, with all my heart," she says taking hold of Daniel's hands.

"Then you can. Let's finish eating. What are we doing next? Did you say a movie? I have never been to one."

"I know. I am taking advantage of your *rumspringa*. We're going to see 'Legally Blond'. It just came out. It's a comedy."

"*Gut*, I can pay for this," offers Daniel.

"Daniel, no! Please," rebukes Mary.

"*Jah*, I know, just have to tell you that I am prepared."

"This is my night for you Daniel Hersberger." Mary looks into his eyes. The two finish eating and walk out to the truck. Daniel walks over to his side.

"Heh, a lady still expects for a gentleman to open her door, even if she is driving." Daniel smacks himself up the front of his forehead, again.

"*Dummkopp!*" He runs around to her side of the truck and opens the door right into his head.

"*Ach*!!"

"You alright? That's red. Are you ok?" questions Mary, now concerned about Daniel's head.

He responds, "Jah, just feeling dumm." With that, Mary stands tippy toe and kisses his forehead. Daniel cradles Mary's face and kisses her cheek, softly at first, then strongly on her lips.

Mary reaches around his neck and returns the long kiss. Nothing else is said. Daniel helps Mary into the truck, runs around the front of it, and jumps in the other side. Before putting on his seatbelt, he leans over and, placing one hand on Mary's right leg to steady himself, kisses her once again, sits up with a smile, and puts on his seat belt.

"Legally Blond, *gut!*" he says again.

Mary just looks inquisitively at him and shakes her head with a smile, mumbling to herself, "And you're not dumb."

Mary pays for the movie. As they enter the theater, Daniel carefully opens the door without hitting his head.

Mary leads the two of them hand-in-hand up the stairway to the back of the theater. After sitting, Daniel takes Mary's hand in his. Mary looks down and is rubbing her thumb over Daniels hand.

She places her other hand on top of both, sliding up his arm, and clutching it strongly. Looking into each other's eyes, they are interrupted when the screen lights up. They settle back and begin to watch the upcoming movies.

Throughout the movie, the young couple steals glances at each other. But nothing else happens beyond holding hands and having longing looks. At the Ice cream shop, they start to talk about what each other like. Both like vanilla ice-cream; Mary with chocolate jimmies and Daniel discovers he likes the chocolate dipped shell. As they arrive back at the ranch, it is close to midnight.

"Daniel, it is late. I don't want ya goin home at this hour by buggy"

"I had a great evening Mary, but I must go home."

"Daniel, no, it's late. Please," a worried Mary now pleads.

"But what will I do, I cannot bother my Aunt Mary."

"You can stay here. I'll get ya a pillow and a blanket and ya can sleep on the sofa."

Giving in, Daniel whispers, "*jah*, ok, but let your *mamm* and *daed* know, ok?"

"Ok. Come in now." Leading Daniel, she opens the door to the kitchen of the Dawdi house. He looks around remembering when he had been there in the past as a child.

"Wait here, I'll be right down." After she reaches the top of the stairs, he hears whispering, and as quickly as the whispering stops, a little rustling around and Mary is tip toeing down the steps in her bare feet. She sets up the sofa.

"There ya go. All set. I'm going up to get ready for bed and will be right down to check on ya and say good night."

Ten minutes later, Daniel is under the covers and the sound of light barefooted steps can be heard coming down the stairs. Daniel looks up and Mary is standing above him in a floral night gown with her hair out of her pony tail and around her shoulders. As she sits next to him on the sofa, he scoots over.

"I love you, Daniel." Bending over, she kisses him softly. He can feel her warmth through the night gown as he looks her over and runs his hands from her hands up her arms to her face and returns her kiss.

"*Gut nacht liebe*" Mary softly says. Daniel just stares.

"*Gut nacht*, I love you, your German is gut." Daniel says still staring.

"*Danki*." Mary kisses Daniel one more time and stands and leaves.

ॐॐ

As Mary and the kinner sleep, a scream is heard through the house. Mary runs into the girl's room only to find the two girls just starting to stir from the scream. As she backs out of the room, Caleb is heard yelling. "*Mamm*! *Mamm*!" Mary hurries to his room to find him standing, soaked in sweat.

"It's *daed*, its *daed*. Something happened to *daed*."

"No Caleb, it's a bad dream," reassures Mary "It is ok Caleb."

"*Jah*, it's a bad dream, but it was real," cries Caleb, as he continues to look over at his *mamm* with tears drenching his face. He cries out in horror. "*Mamm*, its *Daed*!"

Chapter Twenty One

Caleb spends the rest of the night in his mamm's bed. Though he is restless, he sleeps, as do the girls. Kathryn climbs into Rachel's bed, which will be the first of many times. Mary wakes to another headache. There is no medicine that can be taken with her pregnancy. She finds tea helps her with the headache and ice to her forehead when it is really bad, but tea is good also with the nausea, which is much less frequent now.

Ach, another headache, no sickness though. I will let Caleb sleep. I hope he does not remember last night. Samuel, God please be with my husband. Find him safety where ever he may be. I must start breakfast.

As Mary prepares breakfast, she peers out of the kitchen window and finds Daniel and Mary standing on the back porch with their arms around each other.

They must not think anyone else is awake this early on a Saturday. They shouldn't be so much in public. Ach, they love each other, does it matter? I miss Samuel so much and I haven't heard from him. Where could he be? They remind me of us and make me miss Samuel, his touch, his kiss, his body next to mine. Where are you Samuel? What do you do?

ഇരു

Daed will be out in the barn when I get home. I hope he is not too angry with me. I love Mary, I want to marry her, when should I do this? There is the drive. Ach and there is daed!

"*Guder mariye Daed*. I'm sorry I did not come in last night," says Daniel preemptively and very serious. He appears scared.

"You are *naerfich, sohn*. Did you do something wrong?" asks Daniel's *daed*, though sounding uncharacteristically understanding.

Daniel, being a little braver, answers, "No daed, I am afraid you would be angry."

"*Kumme*, when you are finished with the horse, *kumme* in to the house Daniel."

"*Jah daed*."

❧☙

Inside the house, Jeremiah sits down with two cups of coffee after kissing his wife on the cheek.

"Erica, Daniel is home and I want to speak to him with you here. Where are Jeremiah and Katherine?"

"They are out tending to some chores I have for them." Daniel comes into the house, nodding his head to his mother and, smiling nervously, begins with his daed, "*Jah daed*."

"Sit *sohn*. You have missed breakfast, but here is coffee and mamm will bring you a bun, ok?"

"*Danki Daed*." Jeremiah sits back and takes hold of his cup.

"You are no longer a *buwe*, Daniel. We mistakenly thought you were going wild on your *rumspringa*; we were wrong. It troubles me that I make you *naerfich*. You have become a *gut* man. When you did not *kumme* home last night, I was a little *naerfich*, but I knew you were out with Mary. I knew you were ok. I must also have more trust in the Lord and you. Please do not be *naerfich* anymore, ok?"

"*Jah* daed. *Danki*!"

"So tell me, how is Mary?" Jeremiah brightens.

"*Wunderbaar*!" Daniel is now smiling. He looks over and sees his mother as she grins, bringing a plate to him.

"Do you have any plans? You love her very much, *jah*?"

"*Jah*, I do."

"Well, I told you I need to learn to trust you and the Lord more. It begins now. I am glad you have someone in your life, Daniel. You are both faithful and *schmaert*. You will work out all that there is." He looks over at Daniel as he takes his first bite of his Aunt Mary's left over apple strudel.

"*Jah daed, danki*," responds Daniel.

"When you are finished, you have chores sohn. I will meet you outside."

"*Jah daed*."

∾)(∾

"Mary, Daniel did not eat when he left."

"Yes mom. He was really nervous about getting home. He wasn't hungry. Mom, may I speak to you and dad?"

"Of course. When?" As Mary's mom's eye look up.

"Now is ok. I'll get dad."

"I'm right here. What's up there young lady." Mary's dad comes from the back of the house. Stepping into the kitchen, he pulls out a chair and sits down. Helen pulls out a chair next to him.

"Mary, sit down. We're here. What do you want to talk about?" invites her mom. Mary sits down across from them.

"You know I'm in love with Daniel?" begins Mary.

"Yes, we may not speak that much, young lady, but I do see. And yes, your mother and I speak. And yes, I do know that you two are in love."

"I want to become Amish." Everything in that moment becomes still and quiet.

"Hmmm, I see. This is very serious Mary. We know that if you stay with Daniel, you will either have to join or he will have to leave. What do you think, Helen?" asks her father.

"Mary, we, you and I, have had many conversations. This was not one of them. This is not like joining something and leaving it. This is a lifetime. It is a commitment. You do realize that?"

"Yes, mom, I have given it a lot of thought. I briefly spoke with Aunt Mary about it. She said I would have to speak to you first and she will speak to Uncle Samuel."

"Well now, did you give this some thought?"

"Yes dad, I would like to spend more and more time with Aunt Mary, learning their ways. I have already begun going to church with them. Their faith is what is most important to me."

"You sound as though you have given this much thought. It isn't what we would have in mind for you, we're Lutheran, but it is your life. Just like your brother, Roy. The military is not what we had in mind for him, but it is his life." A doubtful but reassuring dad speaks up.

"How ironic the two of you, you and your brother. Totally opposite places you are in. Your Uncle Samuel will be pleased. I know he wasn't when he heard about Roy. You could tell he was against him being in the military. Just shook his head no, turned around, and left. The Amish are all about peace. Still confuses me what he has to do with what's going on with him and Chris Hutchins all this time. This aspect of his business I just don't know about. Well, listen to me just babbling on like a creek. I'm sorry sweet pea."

"It's ok, dad. You and mom are ok with my decisions?"

"Mary, your father and I raised you and your brothers right. Though we are not pleased with this decision, we respect it. We will support you in whatever you must do. We are sure we will learn to like it as time goes."

"Thank you both. I love you mom, dad." With tears in her eyes, Mary stands.

"Heh, we love you too sweet pea, very much," her dad says as he stands, going over to her and hugging her, followed by her mother.

"Thanks daddy. Ok to go over to Aunt Mary's? Mary's dad smiles at her and just shakes his head yes.

൭൫

Mary goes straight to her Aunt Mary's house to share the news. Knocking on the door, Kathryn answers right away.

"Hi Mary, *mamm* don't feel good, she's lying down, shall I get her?"

"No, let me see if she is ok, Kathryn." She comes in taking Kathryn by the hand and they proceed upstairs. They find Mary upstairs lying down with ice on her head.

"Aunt Mary, it's me. Are you ok?"

"*Jah*, I will be, *danki*. I have another migraine. I have more since becoming pregnant. It's almost gone. Can I get you anything?" she asks while trying to get up.

"No, I should be getting you something. How about if I make you some tea? Lay down now," says young Mary, taking charge.

"*Jah*, ok, that would be nice, *danki*."

"Kathryn, come with me. Let's get your mom some tea."

"My *mamm*, Mary," corrects Kathryn.

Mary laughs and follows with, "Yes, your *mamm*." The two go to the kitchen and Mary begins to boil water. *I think I'll wait on speaking to her about my conversations with my parents.*

൭൫

It's Sunday and Mary is over at her Aunt Mary's early. It is a church weekend at the end of September. She helps out with the kinner and her dad hitches up the buggy for the group for church. After church, they go to another part of the community for the common meal they share. Mary is at a new person's home and she notices for the first time that she is being glanced at.

The time is coming to dress plain. I need to speak with Aunt Mary.

Chapter Twenty Two

October arrives with no word from Samuel. Everyone begins to have fears, although it is not verbalized. He has only been gone for a little more than two weeks. There is no news on an Amish farm or the Hersberger Ranch. At least not instantly, in the English sense of television and radio. There are not even questions regarding what he does any longer. No one speaks of him, but everyone misses him.

Mary climbs the back steps to the house, looks down, and sees a lowly rose.

The last rose of summer. Stepping back down, she bends over and gently cradles the bottom of the bud as she breathes in, taking in its fragrance.

For a moment, she is back in time and remembering. She sees Samuel's face smiling as he looks up at her while planting the roses. She remembers his warmth while holding hands. She remembers walking along the fence line, arm in arm, while feeding their horses together.

Then she comes back to the loneliness of empty arms, empty hands, and longing hearts. She climbs back up the stairs. Her boppli with Samuel is nearing four months and she can feel the new life moving inside of her.

Young Mary, in one way learning the ways, patience, and maturity of a young Amish woman, still holds onto her very English impatience and still finds herself a fiery English girl.

Letters are the mainstay for Roy now. He calls his family on his dad's cell Phone; the reception is not always good. The cadet sergeant is kept busy with his duties at this time of year with new plebs called rats.

He is even tempered and gets into their world in an otherwise very clinical fashion. Not getting much time off, he has not seen Lindsay since their visit in the middle of September. Thinking of her often, he has no time for the emotional longing of two young people in love.

ℰↄ ℂℛ

Saturday, the sixth of October, harvest and canning is now over. It is an overcast day with some rain. All the trees have turned beautiful bright colors of reds, oranges, and yellows. Mary has settled the children and they sleep quietly.

Mary begins to sleep soundly and she begins to dream of Samuel; dreaming of intimate times alone. Mary continues to dream, she turns and sees Samuel, covered in blood. She awakens, shaken and crying. Quieting herself, she checks on the children; all are quiet. She checks the time.

Three a.m. Ach, I must get some more sleep. I will surely wake with another headache. Mary falls back asleep quickly.

It's three thirty in the morning. The Hersberger ranch remains quiet on this morning of a church Sunday. The door of the home is never locked, an easy open for the unexpected. Coming in through the kitchen door, he gets a glass of water. There are soft steps which make their way up the stairs and into Mary's room. An unsuspecting Mary opens her eyes, face to face with the familiar figure, and blinks.

"Samuel," she says in a whispered voice…she continues, "Am I dreaming?"

"No *liebe*, I'm home," says Samuel as Mary jumps up, her arms grabbing Samuel and hugging as if she will never leave go. As he was spirited out, so he was spirited back.

"I've missed you, Samuel. I've missed you so much," she whispers in his ears.

"I've missed you also *liebe*. I want to see the kinner," he whispers back. Continuing to whisper, Mary says, "Jah, they will be surprised."

He makes his way to the girls' room first. Both girls are in the same bed. As Mary stands in the doorway, Samuel stoops, sitting on the edge of the bed, looking straight down on them. Both girls open their sleepy eyes and stare briefly, as if in disbelief, and at the same time say, "*daed.*" They leap at their dad, both hugging him without words. Without speaking, they all as a family go into Caleb's room to see him. Repeating his previous movements, Samuel sits on the side of Caleb's bed and brushes back the hair of the sleeping child.

Caleb opening his eyes, just stares, then he cries, "*Daed, daed, daed.*" Sitting up quickly, he takes his daed around the neck and continues, "*Daed,* your ok."

"*Jah,* I am. I love you all and have missed you all, also." All the children are now hanging on daed's neck.

"We missed you, *daed.*"

.....And they shall see us;
and we will fall upon their necks
and they shall fall upon our necks
and we will kiss each other
Moses 7:63

"*Jah* Samuel, we missed you," whispers Mary as she leans over and kisses Samuel on the head.

"What happened? Why are you suddenly home?" asks Mary in relief.

Samuel thinks back to the conversation of the previous twenty four hours. *"Well, Sam, like I said, your work for now is coming to a close." "There is a part of me that wants to be there, you know that,"* he tells Chris. *"And the other part has a new wife and children,"* responds Chris, now with a smile.

"Well, it was time for me to come home; my work had finished. Shouldn't we be getting some sleep? I believe it is a church weekend, is it not?"

"*Jah liebe*, everyone will be so surprised to see you," says Mary, smiling as she wipes away tears then picks up Kathryn.

"*Kumme* Rachel, back to bed. Must get some more sleep Caleb," directs Mary.

"Ok, *mamm*," he says as he gives one more squeeze to his daed.

"*Gut nacht daed* and *mamm*." Caleb drops down bouncing into his bed. The other two *kinner* are put to bed and, before long, they are all asleep.

As soon as they enter their room, Mary turns to Samuel. First, embracing him again, and then kissing him. Afterward, she steps back. Looking into her husband's eyes, she reaches up and begins by unbuttoning his shirt. As she finishes, she slides back into bed, reaching for his hand and pulling him into bed behind her.

Once in, she lays on his shoulder, allowing him to hold her until she falls asleep. Samuel then slides out and rolls over toward Mary and kisses her before settling in and cuddling with her, his arm around her waist.

"I have missed you and love you very much *liebe*," he whispers to his sleeping wife.

Chapter Twenty Three

The next morning, after an early morning breakfast, the newly reunited Hersberger family steps out into the crispness of the fall Sunday air. As Samuel looks around, he freezes at the site of Mary coming from the Dawdi house. Mary, now spotting one additional familiar figure, also freezes in her steps.

"*Liebe,* that is Mary," says a dumbfounded Samuel, standing there bewildered.

"*Jah,* it is Mary. She is dressed plain," he says, as his bewilderment continues.

"*Jah*, much has changed since you left Samuel. Mary is becoming Amish."

"She is what? Things have changed. *Guder mariye,* Mary," greets Samuel.

"Uncle Samuel! Good morning." Mary, holding up her dress, forgets about walking genteelly and excitedly begins to run towards her Uncle. Samuel, one step at a time, reaches the bottom step as she reaches him. Jumping up she hugs him.

"We have all missed you, uncle. Everyone is going to be so surprised. This is wonderful!"

Samuel, smiling, takes one step backwards, holding Bill's daughter at arm's length and looks her up and down. Then teasingly states, "You look plain, jah."

"Uncle Samuel!" Young Mary begins to laugh.

"Does anyone else know you're home? When did you get home? What have you been doing?" Excitedly, Mary babbles on like a brook until stopped by her Uncle.

"Whoa, Whoa, Whoa! Mary. There is time for all the questions later. First church."

"Ok, Uncle Samuel. Good morning, Aunt Mary, how do I look?"

"*Gut.*" Mary says, smiling.

ℰↄↃℭ

The small Amish community of Honey Brook is gathered outside the church talking in small groups of men and woman when the Hersberger buggy arrives. With his wife Erica, Jeremiah, not initially seeing his brother, walks over to help Mary. As they near, Erica spots Samuel first.

"*Ach*!! It is Samuel! Samuel is home!" With that, everyone in Samuel's extended family stops what they are doing and congregates around the horse and buggy. Mamma makes her way forward through the crowd and, without a tear, reaches up as Samuel leaves the buggy, hugging him and says, "*Willkum* home *sohn*." Then she smiles calmly as though she knew to expect him this day.

Samuel, looking around and taking it all in, looks the same as when he left, with his long hair cut straight and his beard. He is still dressed plain. Nothing has changed except the world, which he left twelve hours prior. On this day, the world has changed again.

After church, Samuel spends a long time away from his immediate family, choosing instead to be with his extended church family, catching up on the latest news and reassuring the community by his appearance, that he has not changed and he is exactly what he was when he left, by their eyes, a farmer.

ℰↄↃℭ

Back on the ranch, some of the typical daily chores are on their way to completion. Bill is out in the corral when the familiar clip clop of the Hersberger horse and buggy is heard nearing the drive. Stopping, he walks over to the edge of the fence. Climbing, he pauses half way through as he catches site of his old friend and mumbles to himself, "Well I'll be, Helen! You'll never guess who is home! Sam, when did you get back?"

"Early this morning, how is your family? How is the ranch?"

"The family is well. You can see some of the changes in the buggy with you."

"*Jah*, dressed plain," says Samuel as the two old friends burst out laughing.

"The ranch is fine and business is good. We had some more sales."

"*Gut, gut…..*" By this time, Helen is making her way out of the dawdi house, wiping her hand on her flowered apron.

"Samuel, it's good to see you. This is a surprise! You better stay from now on. You've put your wife through enough. You do remember this woman, your wife. You know this one, she is expecting?" Mary comes up; holding her boppli with both hands, then reaches up from behind Samuel and hugs him around the waist. She steps around and greets Helen.

"*Wie gehts* Helen?"

"Fine, Mary, and I know you're fine." Smiling at both Mary and Samuel. Helen understands many of the small Pennsylvania German words and phrases, though she does not use them, she just responds to them.

๑๓ฌ

Back inside their home, Samuel and Mary sit down for a cup of tea, preferred by Mary now. Young Mary takes the children upstairs to occupy them as their parents speak and catch up on what has been happening.

"Sooo, why is Mary dressed plain again?" Samuel inquires, smiling.

"She wants to become Amish. First, she is very faithful to our Lord. She feels and hopes she will be married to

Daniel someday and wants to be a gut wife in our way. She is very mature, Samuel. She sat down and spoke with me and then her parents of what was in her heart."

"What do Bill and Helen have to say?" asks a concerned Samuel.

"They are supporting her decisions," reassures Mary.

"*Gut*, one of your dresses?"

"No, we made one together. Then we bought everything else she needed." Changing the subject, she continues, "Samuel, this is a letter from Kathryn's grandparents." Pausing, Samuel takes a moment to read the short letter. After reading he stares at the letter, deep in thought, before being interrupted by Mary.

"I did not know when you would be home so I hope you don't mind, but I answered the letter inviting them for Thanksgiving."

"No *liebe*, this is *gut*. You have done very well while I was gone. They have never met their granddaughter." Samuel, very supportive, gives a weak smile, worried.

"They will arrive the Wednesday before Thanksgiving," continues Mary, noticing his expression.

"*Gut!*" Samuel is now shaking his head. Mary reaches up and caresses her beloved's face as she looks deep into his eyes. Samuel appears far away as he gives Mary another weak smile.

Mary continues to speak carefully, "The *kinner* had a bad time while you were gone. They were well behaved but were very upset at times."

Samuel again paused, remaining in deep thought before responding, "I'm very sorry. I understand it was very hard for you. I'm very sorry."

Mary, sensing that Samuel is troubled, places her arms around him and pulls him close to her and begins to whisper,

"Know that I truly love you Samuel. I will go through whatever I am called to go through for you and our marriage." She stands up and leans over, kissing Samuel on his cheek.

"I know *liebe*. Hopefully I will not ever have to do this again," says Samuel.

දා ඇ

Roy is on leave this weekend. Waiting for the most opportune time early this Sunday, he finds Lindsay's father alone in the back yard. He is dressed in his gray uniform in preparation for morning services.

Making his way through the color of dry autumn leaves, he can hear the crisp snaps under his feet. The weather is beginning to cool quickly high up in the mountains of this part of Virginia. Though cool outside, he finds himself a little warm as he arrives in the back yard. Drawing attention to himself, he runs a finger between his collar and neck and clears his throat. He politely begins speaking to Lindsay's father.

"I beg your pardon sir." His eyes widen as he noticeably pays attention.

Roy continues, "As you may be aware, Lindsay and I have been seeing each other for over a year. Well sir, I'm in love with Lindsay and would like to have your blessing to marry her." Roy, standing at attention, stares straight ahead. He draws a smile from her father, who speaks quickly to put him at ease.

"Relax Roy. So, you want to marry Lindsay? I was wondering when you were going to get around to asking." Smiling broadly, he holds out his hand to shake.

"We have spoken about this, her mother and I. We would be very proud to have you as our son in law. We are both proud of you Roy. Yes, of course you have my blessings Roy, congratulations."

Roy is momentarily speechless as he pauses then responds, "thank you sir."

Roy is beaming and appears much more relaxed as his shoulders drop. Lindsay's father questions, "When do you intend to ask her?"

"Now, before we go off to service sir," responds an excited Roy.

"Well, let me get her mother. We'll be in the living room," plans her father.

"Yes sir, thank you again." Roy goes off and finds Lindsay looking for him in the front yard.

"There you are!" calls out Lindsay to him as he comes up the side of the house.

"Where have you been?"

"Lindsay, we need to speak. I was in the back yard with your father."

"Oh no, what is it, what happened?" Lindsay's face turns pale. Roy, ignoring her concerns, proceeds with his plans. He takes her hand and leads her to a seat on the front porch.

"Roy, you are scaring me, what is going on?" questions a now wide-eyed Lindsay.

"Lindsay, you know how I feel about you. I have to tell you that in this past year and a half I have come to love you very much!" Roy pauses briefly. *This is not how I pictured this.*

"Lindsay, I'm in love with you." Sitting next to Lindsay, he reaches in his pocket and produces a small black, felt covered, hinged box. Looking into her eyes, he continues with his proposal,

"Lindsay, I truly love you with all my heart. I want to spend the rest of my life with you. Will you do me the honor of being my wife?"

With her hand over her mouth, Lindsay barely audible, asks, "Oh my God Roy, did you just ask me to marry you?" She is now smiling and crying at the same time.

Smiling, Roy turns a little more with the diamond ring in his fingers, preparing to put it on her.

"Yes Ma'am!" Lindsay barely audible squeaks out.

"Yes, Yes, I love you, too, Roy." Lunging out, she takes him around the neck and quickly leaves go and leans back holding out her left hand, as she continues, "I have to tell my Mom and Dad."

She calls out, "Mom, Mommy! Daddy!"

Roy slides the ring on her finger, which is just a tad bit loose, but otherwise perfect in his way of thinking for not looking for a ring together. It is a princess cut half karat on yellow gold. Roy saved for this ring for six months and all through the summer. He could hardly wait to give it to her and knew holding it in his room was the safest place until the given date that he had been planning; this fall date.

Chapter Twenty Four

"They're in the living room, sweetheart," says Roy.

"Your father told me they would wait for you there."

Looking very surprised, Lindsay speaks up again, "Oh my, is that what you were doing in the back yard with my father?"

Smiling, Roy reaffirms, "Yes ma'am." Roy is smiling even broader now. As the two of them quickly stand, she engulfs her newly betrothed again around the neck, kissing Roy ever so carefully and gently. Roy has her around the waist, pulling her up, and looks into her eyes. Giving one more smile at each other, they act in unison and burst into the house through the front door.

Lindsay's father is the first to speak, "Well, I take it you said yes young lady." Lindsay is no longer speaking, just crying as she nods her head up and down.

"Congratulations you two," says Lindsay's mother, as she walks over and hugs Roy. She then quickly moves to Lindsay, holding her around the shoulder as they look at her ring. Her father shakes Roy's hand again.

As he has his hand, he looks him in the eyes before cautioning, "Roy, you are in one of the finest military schools in the south. Do not let this stand in the way of your studies. We have a tradition of fine young men from the south graduating from there. I want to see you a part of that long gray line. Do you understand?"

"Yes sir, thank you sir," reassures Roy, standing at rest with his left hand behind his back and shaking his future father-in-law's hand again.

ഇ⊃Cଃ

The grayness of November settles in over Honey Brook, Pennsylvania first, then Rural Retreat in southern Virginia a little later in the season. Lindsay and Roy, having spoken, decide to let his parents know in person while on his Thanksgiving furlough.

Lindsay goes to scheduling to request time off to travel to Pennsylvania. She is told that she can go, but will have to be back for her weekend. In the midst of debate, she finds out they will not give her off the entire weekend. She makes a decision to give her two weeks' notice. Almost immediately, she applies for and gets a job at the hospital in Lexington, Virginia. Initially, she makes living arrangements with her aunt in Lexington, where she has stayed in the past. This is where she met Roy, her aunt and Uncle having been a host parent for him.

ഇ⊃Cଃ

November nineteenth comes fast and the last of the arrangements are made for Kathryn's grandparents. A sleeper sofa is bought and moved to Samuel's office. A leather sofa, it fits Samuels's personality. Mary likes how the mattress feels. Furniture is moved about to allow for everything to fit.

One huge Thanksgiving feast is planned for Samuel's family and extended family, along with Bill and Helen and their family.

The old barn will be used. Kerosene space heaters will be used to ward off any chill. The personal horses will be moved to the corral. Stalls are to be mucked and cleaned. Picnic tables will be lined up. Fresh turkeys have been purchased. Other tables to serve the food will also be set up. The meal, on this solemn occasion, will be at one o'clock, after church service is held by Amos.

Wednesday arrives with the men working to make last minute arrangements outside. The women work inside, bringing freshly canned corn relish, fruits, jam, and pumpkin and they start preparing the filling to fill three birds a day ahead of time. The birds will be stuffed at six in the morning. Ovens from the Bunk house are to be used, as well as what once was the dawdi house and also Samuel's and Mary's home. The women of the family start preparing for the day at five a.m.

As the day progresses, the first of the two expected cars arrive late in the morning that Wednesday. Roy arrives, pulling down to the front of the corral. Running to the other side of the car, he opens the door for Lindsay, his fiancée. Expecting her oldest son, Helen spots the car coming down the drive. She is calling toward the car as the two open their car doors.

"Roy, is that you? Bill, Roy's home!" Helen hollers down to the barn. The two converge on the car from different directions.

"Lindsay, this is a pleasant surprise, joining us for Thanksgiving. This is wonderful," calls out Bill.

Roy, smiling, greets his parents, "Hi Mom and dad. Where are Travis and Mary?"

"Well, there stands your sister with Samuel and Mary's young un's"

"Where dad?" Looking at the back of a plain dressed woman, he does not realize she is changing her faith.

"Mary, turn around so your brother may know ya now."

Mary turns and yells, "Roy!"

Roy, looking dumbfounded, speaks up, "Mary? What are ya wearen?"

"I'm becoming Amish, brother." Laughing, he goes over to her and hugs her. As he does, Travis comes out of the house and runs down and hugs them both.

"Both my brother and sister are with me together. Now this is great!"

"Come on you two, I have something to tell ya'll." Roy beckons.

"Ya'll know Lindsay. May I now introduce my fiancée."

Mary is the first to scream, "Lindsay! We're going to be sisters!" as she hugs Lindsay.

Helen has tears as she moves towards Roy, speaking in a low tone, "My son is engaged to be married," and she hugs Roy.

Travis, with a smile, simply says, "Way to go brother." He nods his head yes.

And finally, Dad weighs in, "Let me at this young lady. Ya'll make an otherwise older southern gentlemen a very happy man." Lindsay's petite frame is swallowed up by Bill in a bear hug.

"Sam and Mary, where are they?" He yells, "Sam!"

Sam and Mary come out the door. Samuel responds in kind, "Bill, *Jah!*"

"Roy and Lindsay are engaged," says Bill.

"Wonderful! Seems many of your children will be married soon, Bill," says Samuel as he and Mary make their way toward the group now congregating.

Daniel is next to come up from the barn. "*Wie gehts*, Mary?" He is a tad bit dirty from working in the barn.

Mary excitedly introduces Daniel, "Lindsay, this is my Daniel. Daniel, this is Roy's fiancée. He just told us. Lindsay is going to be my sister. I am so excited."

Daniel pulls off his glove and extends his right hand, "Lindsay, it is nice to meet you."

Bill interrupts, "Well, if ya'll excuse us, it's time to go inside."

"*Jah*, says Samuel, good seeing you again, Lindsay."

෨ C෬

The Kramer's go indoors to celebrate. A rental car comes slowly down the driveway. Coming to a stop, an older couple, tanned with white hair, get out and stretch. Looking all around, they take in the beauty of the ranch with the gray of late fall all around them. Samuel spots their guests from the kitchen window.

"Mary, where is Kathryn and the other *kinner*? The Garrett's are here." Mary comes into the kitchen in a rush.

"I'll get them *liebe*." She goes upstairs to help them finish cleaning.

"Caleb, *kumme*!"

"*Jah mamm*!" Caleb quickly comes from his room. He comes to a stop with his *mamm* in front of his *schweschders* room. "Rachel, Kathryn *kumme*, Kathryn your *grossdaadi* and *grossmudder* are here."

"*Jah Mamm*." Kathryn looks up with a smile and bright eyes.

$$\mathcal{SO} \mathcal{CR}$$

Outside, Samuel meets Kathryn's grandparents. Though he doesn't actively think of it, it lies in the back of his mind that they were once his former in-laws that he has never met.

"Lou and Kathy, hello. I'm Samuel. I was married to Sandy. I am Kathryn's father. How are you and how was your trip?"

"Samuel, it is so good to meet you finally," says Kathy.

"We had a good trip, a little bumpy on the flight up, but nothing to speak of. The drive from the airport outside of Harrisburg seemed a bit long, but it is a beautiful drive coming up through the country side," says Lou as he finishes speaking. He looks up at Mary as she comes out with the kinner.

"Lou and Kathy, this is my wife, Mary, and our *kinner*, or children, Caleb, Rachel, and Kathryn. Kathryn, *kumme* meet your *grossdaadi* and *grossmudder*." Kathryn instantly becomes shy. Holding unto her *mamm's* skirt, she hides behind her.

"Hello, sweetheart, I'm your grandmother. We don't know each other, but I have for a very long time been waiting for this," begins Kathy as she talks to Kathryn while stooping to her level. Mary stoops down also, bringing Kathryn around to the front of her.

Kathryn, who is looking down at the ground, is staring at her grandparents when she breaks her silence,

"*Mamm*, this is my mommy's mommy and daddy?"

"*Jah, liebe*," reassures Mary while giving her a kiss on the cheek.

"*Guder mariye, Grossdaadi* and *grossmudder. Wie gehts?*" Kathryn says as she impresses her daed and mamm. Her grandparents look on in astonishment.

"What did she say? And what language is it?" Lou asks.

"She is speaking in some German, which she is obviously picking up quite well. She said good morning grandfather and grandmother and then she asked how you were."

Her grandmother responds cheerfully, "That is so sweet, come darling." This time, Kathryn goes right into her grandmother's arms. Picking her up, Kathy is held at arm's length by Kathryn while she studies her then, while smiling, hugs her. Kathy at that moment has tears.

"I have truly waited a long time for this. I don't know you that well sweetheart, but I do love you all that much more." And as she gets used to holding Kathryn, Kathryn looks over at her grandfather and reaches for him. Taking her, he says, "Oh my, look at you angel. Aren't you just so special?" Taking Kathryn and hugging her.

"Mary, your children are simply adorable. We have brought you all something from Florida. I hope you don't mind."

"No, we don't mind," says Samuel, speaking up.

"You didn't have to. It is most kind of you though," adds Mary.

"We should get your things out of the car and get you settled first." At about that moment, Bill shows up with a ranch hand and Andrew and interrupts, "Howdy folks."

Turning to his friend, Samuel introduces him and the others to his former in-laws.

"I would like to introduce my good friend and ranch manager, Bill Kramer. This is Jim, one of our good hands, and my niece's husband, Andrew." All shake hands and say hello except Andrew, who politely nods.

"Jim, can you help with the luggage?" asks Samuel.

"Yes sir," says Jim as he walks with Lou towards the car. Jim takes hold of two small pieces of travel luggage, red in color, and heads toward the house.

"Jim, if you could put that in my office, it would be appreciated, thank you."

As Bill and Andrew retreat to the corral, the Hersberger family makes their way to the house and the kitchen. Lou and Kathy follow Jim to Samuel's office. There they find against one wall a full size leather sofa bed with a thick mattress.

After quickly looking around, they thank him for his help. They take out small gifts for the children, Samuel, and Mary. Then they return to the kitchen. Mary is at the end of completing dinner. She decides to hold it for Lou and Kathy. Returning from their 'room,' they enter the kitchen and lay the gifts on the table.

"We thought you may not have been to the sea, children, so we brought you some things from there." By this time, the kinner are on their knees, leaning forward, their arms and elbows on the table.

"First is a container of sand from the shore. See how white it is? You can open the container and feel it." The children are speechless as they feel the softness of the sand.

Diverting the kinner's attention, she continues, "Next are star fish. We found three, so you can each have one. And this is a Conch shell. If you put it up to your ears, you can hear the ocean." She demonstrates by holding it up to her own ears. While holding it to his ear, Caleb nearly screams, excited to get his parents attention.

"*Mamm, daed*, listen. There is a whispering noise coming from it."

Caleb is excited, as first Mary takes it and listens, then Samuel, as he talks to the *kinner*, "*Jah*, this is special. God has put the sound of the sea into the shell for people who have not been there to hear it." Samuel then hands it to the other child.

Kathy smiles at him saying, "You are a good father, Samuel."

"Ooohhh listen, Rachel, it's *wunderbaar*!" explains Kathryn.

"*Jah* it is making a noise!" also explains Rachel.

"And this is something small for the both of you. It isn't much, but it's sweet." Lou finishes.

Kathy follows, smiling and looking down at Mary's belly, she says, "I think the baby might like salt water taffies." The children look at her longingly for the candy.

"Is it candy, *mamm*?" asks Rachel, excitedly.

Mary interrupts, "*Kinner*, go wash for dinner, schnell!" All the children at once say "*Jah mamm*!" They scurry off toward the first floor bathroom.

"You can have a piece of the candy after your dinner," calls out Mary behind the three kinner as the water is heard turning on.

Samuel begins explaining the day's events to the Garrett's.

"Tomorrow, we start early. You will have some idea of an Amish day. We wake up late tomorrow, about five thirty in the morning. Our families will begin to arrive around six in the morning. We have three turkeys to finish preparing. Just before you arrived, they left from a morning of preparing the food and cleaning the barn for tomorrow. Thanksgiving dinner is at one o'clock. It'll follow a short service given by my brother, Amos. We hope you find your accommodations comfortable. We have more than a typical Amish home of the old order. We have electric and plumbing. Some old order homes don't have modern plumbing. Some do. We have modern bathrooms. When I came from my life amongst the English, I was given this farm. I turned it into a ranch prior to getting married. Mary and I have turned it into a home."

The children come back downstairs promptly, motivated by the salt water taffy. They sit down and say grace by Samuel. Dinner consists of roasted pork, corn on the cob, and baked apple crisp. As they begin to eat, Kathy continues speaking with Mary,

"Mary, is this your first child with Samuel?"

She swallows hard and answers, "*Jah*, we are expecting our first *boppli*."

Kathy continues, "How many months are you?"

"We are due March of next year, about four months, *jah*." Kathy asks, "*boppli*, is baby?"

Smiling, Mary eagerly answers, "*Jah*."

"I will leave here with a new language also," says Kathy, smiling and then everyone laughs.

As promised after dinner, the children are shown the different colors and flavors of the salt water taffy. Caleb picks lemon; Rachel wants peppermint, and Kathryn, vanilla. Samuel knows what he is looking for and gets out a chocolate for Mary, "Here *liebe*, this is chocolate." Samuel smiles at her.

"Someone has had these before!" laughs Kathy.

"*Jah*, while I was in...at the shore one time, on vacation." Samuel slips. *I just about poured out everything just now. The power of candy. That was dumb.*

Then he finds another piece for himself as Mary finds another piece for herself.

"Lemon, *Jah*!" and Mary holds it up to Samuel, laughing. With a piece of chocolate in her mouth, she unwraps the second piece. Mumbling with a mouth full, she says, "this is for the *boppli*."

&)CR

Thanksgiving comes in an organized hustle. All that needs to be done is done quickly and with little difficulty. As things subside for preparation, the rest of the day is restful and thankful as the day should be.

Six picnic tables are set up by two's. Three sets in a row. A large turkey is placed on each table. Tables are finished with what is supposed to be served for that day.

The barn scent of hay and straw that is left over is quickly overtaken with the smell of hot foods and the space heaters. Jeremiah, who arrives early, appears as though he wants to speak with his brother, but continues to help out with the horses and buggies. Daniel quickly seeks out Mary. He will do whatever he can to allow him to be near Mary.

As it nears noon, all gather for the service, which Amos has prepared for that day. It is another day of Thanksgiving in the Amish community in Honey Brook. There have been many days of thanksgiving and there will be many more.

"Daniel!" calls Mary. "Can you sit with us? I need to sit with my family, but I miss you."

Daniel, looking and smiling, responds cheerfully, "Jah, I am sure it will be ok. I will let my daed know."

"*Danki*, Daniel," she whispers, taking hold of his hand and giving it a squeeze while looking into his eyes and smiling.

The Garrets pitch in and are made to feel at home. They take in all the activities of families arriving by horse and buggy; some with cars and drivers. They are introduced to all of the families.

Learning about who they will be visiting, they are polite in not taking pictures while they are there. They put to memory even the face of Kathryn, who has Kathy's name and their daughter Sandy's features. This makes for a bittersweet time for them. She reminds them of their only child who has been lost. But it is also a full and rewarding day with many blessings for them in seeing their grandchild for the first time.

All of Samuel's family have arrived, though some are late in the morning because of transportation difficulty. At two sets of tables are Samuel's extended family and Kathryn's grandparents, sitting next to them. There is Jeremiah and Erica with their kinner, Jeremiah and Catherine. Daniel goes to sit with young Mary.

Becky and Daniel and their kinner, Esther and Deborah. Amos and Elizabeth have all five of their kinner on one side of two picnic tables. Emma and Solomon sit on the other side of the same two picnic tables. Mamma, with Katie and Andrew, sits with Samuel next to Kathryn's grandparents.

At another table is the ranch cook, William, and his family. This day he is deliberately kept away from cooking. It is his day to rest. The ranch hands who did not return home for the holidays, stay and eat with everyone else and are made to feel like family. Bill's family also sits with them.

"Daniel, this is so special. I never want to live in any other way. I love all of this." Mary is whispering as they eat. Her mother hears her and smiles.

"Mary, come next year, I will join the church. I will be baptized next fall. We have different ways of doing things. Though you are joining our community, is there something I should do when I want to marry you?"

"I would like it if you ask my father for his blessing. This is the only thing."

"You're *daed*?" asks Daniel.

ℰℂℛℬ

As the day comes to a close, Samuel finds himself lost again in his own world, deep in thought. *Our children allow us to realize how much we have lived life. I understand now daed; you have realized life through us. Yes, you have realized a full life, though I do miss you, daed.*

Chapter Twenty Five

"Samuel, can we chat?" calls Bill from the back porch of the *Dawdi* house.

"*Jah*, what would you like to speak about Bill?"

"Christmas." Bill is smiling on the day after Thanksgiving.

"Already?"

"Yep, even you can't avoid it there, now buddy. How do you do Christmas?"

"*Gut* question, Jah. I think I will let Mary handle this. Let me get her. Get Helen why don't you." Samuel goes into the house and returns with Mary, as well as Kathy and Lou who were with Mary. As they come out, Helen and Bill make their way over to the drive.

"Let's sit at that picnic table." says Samuel, as they all head over to the table and sit.

"We really enjoyed ourselves and dinner with your families yesterday." Lou starts.

"You are always more than *willkum*." invites Mary.

"Helen and I don't know anything of the cultural differences regarding how to celebrate the holiday. So, if you can help us out, we would be grateful." Bill is now looking at both Mary and Samuel.

"Mary, I don't know how we are to do this. I have been away too long, so if you can handle this, it would be gut." Mary nods her head, then sits up and looks out in deep thought.

"It is our most important holiday. Christmas day is a day of prayer. We do not celebrate as you know it with big meals and gift giving. We will do all this on the day after.

We put up a Christmas tree… Santa Claus does not visit… We don't have Santa. We do have gifts. They are something of the heart that is given. They are not many but very meaningful.

Christmas can last a few weeks with visiting other families every weekend… Another important part of Christmas is that the kinner act out the nativity at school. They have already begun this at the beginning of the school year. All of our community come together at the school to watch this."

"Don't the children miss Santa Claus?" asks Kathy.

"No, they never had him to miss him." responds Mary with a smile.

"Well, this sounds grand. All the meaning without the trappings of commercialism." Helen quickly interjects. "We will celebrate it just that way. I like it! I like it a lot! What do you say Bill?"

"I'm with you sweetheart. Sounds good to me!"

"*Gut*, I will help you in any way I can," says Mary as she shakes her head.

Samuel, looking at Kathy and Lou, interjects, "Well, I have something special I would like to do with you two." Everyone looks at Samuel as he grins. They can see what he has planned as the first two of saddled horses are brought out.

"We are going for a ride and take a look at the ranch." Kathy gasps as she brings her hands to her chest, "I haven't ridden in so long. This should be a lot of fun!" With that, Samuel's three children exit the stables atop their own horses being led out by ranch hands. Andrew has Samuel's horse and is leading it out.

Last but not least comes young Mary and Daniel atop their horses followed by Lindsay and Roy.

Roy hastens everyone, "Ya'll ready?" The day is cool and dry. After Kathy and Lou get in the saddles they head out into the field, which now lies brown. Samuel, tugging on his reigns, brings Travelor around to meet up with Kathy and Lou who are smiling.

Thanksgiving weekend comes and goes. With the holiday goes Kathryn's grandparents, in an otherwise tearful farewell.

Roy and Lindsay return to Rural Retreat on Saturday. She packs only clothes to begin with for her move to her aunts in Lexington, Virginia on Sunday.

She will begin work on Monday and start looking for her own apartment that week. Lindsay's priorities have shifted to someone she is promised to.

ℰℭ

December fifteenth arrives at the Hersberger Ranch. It has been a busy week with the birth of another foul and the selling of four more horses. The horses are also being trained for local use and pulling buggies. This is Andrew's idea and his new job, which is proving to be quite profitable for the ranch.

All have been very busy preparing for the big day in a week. It is even a more special time that Christmas will be spent thinking about Christ's birth and others the day after his birthday.

Mary and Samuel find a plastic ranch set complete with horses, house, barn, and corral for Caleb, who loves the ranch and horses. Since he is getting older, he gets his first toolbox with a hammer and screwdrivers. In a separate package are wood nails and screws.

Kathryn gets her own dolls. The girl doll has a blue gray bonnet with matching coat over a blue dress. A dark blue ribbon hangs down from the bonnet. The boy doll wears a blue shirt and black pants and black hat. The dolls are dressed 'plain' and do not have faces.

Rachel gets her own push pedal sewing machine and a sewing kit with all that one needs to do quilts. There are many scraps of cloth in another package.

A special gift from Samuel and Mary for young Mary is her own Bible. From her parents, Amos is hired to build a hope chest made of cedar. This is the beginning of the gifts as the planning and secrecy continues.

That Saturday held something very special for Mary as the morning sun came up on the grays and browns of the ranch. She waited for Daniel for another outing from the back porch of the dawdi house. It was 10 a.m. when the barn door opened and out came Daniel with Mary's father, leading the horse and buggy out.

"*Wie gehts* Mary," called out Daniel with a smile on his face.

"*Guder mariye.*" she responds with a curious look.

"Are you ready to go Mary?" he asks.

"*Jah*, where are we going, Daniel?"

"Back toward my place."

Mary gets in the buggy with her dad's help who just smiles at her. "Have a good time sweetheart."

"Thanks Dad." Daniel takes the buggy out onto Horseshoe Pike heading east, turning right onto Birdell Road, then turning right onto Beaver Dam Road. He pulls off the road onto the family drive on the right. In a small clearing on the left, inside of the wooded area of the drive, he steers the horse and buggy. The horse and buggy rustle through the colorful dry leaves. The horse whinnies with doubt as he is lead forward and deeper into the wood line. Mary looks around curiously and she asks, "Where are we going Daniel."

"Ahh, we're here. I use to play here when I was younger. It is quiet; a gut place to talk. Jah?"

"*Jah.*" Mary responds.

"We have spoken a lot of our future Mary. You have made a lot of changes. I will be baptized into the church next fall." Mary now holds her fingers up to his lips.

"So will I. I have been taking lessons from Samuel's brother. I will also be baptized at the same time." Daniel is just staring at Mary… quiet.

"Mary, I have thought a lot of where I see God wanting us in our lives. You are very special to me. I have never witnessed anyone work so hard at anything."

He is interrupted by Mary as she says, "Daniel, though I love you, I first did it for Jesus. I did this for my relationship with God. I follow what is my calling."

Daniel now holds his fingers up to her lips carefully, gently. "I know… I am very much in love with you *libeling*." It dawns on Mary what may be going on and she begins to cry softly.

"I want to spend the rest of my life with you and care for you." Some more tears from Mary as Daniel in all his manliness begins to cry also.

"Mary Kramer, will you marry me and become Mary Hersberger?" Mary, speechless, continues to look into Daniel's eyes crying. Daniel cradles her face with both hands, leaning forward he kisses a single tear away from the many that have fallen.

"Shhh. There now Shhh…" he pulls her in and holds her close in an embrace. The horse whinnies again. Mary picks her head up and laughs amidst her tears. Looking at the horse, then back at Daniel, she hugs him again resting her head on his shoulder with her face and lips on his neck. Slipping back into her southern accent, she tells him in a whisper.

"I'd be right proud to be your wife, Mr. Hersberger. My answer is yes." She then kisses his neck one more time. The *kapp* on her head is a tad bit mussed now.

Grinning, Daniel picks up the reigns and cajoles the horse, "Get on up now, come on horse!" he says as he pulls the horse and buggy around to the drive again. He points the horse in the direction and heads down toward the house he grew up in.

Standing out on the porch is his family.

"Daniel," his father says.

"*Daed, Mamm*, Mary and I are to be married after she and I both are baptized next fall."

Looking seriously at the pair, Jeremiah, his daed, begins, "Daniel, it is obvious the two of you have spent a lot of time thinking about this. This is *gut. Jah.*" Smiling, he shakes his head. Stepping down he shakes his son's hand. He only looks at Mary, smiling and nods at her. By this time, one smiling mamm comes down and hugs Mary.

ɞɔɔȝ

Bill and Helen got Samuel and Mary and all sat at the picnic table, dressed warmly on this cool day. They tell them that there may be news coming down the drive.

As they sip coffee that Mary has made, they hear the familiar clip clops of Daniel's buggy, which had only been gone an hour and a half. Behind it is another horse and buggy. They both pull into the drive. First to arrive are the smiling faces of Mary and Daniel as they pull up to the corral's fence. As the second buggy is making its way around the corner Daniel bounds out of his and ties off his horse.

Jeremiah arrives closely behind and Daniel ties off his horse while Jeremiah helps Erica out of the buggy. All walk up to porch.

"Daddy, mom, Daniel has asked me to marry him. I said yes."

Helen's eyes water instantly as she scoots out from under the picnic table and runs down the steps. She quickly takes Mary into her arms.

"This is a wonderful Christmas. Just wonderful." Bill comes down and congratulates Daniel. Samuel and Mary are now standing at the top of the steps.

Mary, Samuel's wife, steps away as she begins, "Mary, you came to me not too long ago because you wanted to be a gut Amish wife. I knew there would be a time to start teaching you. This is that time, with your mamm's permission of course."

"Yes Aunt Mary, *danki*!" turning her attention to her mom again saying, "Mommy, I'm so happy!" As she hugs her tight.

"I can feel your happiness; oh yes, I can feel your happiness!"

Samuel and Jeremiah enjoy a small reunion. Plans are made for Jeremiah and Erica to make the formal announcement to the community at an opportune time during a Sunday service. The wedding will be held on the ranch.

෨෦ඏ

Christmas becomes a very special time for Bill and Helen. They have not attended church in a long time. Reflecting back at their many blessings and how the family has grown, they see that they are no longer the same.

They have neglected their personal relationship with their savior. This Christmas marks a time that they have begun to attend worship again themselves. Christmas Eve, midnight, Bill and Mary mark that change by going to worship at the Lutheran Church down the street from the ranch on Horseshoe Pike.

෨෦ඏ

Christmas night, the family of Samuel and Mary sit around the fireplace. Samuel reflects back and tells Caleb and Rachel again how pleased he and his mother are of them and their parts of the Christmas play. He talks of the birth of the Christ child this night many years ago.

The fire glows brightly as the smiles on the faces of the kinner that Christmas night. At the completion of a short prayer the children are off to bed.

Samuel and Mary return to sit in front of the fireplace on the sofa, Mary in Samuels's arms. All they hear is the snaps and pops of the fireplace.

The flames in multiple colors dance to the wind outside. Samuel thinks back during this silent peaceful time. *I can see the hands of the father at work on all that is good in this world...and I am thankful... daed!*

Chapter Twenty Six

Christmas being a holy day, the kinner have to wait until the day after for gift opening. They wake early the day after Christmas. Beneath the tree, decorated with stars and angels all made by the three kinner, are the gifts decorated colorfully for this special day.

Mary has started the dinner for the family to be at noon today. It will be a fresh large chicken and ham with mashed potatoes, green beans, corn, and different relishes that were canned that fall.

After breakfast of pancakes, jam, and syrups, the children open their gifts. Mary and Samuel's first Christmas together, watching as the children's eyes glow and listening to the ooohhhhs and aaahhhhhs!. It was indeed a very special time.

Mary comes down with Samuel's gift. After carefully opening the box from its light blue wrapping of a snow scene, Samuel pulls out a bowl with a lid and an attached note.

Mein Liebling Samuel,
Thank you for coming into our lives
and changing them.
You have brought more joy than a woman with kinner,
Or one child, could ever ask for.
I Thank our dear Lord
Each day
For your life.
This bowl is storage,
for all that is in your past

that you hold dear,
inside of you.
It is also for these candies
that your children
and I have made for
you
With all my love
Mary.

Samuel, the toughness in him melting, smiles with tears.

"*Danki, mein liebe.*" He holds it close to his heart then, laying it aside, hugs her and kisses her. "I have a special place for this... Wait my turn." As Samuel scurries off for his gift.

Returning with multiple gifts in his arms, he sits cross legged on the floor in front of her, placing the gifts in between them. The children gather to watch.

"Open this first," he says holding a package up to her. "I know it is not our way, but I dream of us riding together." As she opens up the first package it is a yellow, plaid cotton shirt with a pair of jeans underneath. "I guessed the sizes. Or should I say, found someone your size to help me find these."

"Samuel!" Mary begins to protest, and then, looking down at the children, she holds her finger to her nose. "Shhh," she smiles and holds up the shirt in front of her.

"Who helped you?" asks Mary.

"Mary," Samuel responds, as they both laugh.

The next box is heavier. As she opens it, she finds boots with fancy designs on them and they flare at the top.

"Men's boots, Samuel?"

"No *liebe*, women's boots for riding!" Samuel responds, panicked. Mary tries them on and says. "They fit *gut!*"

With two packages left, she is handed a big square package. Opening it, she finds her own Stetson. "I know you will not get a chance to wear these often, but this is for us for our time." Samuel smiles at her then hands her the last of her gifts.

226

"Samuel, you have given me too much!"

"Never could I give you too much *liebe*. You have changed my life in ways you can never understand. You and the kinner are my life. I also thank our dear Lord for every breath you breathe."

Mary opens the last very large box and pulls out a very large, queen size, baby blue quilt. On it is a scene of their ranch with everyone in place. There is a house, a *dawdi* house attached, horses, corral, bunk house, Amish buggy, and little figures of Samuel, Mary, and four children. And as she counts, she says, "There are four *kinner* Samuel," then remembering, she holds her unborn boppli and begins to cry, holding the blanket to her bosom and placing her face on it.

Shortly before dinner, the Kramer's, who were invited, arrive carrying gifts, some bigger gifts. Sitting down, Samuel starts by giving them theirs.

"Roy is not here, so I shall give you his. And… this is yours Helen, from Mary and I." Mary opens it up to the quilt she had made.

"Oh my Mary. This is what you have spent a lot of time on. Oh my, I don't know. This is so special." She too holds it up to her, burying her face in it.

Bill, opening his, finds large homemade handkerchiefs in reds, greens, and yellows.

"My wife has many talents." Samuel says.

"Thank you Mary. This is special." Says Bill quietly.

"Travis, this is something we knew you could use since watching that horse trample your old one."

Travis opens up his box to a new tanned color Stetson. Putting it on, he smiles. "Thank you Uncle Samuel, Aunt Mary."

"And Mary, this is for you."

Mary opens up her gift to a small white Bible on top of a family Bible, and a note.

To a very special niece:
This small bible is for your

Very special relationship to our Lord.
Use it for your growth.
The larger is for you to grow your family.
Use it wisely to grow your family on it.
You can write in it as your family
grows and changes.
With all our love
Aunt Mary and Uncle Samuel.
Mary clutches it and smiles warmly.

"This is the best Christmas. I have my family, my new family. I have our Lord Jesus. And in everything, I have him to thank."

There was one very special gift that went to John, his 'English brother' a handmade plaque. An emblem and a note written inscribed in brass. It begins, to my special brother.

Chapter Twenty Seven

The two snow storms for the New Year fall on non-church weekends. They are not lost to the Hersberger kinner, and also it is not lost to Samuel as he goes outside to shovel following the snow storm, which is now ending this Sunday morning.

As he steps out, he notices it is snowing big flakes. The sun is trying to break out as the clouds carrying their own form of beauty pass overhead. Looking up, one falls on his face. It feels cold and clean. He doesn't wipe it away. He just looks down again and out at the whiteness all around him.

The horses are whinnying in the background as they are removed from their allotted spaces. Samuel knows their stalls are being mucked. Life continues on his family's ranch. There is no one outside but himself for the moment.

This is good. It is something he likes. It is his special time alone with the Lord. *It is another gut day Lord, Jah a gut day. Today we will have my mamma over for Christmas and also Katie and Andrew and their boppli. Bill has done a gut job with the driveway. All I have is some steps and a path to shovel.*

As he finishes his work, Mary, all bundled up, comes out into the briskness of the winter air. She is smiling broadly as she steps out onto the wood porch carefully holding onto the railing with one hand and her belly with the other.

Samuel, catching site of her, hurries up the steps and to her side and questions her, "*liebe*, what are you doing out here?"

Mary, looking up and taking hold of Samuel's arm says, "fresh clean air."

"*Jah* it is!" says Samuel, quick to agree. He helps her carefully down the steps and cautions her, "you must be careful *liebe*. You might slip and fall like… this."

At that moment, a playful Samuel takes hold of his love, holds her tightly and falls back with her into a freshly made high snow bank.

"Accchhh! Samuel! What are you doing?"

Samuel, laughing, picks up snow and throws it over on her. As she laughs, she scoops up some fresh snow herself and throws it back whispering,

"You are such the *kinner* sometimes Samuel Hers… Hmmmmm." She is cut short as he kisses her softly and she returns it.

Pulling away, he looks at her from above and thinks to himself, *A playful push, a laughing fall, a sudden rush, you softly call, a quiet hush, we kiss, lying softly in the snow.*

"I am so in love with you Mary," he says.

Mary stares at him, still smiling and breathing heavily. She reaches up with her right hand and brushes away snow from Samuel's beard while stroking his face lightly. Then she leans up slightly, kissing the one who shares a new life within her.

"I am also very much in love with you Samuel." They lie back in the snow looking at each other for a few moments like a couple of kinner.

Yes, Samuel has brought something new to this small part of the Amish community. He brought playfulness and an openness of his love for his wife.

"Samuel, we are so very happy; can this last?" asks Mary as she looks over at her future looking at her.

"*Jah*, it can *liebe*." With those words, Mary leans into Samuel and kisses him again.

"I didn't notice but it is getting cold," says Mary, leaning up. Samuel bounds up then quickly reaches down and, cradling his wife, carefully begins to lift her from their loft in the snow, but not before she does one more thing.

"Wait Samuel, I haven't done this since I was a *kinner*." Lying flat she waves her arms in the bank up and down. Smiling she looks at Samuel and says "Ok, now carefully, lift me."

Samuel smiling lifts her carefully. They both look at Mary's carefully made angel in the snow.

"Who is like the *kinner*?" snickers Samuel. Mary, initially giving Samuel a small push, holds onto his arm. They look out onto the white fields.

Samuel, taking hold of Mary's left hand, begins to lead her on a walk down the long drive. They don't make ten steps when Mary takes hold of her husband's right arm with both of her arms and leans her head into his shoulders.

"It is a beautiful day *liebe*," she says.

"*Jah*," responds Samuel.

On their return to the house the children are seen coming from the barn, laughing.

"We cared for our horses *daed*," says Caleb spotting his mamm and daed.

"*Jah*," says Kathryn, smiling happily while walking in the snow.

Rachel reaches down and makes a snowball, and throws it at Caleb, he yells, "Rachel, I didn't see that coming!"

"No, you didn't!" she laughs.

Caleb makes one and throws it back as Kathryn, not to be left out, throws one catching her bruder on the back. She laughs heartily and is joined by Caleb calling to her, "You, too, Kathryn?" She continues to laugh, as Rachel hurls another, just missing the two of them.

Rachel screams as Caleb begins to chase her and Kathryn follows while calling out to her sister, "Rachel I'll help you!" Quickly she makes a snowball, which falls apart when she throws it.

Caleb, not making snowballs any more, scoops up snow and throws it on his sisters. They scream and begin to throw snow back.

"*Daed*, can we get out the sled," calls out Rachel.

"*Jah*," he calls back, as he and Mary laugh at their children playing.

"We are so blessed Samuel."

Samuel again says simply, "Jah."

The sled comes out being pulled by Caleb. It is an older sled made of steel rudders and wood.

Kathryn is on top of the sled with Caleb and Rachel pulling. Kathryn is laughing and yelling, "Faster! Faster!" They begin to run as Kathryn summersaults off the back and, while sitting in the snow, just looks around and laughs.

"My turn," calls out Rachel as she sits on the sled. Kathryn jumps up and grabs the rope with her bruder.

"Pull fast Caleb!" And before Rachel has a chance to take hold she is also somersaulting off the back.

"*Ach*, Kathryn you are being *kischblich*!" yells Rachel. Kathryn calling back says, "No I'm not being silly! You're all white like I am Rachel!"

"Caleb's turn!" laughs Rachel diverting her attention to their brother. "No, No!" he responds.

They continue to play, changing their play, for the rest of the morning until a gray over black buggy is seen coming down the driveway.

Their cousin Amos is first to come off the buggy and comes around, taking hold of Samantha as she is passed from Katie. Katie then takes their boppli back. Amos then helps Katie's grossmudder down from the buggy.

Kathryn is the first to call, "*Guder mariye*!" The other two, not saying anything, run up and give hugs. Kathryn is lifted by grossmudder and hugged.

After arriving to the warmth of the inside, they have dinner then retreat to the parlor. Christmas gifts are exchanged again as a very special tradition continues. After the gifts are exchanged, everyone settles for pie and coffee or tea. The kinner enjoy whoopee pies.

Kathryn enjoys what becomes a new tradition of her own, holding Samantha while she sits. She explores the boppli's tiny fingers as she holds onto Kathryn's finger. She looks up into Kathryn's eyes. Kathryn, hearing ahhhs, thinks that she is talking, "Samantha is talking to me!" Samuel, Mary, and Katie who are there and hear her, just smile and look at each other. At that very moment, the baby shakes both arms in the air back and forth laughing.

"She is happy, *mamm*."

Mary answers, "*Jah*, she is very happy to have you holding her."

ॐ

Daniel, sitting back on the sofa in the Kramer's living room, has young Mary rest back against him. Mary is reading aloud, softly. Daniel's eyes begin to close as his head falls back, awakening him. He springs back up to Mary who looks around at him smiling and asks, "Am I putting you to sleep?"

Daniel responds with sleepy eyes, "More like relaxing me."

He then smiles and continues, "I want to have you where you are forever." Daniel pulls Mary in close and then kisses the top of her head.

ॐ

Roy is with his fiancée, Lindsay, down at her parents' home in rural retreat. It is one o'clock, dinner is done, and the two plan their return to Lexington where Lindsay must return to work and Roy to his education and duties at the Virginia Military Institute.

They stand on the front porch. Roy leans against the wall of the front of the house and Lindsay leans against him, wrapped in the warmth of her loves arms. Roy's face is buried in her hair. He takes in the slight fragrance of lavender as he kisses her.

ॐ

Bill and Helen sleep quietly until Bill awakens to an unknown uneasiness. Sitting at the edge of his bed, he begins to think of his children growing and realizes that he is losing them. One by one they grow and leave. One day they will be like he is, older and approaching the night time of their lives. He cries softly. The hardened man breaks down, remembering little children about him, calling to him, daddy-daddy. Helen is not aware of anything that is going on. Bill sniffs his anguish back once more and lays his head down and falls asleep.

Time has begun to hide Samuel's secrets well. It begins to hide it as the ground is hidden under the freshly fallen snow. Through the late fall and into the winter, there is no news of the outside world, only peacefulness, which Samuel has so richly deserved. The only things that come back are his thoughts of his daed.

Chapter: Twenty Eight

Christmas will continue until January twenty-sixth, a church weekend. Arriving home in the early afternoon, after dinner at Jeremiah's home, the children go off into the house followed by Mary, then Samuel.

Mary sits at the kitchen table. As she holds her head, she looks up, "Samuel." He looks at her as she says, "I love you." Mary then collapses from her chair onto the floor.

"MARY!" Yells Samuel. The children come running,

"Mammmmm!" can be heard the screaming of the kinner,

"Mammmmmmmm!"

Terror grips the family. Samuel snaps out of the initial horror and begins to give orders, "Caleb, get my phone off my desk! Rachel, go get Mr. Kramer!" He then dials 911. Bill, Helen, and a ranch hand follow a hysterical Rachel into the house. Samuel, looking over his shoulder, informs them as to what he knows, "She collapsed. She is breathing, but she is not responsive! I called an ambulance!"

The ranch hand quickly volunteers, "I'll go out to the road to flag them down." Samuel, after feeling for and finding a pulse, rolls her onto her side.

In the distance a siren is heard. Helen returns with a blanket and covers her. Bill says, "I hear them, I'll meet them outside Sam."

"Gut, Bill, danki," says Samuel, solemn.

There is one more scream of the siren that is cut short and then a truck is heard approaching. As the doors of the ambulance are heard, another two sirens are heard approaching. They stop as a fire truck comes down the driveway followed by a police car. Organized chaos ensues as firefighter paramedics and a police officer enter the kitchen. Other firefighters are taking the litter out of the ambulance.

$$\mathcal{EO \, CR}$$

The ambulance brings Mary to the hospital. After she is seen in the emergency room, Samuel is taken off to the side by the doctor.

"Mr. Hersberger, your wife has suffered a stroke. Now, we can save her and there is a good chance of your wife recovering fully. We want to give her TPA, Tissue Plasminogen Activator. It is highly effective in reversing strokes, but it could kill the baby. If we deliver the baby, it is not to term and there is the possibility the baby will not survive. The baby needs special attention that we do not have here. We do not have a neonatal intensive care unit. Then there is the cause of the stroke. Mister Hersberger, what would you want us to do?" Ashen in color and wet with perspiration he is staring straight ahead as he thinks to himself, *My dear lord, we have not come this far for this. What is your will lord. Mary could not survive this to the detriment of our child. Could she forgive me for any choice that I make. What are my choices. Chris. My blackberry. Maybe he can help.*

"Doctor, *danki* for all that you are doing. How much time do we have?"

"The first hour is critical. We have three hours to reverse any residual effects."

"*Jah*," says Samuel responding while pulling out his blackberry. The doctor looks on in amazement. Samuel calls his old time friend and boss. Chris answers right away,

"Sam, it hasn't been that long, how've you been?"

His voice breaking, Samuel tries to talk.

"Chris... It's Mary... she's suffered a stroke. I need help. Without proper treatment, I could lose her or the baby." Chris yells over the phone.

"Damn it, no! No! How is she right now? Where are you?"

"She is unconscious and critical. So far the baby is ok. But it is too early for the baby. And they don't feel as though they can treat her without harming the baby. We are at a local hospital here outside of Honey Brook, Cherry Tree Hospital. It is along the Route 30 bypass."

Chris cuts in right away, "Sam, give me a couple of minutes, Stay with your blackberry, I'll call right back."

"Got it!" responds Samuel as he ends the call.

ℰℛ

"Heh Michele, doing anything?" Asks the black hawk pilot, Lieutenant Colonel Jake Simmons, while putting his blackberry away. Michele is hanging out with the medevac crew on her time off again. Urgently, he asks, "Are you doing anything!?"

"No, I'm off until tomorrow, why?" asks Michele who is pacing Colonel Simmons as they walk quickly to the bird, which is a hundred feet from the hanger.

"We just got an urgent call, emergency transport of a stroke patient to Washington." As the pilot and the nurse talk, they close quickly on the helicopter.

"Ok, why not civilian air?" Michele asks as the crew chief awaits them to see what is going on.

"There's something else, she's pregnant," says Simmons, looking over at her.

"Oh my, she's young. Somebody's wife?" asks Michele.

"Mission!" The pilot is yelling to the crew chief now as he nears the aircraft, he continues, "We have to go, we're starting it up." He turns to and answers Michele's question, "Don't know Michele, must be important. The call came from Bragg. Washington is already expecting us!"

"Yes Sir!" yells the crew chief as he continues. "Get these blades fired up!" The co-pilot is already in the Blackhawk seated and reaching overhead, the turbines start to whine. The copilot yells out, "CLEAR!" as the rotors overhead and the tail begin to turn, slowly at first. The crew chief pulls the chucks away from the wheels. Now fastening his belts, the pilot yells out!

"WE HAVE TO ROLL, QUICK!"

"Looks like I was meant to be here," sighs Michele, dressed in her battle dress uniform. She jumps into the back of the Blackhawk.

The crew chief slides the door closed behind her. The turbines and the blades are now at full pitch, ready to lift the Black Hawk Helicopter.

Once inside, the crew chief puts a helmet on Michele adjusting the mouth piece. As he plugs her helmet into the console, she can hear the pilot speaking as they are preparing to lift off.

"Tower, this is Dust-off-Romeo-Tango-Whiskey-four-niner-eight requesting priority clearance" The bird is now hovering and moving away from the hangers.

"Dust-off-you-are-cleared-to-one-thousand."

Responds the tower.

Michele, a critical care registered nurse on a joint Pennsylvania Army National Guard and Eighty-Second Airborne Division FTX (field training exercise) with her field hospital, begins going over all the equipment with the flight medic and the crew chief. Inside a matter of seconds, the helicopter lifts and noses out quickly into the air.

"Major!" The medic instructs, "This is a real quick review. This is the Carousel, it holds the litter pan which holds the litter. When we get her, we will move her to our litter. It'll be easier. Then she quickly points out the location of everything: IV solutions, O2, EKG monitor, pulse ox , Aid bag, hearing protection for the patient, extra blankets.

I'll deal with all the technicalities and equipment. You take care of the patient. Medicine and equipment wise if you need it, I'm your go to person. The crew chief and I will deal with loading the litter, he'll get the head end and I'll get the feet. You and the co-pilot, Mr. Reynolds, will help with the sides if we need it. Got all that?"

"Yes, Sarah, I got it."

"Major" The crew chief cuts in quickly.

"If this bird is forced down, wait till all movement stops. Go straight out at either nine or three o'clock. KEEP YOUR HEAD DOWN! Always exit the aircraft straight out. Do not go past the cabin either forward or to the rear, otherwise, follow my lead, everything will be ok. Do you understand me?"

"Yes sergeant, thank you!" At that moment the pilot breaks in.

"Michele, the family's name is Hersberger, we're looking for a Samuel Hersberger, that's the husband, her name is Mary."

ΩΟΩ

Four minutes later, the blackberry is buzzing on the counter top of the nursing station. Samuel answers on the first buzz.

"Sam, we have air assets in the area. They will be in the air in five minutes and at your location in ten. Have Mary ready! Don't allow them to let any grass grow under their feet! You understand? Air assets are inbound!"

"Yes sir." Samuel turns to the nurse while ending his call with Chris, "Miss… Nurse!" Samuel speaks with more authority,

"There is a helicopter coming for my wife! They want her ready!"

"I beg your pardon sir. We know nothing of this. Where is she going? How…"

The phone rings at the nursing station. The nurse turns her attention to the phone in front of her, "Excuse me, Emergency room, Mrs. Walters. Yes, this is the nurse. Yes, this is Cherry Tree Hospital. This is who? You're a doctor from where? Yes, we have Mrs. Hersberger. Yes sir. I'll let the doctor know! Doctor Lindfield… that was a doctor from Washington, a neurologist, there is a helicopter on its way to pick up Mrs. Hersberger." The doctor just looks at the nurse.

"That was fast. What is going on? Well let's start getting her paper work ready for a transfer."

Samuel, after seeing his wife again for a few minutes, makes his way outside to wait for the helicopter. Passing the nursing station, the doctors and nurses watch the otherwise humble Amish man as he leaves.

෩෬

While standing off the landing pad, Samuel is approached by a uniformed security guard.

"Sir, you can't be here." Samuel, very stoic, turns and faces the guard.

"There is a medevac inbound to pick up my wife."

"I didn't hear anything about this!" The security guard questions, looking at the man with longer blond hair and beard, dressed plain. Taking Samuel by the arm, he faces him and repeats more forcefully.

"Heh! Do you hear me? You have to come…" At that moment the beat of heavy props can be heard in the distance and closing quickly. Looking up, both men view the horizon and see the large green Blackhawk helicopter approaching quickly and low over the bypass.

This guy is coming in like he's in combat, Samuel thinks to himself. As the green Blackhawk with a white shield and red cross on its nose near, they can see the crew chief with his head hung out the side looking down.

The Army Medevac, its tail down low, nose up, lands fast and hard. Samuel and the security guard, looking at the left side of the Blackhawk, can see the copilot looking over at Samuel giving him thumbs up.

This guy has seen action!

Letting go of Samuels arm, the security guard yells into Samuels's ear. He is barely audible. "Who are you?" Samuel, looking into the security guards eyes and says nothing. He thinks to himself, *And now, all will be revealed! They're here for you Mary! For You! You're going to be OK! Angels daed...Angels!*

###

Dear Reader:

You Matter!

Simple words, yes, but they mean everything to me. I have taken the same attitude I have with my business and brought it here. At my business I always remember that I deal with people. They live, breath, smile, and cry about the same things I do. When they visit and order a sandwich, it is more than fueling up. Times are tough and I realize that if they are visiting me, they are looking for a treat, which means something special to them, especially if they visit with their families. So I shake hands and Thank and feed the troops. I thank a vet. I hand out lollies to children. And visit with my customers if they eat in. They matter!

Thus the same attitude is given when you read my e-book, book, or visit me on face book. You don't have to; your day is full like so many others. So if I am important enough for you to visit me, then you are important enough for me to respond to, in one form or another, to say, Thank You!

The Lord's Blessings to you,

Will

Don't miss Will's next book in the Secrets of the Son Series, Unveiling

Coming out late spring 2012.

Chapter One

As the turbines of the Black Hawk wind down, the crew chief can be seen sliding open the side door. The copilot steps out and to the front of the helicopter as he looks up at the blades. Samuel, now with the security guard standing off to the side, notices part of the flight crew coming toward him. They are the pilot, flight nurse, and medic.

"Are you Mr. Hersberger?" asks the pilot.

"*Jah*, I am Samuel Hersberger."

"I am Lieutenant Colonel Simmons. This is Major Donnelly, our flight nurse, and Specialist Long, our flight medic."

"You are here for my wife?" asks Samuel.

"Yes sir, where is she? She is supposed to be ready for us," cuts in the flight nurse.

"She is still in the emergency room. I don't know what is taking them so long." A subdued Samuel informs Major Donnelly.

Irritated, Major Donnelly, the flight nurse, takes charge.

"Jake, I'm going in for her. Can you have this bird ready to fly when I come out?" The pilot, who is looking directly at Samuel, diverts his attention, looks at the major, smiles, and nods his head.

"Consider it done!" he shouts as he turns towards the helicopter.

"Sergeant!" calls Major Donnelly to the crew chief above the din of the turbines still winding down.

"Can you bring the litter? Sarah get the O2 tank, Ekg monitor, pulse ox, and aid bag. Mr. Hersberger, lead the way. Show us where your wife is. As they head up the concrete walkway, the crew chief and medic dressed in flight suits, with helmets in place, and nurse, with flight helmet in hand, follow Samuel. They cross the parking lot and into the side of the ER as the crew chief holds open the door. Inside, they arrive at the triage station. Speaking to the triage nurse, Michele Donnelly is very clinical and to the point.

"Excuse me, I'm Major Donnelly. I'm a critical care nurse with the United States Army. We're here for Mary Hers..." She is cut off.

"Just a minute." As the nurse is distracted.

"Open the door now!" commands the Major. She is looked at in a huff and the door opens.

"Where is your wife, Mr. Hersberger, show us the way. Specialist, Sergeant, follow Mr. Hersberger and get his wife ready to go! I'll see to the paper work." As they follow him, Sarah spots a gurney, puts all her equipment on it, and motions for the crew chief to put the litter in place with the other equipment. They wheel down to the room where Mary now lies.

At that moment, Army medic Sarah Long takes charge. As she gets out a blood pressure cuff and stethoscope she has the crew chief get the litter ready.

"Heh Jim, put everything on the floor except the litter, let's get that opened up. I'm going to get a set of signs and check her pulse ox." Everything kicks into high gear.

"Jim, write this down. One hundred-forty four over eighty-eight blood pressure,... ninety-two pulse,... twenty-four respirations,... pulse ox ninety-nine. Blood pressure is high, but not too bad. Let's move her first, let me get some help." just then Major Donnelly shows up with an ER nurse, laying her helmet aside she listens to the medic.

"Major, I got her signs, they're stable and we're preparing to move her. Jim, if you can roll that side of the bottom sheet as I do, we're going to move her with it. Major if you can get the head and ma'am her feet please, let's do this! The Sergeant rolls up the sheet and grabs hold and pulls it tight under her. "Mr. Hersberger, if you can wait outside there, give us a little room sir, thank you. Watch the IV! On my command, on three, one... two... three, lift and over." Mary is lifted in one smooth motion to the litter. The medic continues.

"Major can you hand me the IV?"

"Do we have an IV pole?" asks the Major.

The medic responds, "No ma'am, I have it." After she places a pillow under Mary's head ever so gently, she then takes the IV bag and line, and places the IV under the small of Mary's back.

"We'll hang it in the bird. I have an electronic B/P cuff in the bag ma'am. If we can't get that on her, we won't be able to hear in order to take one, nor will it be easy to get a pulse in flight. Is the pulse ox still in place?"

The monitoring equipment is changed over quickly to the portable and placed at Mary's head. The O2 line is disconnected from the wall and placed on the tank, which they position between her legs.

"Specialist, set the flow rate at two liters," says the Major, taking over after Mary is stabilized on the litter.

"Yes ma'am!" Everything is running smoothly. Sergeant Walkins, the crew chief, is seen and heard speaking into his helmeted mouth piece as he presses a button on a radio on his hip.

"Colonel, get the blades fired up!"

"Firing up," comes the response. As they near the door, the whine of the turbines is heard as the blades engage and the beat of heavy props overtake the whine.

ഇൻ

"Mary, place the kids in the back seat with seatbelts. Let's get over to the hospital and see what's going on." Bill says, as he gathers the family. Mary places the three kinner who are still crying in the back seat and does the best she can to belt them in. She climbs in the front, between her mom and dad. Fifteen minutes later, they are making their way behind the hospital toward the emergency room parking lot. As they get closer, they hear the unmistakable sound of a helicopter.

"Do you hear that? Is something coming in?" asks Bill. Everyone is craning their necks, looking up, as they come around the corner to the lot.

Spotting the helicopter first, Mary say's, "It's military, dad."

"Yep, Army, wonder what they're doing here?" responds Bill urgently.

Helen who is sitting on the right side as they pass the flight crew to their right shouts. "Bill, there's Samuel!" Just then Bill's cell phone rings as they see Samuel on his Blackberry.

"He must be calling us!" Mary say's excitedly, as she turns around in the seat looking back. The kinner are now stretching, looking up. Bill pulls the truck into the lot and goes to the back seat, getting the kinner out.

"Mary, can you get Kathryn from that side?"

"Yes sir." Mary responds, already at the back seat.

They get all the children out as they head toward the back of the truck. The flight crew with Mary make their way across the parking lot with Samuel. In a loud voice, to talk above the din, Samuel gestures toward his children.

"Can we stop for just a moment? These are our *kinner.*" The co-pilot exits the aircraft and waits for the litter. Bill, Helen, Mary, and all the kinner look on in astonishment as they quickly close in on Samuel, the Blackhawk flight crew, and the ER nurse.

"I was just trying to call you, I don't have much time. Mary has suffered a stroke and they are not able to fully help her here." Samuel picks up Rachel and Kathryn at the same time, motioning for Bill to get Caleb, who is quickly picked up.

"We are going to Walter Reed. They are waiting for us there. *Kinner,* your *mamm* is going to another hospital. These fine folks are going to take care of her there and care for her *wunderbaar* gut, *jah!*" Rachel starts to cry again.

"*Mamm*", she reaches down.

Michele, now with helmet in place, reaches out for her. Again raising her voice above the din.

"Mr. Hersberger, here let me help!" Reaching over, she takes Rachel from him. "Here you go sweetie, say

246

something to your mommy. She can hear you. Do you want to give her a kiss? Go ahead you can."

Rachel leans down and kisses her *mamm*, "I love you *mamm*!" And she touches her face. The episode is repeated by both Samuel and Bill as they give the other kinner the same opportunity. The crew chief cuts in, "Ma'am we have to go!" Yelling at everyone else, he looks toward them.

"You can follow with the children. Go straight in, follow me." Moving toward the helicopter, the props blow everything around. Young Mary's bonnet is nearly blown from her head.

Mary, Samuel's wife, on an army litter is lifted off the gurney as planned, the crew chief, taking the head of the litter, followed by the medic, at her feet. The flight nurse takes the side opposite the co-pilot. She is slid into the litter pan. The crew chief places hearing protection on Mary. Meanwhile, Samuel is yelling toward the children that he loves them and will be back soon. He reassures them that they will see their *mamm* again soon and admonishes them to pray. Pulling Bill up close, with his arm around him, he asks that he get his mother for the kinner and places his home in his care. He gives a hug to each one of the Kramer's and looks at them one more time as he enters the Helicopter.

The flight nurse and medic are busy readying Mary for the flight. The IV bag is hung and the monitoring equipment is put in place. The crew chief makes sure that Samuel is strapped in. He exits the aircraft and gets everyone away safely.

Running back, he pulls the chucks from the wheels, throwing them inside. Jumping in, he slides the door closed. The crew chief, sticking his head out the left opening, looks down, then up at the blades. Samuel can hear the conversation in his head set.

"Colonel, we're clear." The helicopter rises six feet off the ground, turns clockwise in the opposite direction from which it came and, with a revving of the turbines, the props becoming deafening, and the Blackhawk pitches nose down

247

and very quickly it is in flight, banking hard to the left, in a southerly direction.

ℰℭℛ

Quietly, the children whimper in the back seat. Mary and Helen sit in the back with them, each holding one of the girls in their laps, close. Helen, with one arm holding Kathryn, has another around Caleb, pulling him close to her.

"There now, your *mamm* is going to be fine." Soothes Helen. Mary is rocking Rachel as if she were a baby.

"*Mamm* is going to be ok, she is, she really is." Nurture's Mary, now stroking Rachel's hair.

It was a short drive back home to the Hersberger Ranch. As they enter the drive, they see John's black pickup truck and two buggies. Ranch hands are seen caring for the horses. Andrew is one of them.

As they pull to a stop, Jeremiah steps from the house, appearing somber, mama following close behind with Katie holding Samantha. Jeremiah, appearing to speak for all, closes on Bill.

"Bill, *wie gehts*? We heard ambulance sirens. John came for us. He saw the ambulance leave. Please Bill, what has happened? Tell me everything. I will not judge, just tell us what is going on." Jeremiah pleaded.

"It's Mary, she suffered a stroke." Bill begins and is cut off by Samuel's mother.

"We must go there, be with them."

"You can't. She is no longer at the local hospital."

"Where is she?" Katie questions with tears in her eyes and her voice breaking.

"Apparently, there are complications…" Mama begins to sob as Katie holds her. Jeremiah places his right hand on Bill's shoulder.

"Continue, Bill."

"They could have treated her there with medication to reverse the stroke, but they were not sure of the effects of the medication on the baby. When we arrived, they were moving her to another hospital." Bill hesitates, looking over everybody.

"Where did they take her, Bill, please." Jeremiah continues to implore.

"Samuel has arranged for her to be moved to Walter Reed Army Medical Center in Washington D.C." There is stunned silence. Everyone looks at Bill in disbelief. Then uncharacteristically, Jeremiah asks.

"This is a *gut* hospital, Bill?"

"The best. He must know somebody important. They sent a helicopter with a full medical crew. They should be arriving there shortly. They were very kind to Mary and the children. I'm sure she is in the best hands." Silence falls upon the quietly crying family.

"Samuel is a *gut* man. He cares for his family well, *jah*. This is for our family to pray and to keep close to our hearts. Bill, did Samuel say anything before leaving?" Jeremiah, now breaking the silence, further questions Bill.

"To notify you and ask his mother to stay with the children. He asked that I care for his home and the ranch. Is this ok with you, Jeremiah?"

"*Jah*, I respect his decision and support him in any way I can. *Danki*, Bill. You are a *gut* man also. Samuel is blessed to have you and your family here." While the men are talking, Daniel has come from the barn and come up behind Mary. Taking Rachel, who is now sleeping, he comforts her. Mamma begins to make plans.

"Let us take the children into the front room, so they may sleep close by. It will be dark soon. We should start something to eat. I will need my things from home."

"*Jah*, mamma. John…" John, knowing what is needed, cut's in. "I'll take Andrew and Katie with Samantha home and bring back your mother's things, Jeremiah. Anything I can do to help. Please, if you hear from Samuel, let me know. Thank You."

"*Jah*, I will, John." The children were placed on the sofas in the front room. Meanwhile, John takes Andrew, Kate, and Samantha home, picking up mama's things, and returning with them. Jeremiah remains with his family as Daniel spends time with Mary. Helen also remains with Mama to help out in the kitchen, preparing an early supper. Bill goes for Mr. Schrock, to bring him back to the ranch and explain what happened.

℅℞

The Blackhawk, carrying Mary, Samuel, and the flight crew leave the airspace over Pennsylvania. The flight nurse, Major Donnelly and medic, Specialist Long continue to tend to their patient, as Mary's husband looks on. Lieutenant Colonel Simmons can be heard cutting in on the head set as everyone momentarily looks up.

"Mr. Hersberger, do you remember me?" Pausing for a moment, Samuel looks forward over his wife, taking in the tone and inflection of the pilot's voice and answers.

"Jah, I remember you. Charleston, nineteen seventy-nine. *Jah*, you were a knob..." Samuel is stopped, mid-sentence.

"You gave me a lift back to school. Got me past the guards after I signed in late from leave. I'll never forget that. I recognized you from the moment I saw you at the hospital. We'll get your wife to Walter Reed, sir. She'll be fine. I'm not a very religious person, but I see God's fingerprints all over this mission. I know she'll be fine."

"*Danki*, Colonel Simmons, you've done *gut* in your life, *Jah*, *verra gut*. *Danki?*" Samuel stares straight ahead. Then, looking down at his wife, he feels God's presence with him and his wife and knows in his heart and soul that yes, his Mary will be fine.

###

Will Carpenter is a faith filled family man, happily married for twenty-seven years. His wife Michele, is a master's prepared nurse educator.

They have three children. Matthew a Lutheran pastor is married to Mandy and they live in Michigan.

Lindsay presently lives in Charleston, S.C. where she teaches special education. She is engaged to Eli, who attends the Citadel. He will graduate and be commissioned this May. They will marry this June, and then will move to Fort Lewis Washington in the fall.

Mark their youngest is also a first classman at the Citadel, he will graduate and commission into the Army this May. He will attend flight school this fall at Ft. Rucker Alabama. Mark, following flight school will be a medevac pilot, flying the Blackhawk helicopter.

Mr. Carpenter spent eleven years in the Army as a medical specialist, army recruiter, army scout medic, and clinical specialist.

He is also a retired nurse with twenty-nine years of experience in various settings to include areas of emergency medicine, pediatrics, geriatrics, and child and adolescent Psychiatry.

A business owner, he resides near Honey Brook, Pa., an Amish community. This has enabled him to thoroughly research their deep-rooted faith and culture.

Keep in touch with Samuel and his family on facebook.
http://www.facebook.com/people/Samuel-Hersberger/100001879866459

Keep in touch with the Author
http://www.facebook.com/Will1953

Web Site 'Secrets of the Son
http://secretsoftheson.webs.com/prodigalexcerpts.htm
(Other links can also be found here.)